CW00369193

GEORGIANA

GEORGIANA

To Stephen + Marilyn

With love,

Roger

A NOVEL BY

ROGER DIXON &
SOPHIE DIXON

Copyright © 2018 by Roger Dixon and Sophie Dixon.

Cover Illustration Copyright © 2015 by Suzanne Southerton

PAPERBACK: 978-1-948962-98-8
EBOOK: 978-1-948962-99-5

All rights reserved. No part of this publication may be reproduced, distributed, or transmitted in any form or by any electronic or mechanical means, without the prior written permission of the publisher, except in the case of brief quotations embodied in critical reviews and certain other noncommercial uses permitted by copyright law.

Ordering Information:
For orders and inquiries, please contact:
1-888-375-9818
www.toplinkpublishing.com
bookorder@toplinkpublishing.com

Printed in the United States of America

CHAPTER I

Paris 1985

The Old Clockmakers district is bounded by Notre Dame and the river Seine on one side, and Les Halles, the central Market on the other. Before the War it numbered many Jewish craftsmen and merchants among those who gave it life, but now these are few in number.

Most of the premises in the narrow streets are lock-up shops and art galleries catering for the well-to-do, and the tourists who appear each year in increasing numbers, drawn by the deliberately preserved 'quaintness' which, with the passage of time, becomes less and less like the living, noisy and often dangerous community it once was. But few notice, and those that do shrug: at least the City developers are spending their money; and, after all, it will not be long before they themselves join the long jostling column of those who have already passed into history.

What residents remain are mostly students from the University close by and their landladies. But it was past midnight and the darkened streets were deserted; or so it seemed to the occasional police car cruising past on patrol. Behind the shuttered windows of one of the premises, larger than most, a robbery was taking place. Over the main front entrance a sign read "Lunas International - paintings and fine art."

The two thieves had reached the strong room where the most valuable pictures were kept. They were two brothers from Amsterdam, both in their mid-twenties, Albert and Hans. They were art-dealers themselves, although nothing like so successful as George Lunas, the owner of the firm they had invaded, but this was something they hoped to remedy as they put to one side items of less value until they found the three pictures they were looking for: One Monet, One Matisse, and one Van Gogh. Both the knowledge that these almost priceless works were being kept in the store-room overnight, and the fact that they had

1

been able to penetrate one of the most sophisticated security systems in Paris they owed to Marie Gerrard, the efficient and trusted secretary of George Lunas.

In her mid-thirties, such looks as Marie had once possessed were fading, and there was nothing more exciting in her private life than the annual ocean cruise, for which she saved for the rest of the year. During this she looked forward to her vacation with mounting excitement in the hope that, this time, she would meet and fall in love with someone who would not only satisfy her longing to be loved in turn, but who would look after her in reasonable comfort for the rest of her life. But each year she returned disappointed to the apartment on the outskirts of Paris she had shared with her Mother until the latter died two years ago. And so it was with amazed surprise when the romance she had been looking for arrived from a totally unexpected direction.

The young Dutch art dealer had called into the offices of Lunas International at a time when Lunas himself was abroad on one of his many business trips. In the normal way, she would not have come into contact with a chance visitor, but the Receptionist asked her to see him as apparently there had been some misunderstanding and Mr. Drovy was under the impression he had an appointment with the Boss and had driven from Amsterdam that morning especially to meet him.

Marie was immediately taken with the visitor; tall, very blonde and good looking. And when the misunderstanding had been straightened out and a new appointment made, she was thrilled when he asked if she would keep him Company for dinner that evening as the only friend he had in Paris was also out of town. She was aware, of course, that he was ten years younger, but she saw no harm in accepting the invitation, and indeed told herself on the Metro on her way home to change that Mr. Lunas would probably have expected her to do what she could to make up for a potential customer 's disappointment.

But it was not coincidence that Hans had called while Lunas was away. He and Albert had planned the robbery for some time and had agreed that it would be far too risky and possibly pointless without inside information. And after Albert had made a point of courting one of the junior secretaries of the Firm and pumped her over several dates as to who was who, and Hans had followed Marie home once to make discreet enquiries about her locally, it became obvious that she was the key!

Hans took his time. There was much at stake and arrangements also had to be made to transport anything they did manage to acquire back to Holland then on to collectors in America and the Middle East who would not only have the wherewithal to pay for works of the anticipated value targeted, but could be trusted to enjoy them in secret for the foreseeable future.

He phoned Marie from Amsterdam at her apartment, having obtained her number on their first date: 'He would be coming to Paris next Wednesday on some other business; could they meet again?'

This time she did not hesitate. She had treasured the memory of their evening together. He had behaved like a complete gentleman; almost formally, but they had dined in a wonderful restaurant, and after that he had insisted on driving her all the way home. It had an almost dream like quality about it, but she never expected to see him again and was delighted and amazed that he should ask her out a second time.

The evening had begun as before, and once again he had driven her home. But this time, he accepted her offer to come in for coffee, and from then on things had taken a very different turn. He stayed the night and made love to her, awakening passions she thought her body had long forgotten, and raising her to a level of desire she had never experienced before.

She was shy with him at breakfast, but he was loving and considerate, and before he left made a date to meet her when he next came to Paris in two weeks' time. Marie was glowing with happiness as she watched his car until it turned the corner at the end of the street, hoping he would wave just one last time - which he did.

The days until their next meeting dragged to begin with, but she occupied herself by spending all the money she had saved for the next cruise on clothes, a new hair-do and a complete make-over in a beauty salon. Her colleagues could scarcely fail to notice and Lunas himself congratulated her. She looked ten years younger. No one was indelicate enough to say so, but Marie herself knew it. They all thought it was the clothes, but she was lit from within.

This time he stayed with her a long weekend. They went everywhere and saw everything. He took her to the theatre; to a night club and a long drive in the country. When they next said goodbye Marie knew she was in love for the first time in her life. And the miracle was he loved her too. They started to make long term plans. They wouldn't get married to begin with, but their future lay together. With her experience she would be a great help to him in building up his business.

She travelled to Amsterdam to meet his brother, with whom she got on well, and on her last night he drove her out to Grosingon to see the house where he had been born. On the way back they stopped for a meal and it was here, for the first time since she had known him, Hans seemed depressed.

He pretended he did not want to worry her with his troubles, but she eventually persuaded him to tell her, and it was then he mentioned for the first time how a deal that had seemed so promising had gone sour. He and Albert had thought to make enough to be able to move up market where the serious money was made. But it turned out they had bought a couple of clever fakes, and in order to meet their obligations to their customer, they had been forced to buy replacements at a cost far in excess of what they themselves would be paid.

To begin with Marie was almost happy when he confessed his troubles. She had her inheritance from her Mother untouched. Now she would be able to fully show her love for him. But when he eventually told her how much he needed she was flabbergasted.

He then appeared to cheer up. He was sure he and Albert would find a way through, and he kept this up right to the time he put her on the train back to Paris. But during the return journey and for days afterwards Marie worried about what might happen to him; to both of them. She was part of his life now.

What made things worse was he did not contact her for several days. They had got in the habit of phoning daily when they were apart, but he did not call: and whenever she called him, she only got his answering service.

By the time Hans did phone, she was almost frantic: 'Yes, they were still in trouble. If anything, things seemed to be closing in on them. '

Marie jumped at the chance when he eventually said she might be able to help. He and Albert had been talking. He did not want to discuss it over the phone. They would arrive in Paris the following day.

When Marie put down the phone she could not imagine what it was she could do to help him. She only knew that, whatever it was, she would do it. Life without him now was unthinkable.

When she found out, Marie realized that the Police would soon draw the conclusion that the only way the thieves had been able to gain entry, avoid all the alarms and make good their escape would be with the help of inside information. But she would be only one of those suspected, and by sitting with one of her elderly neighbours until almost midnight, which she was in the habit of doing anyway from time to time out of compassion for the old lady's loneliness, she established an alibi. She was questioned with the others, but, as anticipated, swiftly eliminated from the official enquiry.

It had been purely by chance that Maurice, George Lunas' Moroccan chauffeur/bodyguard had seen Marie in the Rue St. Guard walking hand in hand with a good looking young man, at least ten years her junior, oblivious of everything but the sheer bliss of spending the evening with him. (This had been during the treasured long week-end they had spent together.) Of course, like everyone else who knew her, Maurice had been intrigued by Marie's late blooming, but he worked for Lunas personally and had little opportunity to discuss the matter with her colleagues. In any event, he was someone who kept his opinions to himself unless specifically asked by the Boss, and he never mentioned it. But there had been something odd about them together. He could tell by the way she looked up at her tall young companion that she was in love with him, and a second glance told him that, despite his answering smiles, her 'lovers ' attention was less than total.

Maurice stood on a street corner watching them walking away from him on the opposite side of the street. Had they walked on and round the next corner he would have shrugged and walked away in the opposite direction.' After all, what business was it of his if an ageing secretary threw himself at someone who obviously had an agenda besides love!' But, just as he was about to turn away, they turned into a small restaurant with windows looking out into the street, and driven by something more than idle curiosity, some instinct that had warned him before when all was not as it appeared, Maurice arrived outside just as the couple were seated at a window table, making it necessary for him to step back quickly into a doorway before being seen.

He saw Marie reach across the table and take the young man's hand. Now Maurice could see him full face he recognized him. It was the young Dutch art dealer who had called to see his employer some weeks before. He never forgot a face. So....that was all there was to it. He must have asked her out then....But why?

It was not until weeks later when the police began questioning everybody, including himself, he knew he had his answer. And so he found himself on a train to Amsterdam the following Saturday, sitting one carriage back from Marie who had been looking almost frightened when she passed him unseen on her way to board the train.

It was true. She was frightened. She had never been so nervous in her whole life as she had during the period of the initial police investigation. Her alibi was checked and confirmed. After which she was told there would be no further questions. But she was on tenterhooks until the Police had finally left the building and found it difficult to concentrate on her work. This was so unlike her, Lunas assumed the whole business of the investigation had upset her and suggested she took some time off, but she stuck it out until the weekend.

Hans had said he would ring. She was to do nothing until one or other of them contacted her; but by Friday evening she was beside herself and booked her seat the following morning. Now, one fear piled upon another. What would he say when she arrived at his apartment, having disobeyed his instructions? But she had to see him. To feel the reassurance of his arms around her, and to hear him say that he loved her and that everything would work out.

Hans was not in a good mood. Albert had just returned from seeing their contact to report that they would not be in a position to take delivery or, more importantly, pay for at least another three days. On the open market, the pictures would have been worth at least fifteen million dollars. They had been forced to accept one tenth of this; but it had been pointed out to them, there was a very limited market for such valuable works. The fact that they were so well known, in a bizarre way diminished their marketability.

His anger boiled over when he found Marie waiting for him, having rung the door bell. He and Albert had hoped to be far away before it dawned on her that he had used her and had no intention whatsoever of sending for her. But with an effort of will he drew her inside, before giving vent to his irritation, and even then managed to keep it within bounds, pointing out, not unreasonably, the danger she could have put them all in by coming to see him so soon: 'She should have waited. He would have called her soon enough. After all, if they were to spend the rest of their lives together what did a few weeks matter? '

This last was a master stroke. Marie humbly accepted his rebuke, and having seen him and heard him say such magical words, she was prepared to turn around and go straight back to Paris and wait. But despite the fact that he had no intention of burdening himself with her, she had proved remarkably talented in bed, being quick to learn the things he had taught her, and full of imagination herself, once she had thrown all inhibition to the wind. And so they went to bed for the afternoon and made love until Albert returned in the evening.

Albert was not so good at disguising his shock at finding her in bed with Hans. He had always realized she was the weak, if indispensable part of their plan. And realizing she was certain to tell all once she realized they had dumped her, despite certain jail for her part, he could not wait to be shot of her. But after Hans and Marie got dressed they both tried to reassure him; Hans pointedly pulling faces at him over her shoulder, while she explained that they had decided she would return to Paris the following day.... and be good! (This said with an arch smile up at her lover, confident now, that all was well and still glowing from his love making.)

They went out to dinner together. Then back to the apartment where, for her benefit, they continued to discuss imaginary plans of the life they would soon have together. But, enthralled as she was, Marie was exhausted and started to yawn. She went back to Han's bedroom and was fast asleep before he came back from the bathroom to join her.

Albert had his own room. It was modestly furnished except for a large antique wardrobe, presently locked because it had a false floor, beneath which the stolen canvas waited for their new owners.

Maurice watched the lights go out in the apartment on the third floor. While they had been out he had searched it thoroughly and it had not taken him long to discover the hiding place. Their Security scarcely matched the value of the stolen goods, but, after all, who in their right mind would expect to find a Monet, Matisse and Van Gogh in such a place. The pictures were already on their way back to Paris, but there was one thing left to do in order to carry out Mr. Lunas' instructions to the letter.

Maurice let himself into the apartment again and switched on the lights in the living room. The doors leading into the two bedrooms, the bathroom and the kitchen were all closed. In his right hand the Moroccan carried the automatic he had taken off a dead would-be mugger in Marseilles more than twenty years ago; since this, the two had been inseparable. He knew which door to open first. He had seen the signs of their love making during his previous visit.

Marie and Hans blinked as the ceiling light suddenly flooded the room then sat up, eyes widening with terror as they saw the gun pointing at them and the expression of the dark skinned man who held it in his right hand.

Hans first thought was that one of their contacts had decided to play for higher stakes. Then he heard the woman beside him gasp :

"No, Maurice. Please, don't!"

He shot her a glance. Marie obviously knew the intruder but it seemed of little comfort. Such was her terror, she was not even aware of her nakedness beneath his gaze, which was a mixture of anger and contempt.

"What do you want?" Han's voice sounded strange even to him. But the man ignored him.

"I've already found the three pictures you stole."

"Please Maurice."

"Don't worry. I'm not going to kill you. But Mr. Lunas will be disappointed to have his suspicions confirmed.

"I…."

"He trusted you. You betrayed him."

Hans again managed to find his voice. Have you called the Police?" He rasped.

The Moroccan briefly fastened on him a look such as one might have discovered something unpleasant under a shoe.

"Mr. Lunas does not care to confide his business to outsiders."

"Then why...." Hans began, but the Moroccan interrupted harshly.

"You will both get dressed and leave Amsterdam immediately. Do not return to Paris. Avoid London and New York; anywhere, Mr. Lunas has business. If you are seen, you will be killed without further warning. Is that clear?

Hans opened his mouth, but before he could say anything, he heard Albert's voice through the open living room door.

"Drop your gun. Is that clear?!"

To Marie, what happened next was a nightmare that haunted her for the rest of her life. The Moroccan did not waste time turning round. It was obvious someone had come out of the other bedroom and was probably holding a gun on him. He slammed the door shut behind him and dodged to one side, just in time to avoid the volley of shots which shattered the door beside him.

Marie became aware that while Maurice was distracted by this, Hans had reached under his pillow and was levelling a pistol at the man just inside the door.

"No, Hans!" The shriek was instinctive. But later.... so many times, she wondered if it was this that caused her beloved's death.... until it drove her insane.

Alerted to the danger, Maurice had time to let off one shot, but not soon enough as the bullet from the man on the bed caught him in his left shoulder and half spun him round. Even so, with a street fighter's instinct, he kept his eyes on his assailant and prepared to fire again, but Hans had fallen back on his pillow, a red star spreading in the center of his forehead.

Marie started to scream, and just as Maurice recovered his balance, the door burst open and Albert charged into the room with more courage than wisdom. He presented an easy target to the Moroccan who contented himself by clubbing him to the floor with the side of his gun where he lay, apparently out cold.

Maurice steadied himself then took a deep breath. Marie was still screaming so he took three steps towards her and slapped her hard across the face. She stopped and began to stare at him with a hatred even one of his experience had seldom seen. He said "I suggest you leave at once. Someone is bound to have heard and called the Police.

"You bastard. I'll kill you."

Maurice stared at her for a moment. Perhaps he should finish it here and now? But he pushed the thought to one side. He had his orders. He glanced down for a moment at Albert on the floor, who let out a faint moan.

"And take your friend with you."

As he left the room he saw the woman begin to move. He assumed it was to help the younger man up, but his own wound was beginning to hurt like hell and he could see blood starting to spread through his jacket. If he was going to get to a doctor he could rely on before he fainted from loss of blood he had no time to waste. Even so, as he approached the front door, some instinct made him turn in time to see that instead of helping him up Marie had picked up Albert's revolver and was pointing it at him. He looked at her coldly.

"Put it down. If you pull the trigger you will miss, but then I shall feel free to kill you."

The two stared at each other across the living room, then suddenly Albert appeared in the doorway behind her and made a grab for the gun.

Maurice turned, opened the front door and walked out into the darkened stairwell. But he did not continue on down the stairs. He pushed the revolver into his shoulder holster, ignoring the additional pain this action caused him, then bent down to draw a long knife strapped to his left calf.

Marie allowed Albert to regain possession of the gun. She watched him, as if in a dream, as he ran across the room and out into the stairwell, hoping he would shoot Han's murderer in the back as he ran down the stairs. But there was no sound of running feet. No shot. Just a kind of gurgle. Then Albert appeared in the doorway again. He was clutching his throat and his eyes were staring at her.

"Albert!"

She rushed towards him just as he pitched forward, his blood drenching her naked body which was already stained with that of his brother.

She saw his throat had been cut from ear to ear. In the sudden silence she heard the sound of footsteps going unhurriedly down the stairs.

CHAPTER II

New York - six months later

To George Lunas there was always something magical about Manhattan, particularly in the Spring. And although he had only flown in from Rome the previous evening there was a spring in his step as he walked across the Lobby of the Waldorf-Astoria to the entrance and where he knew Maurice would be waiting with the car to take him to the Adams Gallery in Greenwich Village, one of the more recent acquisitions of Lunas International of which he was both chief executive and principal shareholder.

With dark good looks, black hair, dusted with silver at the temple, and immaculately dressed in pinstriped Saville Row Suit, handmade shirt and shoes he was attractive enough; but it was the sense of power, instantly recognisable, with its underlying mood of controlled violence, that made Lunas irresistible to any woman who allowed her mind to wander in his direction. With men, the choice lay between respect or fear. There were no half measures.

No one knew exactly how old he was. Born in a Paris slum, the son of a laundress and one of a number of possible fathers, his first memories were of the end of the German occupation and how they were unexpectedly worse off as soon as the Germans left.

He had done what he could to help his Mother, earning a little and thieving the rest. But when he was ten she died suddenly. No relatives came forward and so he and his half brothers and sisters were taken into care. But after a few days George escaped, and as nobody looked for him very hard he avoided recapture and began to look after himself. And so it had been ever since - driven by an insatiable thirst for knowledge, and a gut instinct for recognising and seizing opportunities as they presented themselves, many of which in the early days took him into the shadow lands of doubtful legality. But those days were past, and only a few enemies would remind him, in the unlikely event they forgot that 'those whom the Gods would destroy, they first made mad.'

Lunas International extended into Shipping, Textiles and electronics. But Lunas' greatest love was fine art, and in particular painting, a love that had begun when he was still little more than a destitute street urchin and had discovered that Museums and Art Galleries (in those days) were places where he could shelter from the rain and cold in warmth and security. He began to walk around to see what everyone else was looking at, and then it hit him: here was a world he had never dreamed of.... that stayed with him in his memory long after closing time and he had to turn his mind once more as to where his next meal was coming from. He even managed to get hold of some paper and crayons and tried to draw himself. But it was hopeless. What he loved would not yield to him; not even later, when he joined some classes, and for a while he was so devastated he stopped going. But not for long. He was drawn back, and eventually discovered there was almost as much joy in learning to understand what those whose paintings sang for him were saying, and he began to haunt the public libraries as well, devouring everything about art he could lay his hands on. He became knowledgeable.

No one ever knew, but by the time he was twenty, he was as informed as any who held themselves out publicly to be critics; and with knowledge came an even deeper love.

By the time he was thirty he had laid the foundation of what was to become one of the greatest private collections of paintings in the world, and following his instincts, he made a fortune from buying and selling works of art that would have satisfied most people, enabling them to retire and enjoy life. But it was only the beginning, for he had discovered the excitement of business for its own sake. In the next ten years his business became truly international a conglomerate the equal of many large public corporations, but those who made it their business to pry into his affairs never managed to discover who else was involved. Every door they opened, there was Lunas standing alone - smiling sometimes, but always impassable. And despite the fact that the rest of his business had grown to dwarf the original art dealership, nothing gave him more satisfaction or pleasure than to visit his galleries in Paris, London, Berlin and Sydney; and the Adams Gallery had fulfilled a long held ambition to move into Manhattan, surely the most productive place in the world of Art at the present time; it's very atmosphere crackling with new ideas and ways of doing things.

Those who noticed his progress across the Waldorf Lobby, first to leave his key at the desk, then to the revolving doors leading outside found it difficult to look away again until he had disappeared. Some assumed he was a well known actor or politician, but just could not put a name to the face. Whatever, you could no more ignore him than a suddenly awakened memory of things past, or the possibility of hopes to be fulfilled.

If Lunas was conscious of any of these things he chose to ignore them. There outside, at the foot of the steps, was Maurice grinning at him through the car window. The Moroccan made no attempt to get out and open the door for his employer. He was not that sort of driver. But Lunas came down the steps with an answering smile. He had no close friends -just a few long time employees he knew he could trust, and Maurice was one of them. The bond between them had been forged long ago in an incident neither ever referred to. Each had saved the other's life and that put them on an equal footing. But each played the cards life had dealt them with mutual respect for the position of the other. Anything else was unthinkable.

Lunas nodded at the doorman and settled in the back as the other closed the door behind him. The Staff of the Waldorf were not bothered he never tipped them in public, knowing there would be a generous gift for them the day he decided to leave.

Maurice put the car in gear and swung into the down-town traffic. Then Lunas lent forward and gently patted him on the recently healed shoulder.

"It's wonderful to see you behind the wheel again, Maurice. I've missed you. When did you get in?"

"Yesterday."

"Are you staying with your Sister?"

"In New Jersey, yes. I picked up the car last night."

Lunas nodded again. "And the shoulder?"

"It still aches sometimes. But I was lucky."

Lunas paused in silence for a moment. Then he said "What of the Woman?"

The Moroccan glanced at him in the mirror. "Why are you still worrying about Marie?" he said.

Lunas shrugged. "I confided in her too much. I thought I was a judge of character!"

"The Dutchman turned out to be a better one."

"True."

Maurice continued: "After the funeral, she disappeared."

"Perhaps it's as well."

His driver pulled a face. "I don't like loose ends."

Lunas nodded as Maurice continued: "And I was the one that killed her lover, don 't forget!"

"But the Court cleared you completely."

Maurice did not answer for a moment as he pulled up at some lights and the rush hour crowds surged round them like a river parted by a rock. Then he said: "You should have seen the look she gave me when we met outside for a moment after the verdict."

"She was lucky we did not press charges."

"I'm sure we shall see her again one day."

The lights changed and Maurice started down Fifth Avenue again before adding, quietly "I think one day I shall have to kill her before she kills me."

Lunas shook his head. "She'll find another man. She'll forget all about the Dutchman."

"Not Marie," Maurice said quietly. "There will never be anyone else. She knows that. Perhaps she knows in her heart she would have lost him anyway. But now she can tell herself it was all my fault."

The two of them fell silent, each with his own thoughts as the car continued down Fifth Avenue until Lunas glanced up and saw they had reached Washington Square.

"Pull in" he said suddenly.

There was a slot, and Maurice pulled into it before glancing round questioningly. The Boss was smiling again.

"I'd like to walk from here."

He saw the Moroccan's eyes widen.

"It's not far. It will help to clear the cobwebs!"

He opened the door and got out, slamming it behind him, then turned to speak to Maurice through the open window.

"Go on to the Gallery," he ordered. "Tell them I'll only be a few minutes."

Maurice nodded, and Lunas stood back as the car drew into the traffic again, turning left at the next intersection. He then crossed the street and entered the Square through the Arch.

Lunas paused for a moment, glancing round happily at all the activities: Many of the park benches were occupied by Students from nearby New York University laughing amongst themselves before going to join classes. There were young mothers watching their children play while chatting to their friends, glad to be released from the confines of their apartments, some hitching up their skirts in the hope that even the weak April sunshine would do something to relieve their legs' winter pallor.

Lunas picked a path that would take him to the centre of the Square while continuing to take in the passing scene. Here and there were some doing slow motion Chinese exercises. A young man was practising juggling, and a girl was riding around on a monocycle distributing leaflets. She thrust one into his hand with a smile, and was off again in an instant. He glanced down and saw she was advertising a one woman show in a nearby 'loft' theatre (Seating capacity twenty-five; so get there early so as not to be disappointed!)

Not wishing to appear rude he waited until her back was turned before dropping the leaflet into a convenient trash can, but he noticed most people threw them on the ground after a momentary glance.

One or two artists had set up easels and his path took him up to one of these, a girl of about eighteen who was sitting on a stool, concentrating on her canvas, apparently oblivious of all the action going on around her. He noticed she was wearing the usual students ' uniform of scruffy jeans, T-Shirt and sandals. Her dark hair was tied with a flimsy blue ribbon in an untidy bunch off her forehead.

He stopped to glance over her shoulder, curious to see what it was that so captured her imagination. He saw she was painting a tree; one of the oldest in the park with gnarled trunk and branches. He glanced round and saw it was the only one already in full leaf, as if showing its younger companions what was expected of them at this time of year. He looked back at the canvas for a moment then glanced at the young artist herself and saw she was now staring back at him through a pair of eyes the colour of sapphire, although the rest of her features were Hispanic. He saw she was extraordinarily beautiful and was so startled it took him several seconds to snap out of it. In the meantime the young woman glanced away, without interest back to her canvas.

He stepped back a pace, followed her gaze, then said pleasantly: "Where did you learn to paint like that?"

"Like what?" She did not bother to look up.

Lunas put his head on one side as he examined the picture more closely.

"Well, you really seem to have captured the spirit of the tree."

"Huh." She leant forward and touched a spot of blue to the trunk.

"It is beautiful" he said, "but sad. Like an old person who knows they are nearing their life's end, but determined to go out with a flourish."

The girl continued to paint, apparently unimpressed by this until she said "Is that accent genuine?" She still did not look at him.

Lunas smiled. Some response was better than none.' I suppose so,' he said, then paused. But as she made no rejoinder he continued: "The only thing is, the composition. "

"What's wrong with the composition?" She still did not look up, but her voice had taken on an edge.

"Well... no matter how well you paint I mean, a tree, by itself...."

This time she did look up at him.

"You want I should put a dog crapping on it or something?"

Lunas suppressed a grin. "Well, it has been done," he said seriously.

"I don't do what other people do."

"People have painted a tree by itself before", he insisted. "I only thought.. " but she interrupted him, evidently having little wish to hear what he thought "Not the way I'm doing it."

She then put down the brush in her hand and picked up a much larger one. He watched her fascinated.

"Look, do you know anything about painting?" She asked.

"A little," he admitted, modestly.

The girl smiled sweetly and held out the brush to him. "Then take this and go over there and paint your ass green."

He paused for a moment, then burst out laughing, and at that moment a pretty black girl, about the same age as the one challenging him and similarly dressed, came up to them and stopped, looking from one to the other in surprise.

"O.K. I get the message," Lunas said good naturedly, and turned away, quite unfazed. "Goodbye Miss Spitfire!". He continued walking towards the Park exit opposite.

"Go fuck yourself" he heard her call after him. And as the two girls watched him move away they heard him laugh again.

The newcomer's name was Mary Thomas. She was Georgiana's best friend and a fellow student. "What was all that about?" She said, turning back to her.

Georgiana shrugged. "Oh, I get sick of dirty old men pretending to be interested in my work when all they want is to grab my ass or invite me back to their place" she said.

Mary glanced for a moment at the retreating figure of Lunas. "He didn't look like a dirty old man to me," she protested mildly.

Georgiana followed her gaze. "Well, maybe not," she admitted.

The two girls turned to each other grinning and Mary said: "He's elegant. I wouldn't mind someone like that taking an interest in me! "

Georgiana stood up. "Oh, come on," she protested. "He's old enough to be your father!"

"I like the mature type!" Mary insisted defiantly.

"Well, I've finished here anyway." Georgiana started to pack up her things.

"Do you need any help?" Mary offered.

But her friend shook her head with a grin. "I couldn't find anything the last time you helped!"

"Sorry".

"But thanks anyway."

Mary watched until she was ready.

"Do you have a class?" she asked, but Georgiana shook her head.

"No. Parrot face is sick."

Mary nodded. "I've just finished."

Georgiana smiled. "Good, you can walk me over to the Diner".

"O.K." Mary picked up and folded the stool. "I suppose you can trust me to carry this!"

"I guess so."

Mary saw her friend was looking at the tree and knew she was back in a world she could never share, no matter how much they loved each other. Then Georgiana snapped out of it. "O.K. Let's go."

The two girls walked towards the West Side down-town exit, then across 4th Street and continued on down Thompson Street. They walked in silence for a while, then Mary said "How is mother's sister?"

"Aunt Polly? She's still sick. Mom has to go over most evenings to take care of her."

"They're lucky they have you to help Pop," Mary observed.

"I don't mind. He doesn't like her being out late so much, but he's too considerate to say so'.

"Your Pop's lovely. He adores you!"

Georgiana nodded. "I know. I'd do anything for him. But I can't take my mother's place. He gets so anxious about her."

"That's understandable."

"If we didn't stay open so late he'd go over with her, but we can't afford to close in the evening."

The two continued until they found themselves outside Ricki's Diner, named after Georgiana's father, a small brash looking establishment on Thomson Street currently benefiting from all the new construction that was going on, the developers having run out of sites further up-town.

Georgiana turned to Mary. "Do you want to come and say hi? Maybe get a bite?" But her friend shook her head and pulled a face.

"I can't," she said. "I've got to run some errands of my own."

"O.K. Will I see you tomorrow?"

"Unless you're free this evening?"

It was Georgiana's turn to pull a face. "I doubt it" she said. Mom goes over most evenings at present. I have to stay and help Pop.'

"O.K." Mary smiled and handed over the stool. "Til' tomorrow then."

"Thanks for carrying this."

"That's O.K."

The two girls looked at each other, and Georgiana was about to turn away when Mary said suddenly, "Georgie...."

"Yes."

Mary paused for a moment, then she said emotionally: "I don 't know why anyone as talented as you would want a dumb cluck like me for a friend!"

"Hey...."

"But if you ever need me, you know I'll always be here for you."

Georgiana put the arm carrying the stool round her friend's shoulder and hugged her.

"I love you too; you know that," she whispered.

Mary nodded, and Georgiana felt with surprise her friend's tears against her cheek. She pulled back and looked at her frowning.

"Mary! Is something wrong?"

Her friend shook her head, and stepped back, wiping her eyes with the back of her hand, and forcing a smile. "Not a thing. It's O.K. Just me being stupid."

Georgiana looked at her keenly. Mary wasn't what you'd call psychic, but she knew her friend sometimes had feelings about things that had not yet happened, that turned out to be amazingly accurate.

"Is something going to happen?" She asked quickly. And after a moment Mary nodded.

"Yeah. Someday you're going to be really famous. And rich." Georgiana continued to look at her.

"Is that all?"

Mary pulled a face.

"Ain't that enough to be going on with?"

Georgiana relaxed, and smiled. "I guess so. But then I'm going to need you more than ever."

"I hope so."

They stepped forward to give each other a last squeeze, then Mary held up her hand and turned to walk away. Georgiana watched her for a few seconds, but Mary did not glance back so she turned, opened the door and walked into the Diner.

Rici, her father, had come to the United States from Puerto Rico twenty years ago. He had been a hard working young man, with smouldering good looks and a determination to make something of himself. But first, he had to learn English, and that was how he had met Christine, Georgiana's mother, who gave private evening lessons to recent immigrants to supplement her earnings as a school teacher in a depressed neighbourhood. Rici fell in love with her on sight. But she was blond and fair skinned, with cornflower blue eyes and a heavenly figure; so far above him in the social order, seemingly there was no possibility she could ever think of him in a romantic way.

He was wrong. She knew he was attracted to her, but he was so shy she went crazy trying to think of ways to encourage him without making him run off. Eventually, she contrived a date, and managed to arrange for him to kiss her goodnight, thinking it was all his idea. A whirlwind courtship followed and they were married a year to the day Rici had arrived in America.

It was a wonderful dream come true. They pooled their savings and managed to buy a small eatery in New Jersey. Nothing as swanky as Rici's Diner on Thompson Street, but they made money from the time they opened the doors, and after Christine gave up teaching to manage tables, while he concentrated on the kitchen, they never looked back.

Georgie had come along a year later, but it was a difficult birth and the Doctors advised her to be sterilised as it would be dangerous to have any more children. They had both been disappointed, but agreed the operation was necessary. And Georgie was so adorable she made them forget they had ever wanted any more children.

Georgiana glanced round as she closed the door behind her. It was early for lunch, so only half the tables were occupied. Even so, the place had a buzz.

Doris, the Help, was dealing with two customers who were sitting up at the Counter, and her mother was chatting to some construction workers, regulars she recognised, sitting at one of the Booths. She had to admire her mother. She was almost forty, but looked ten years younger. She certainly looked after herself. She wore her skirts short, displaying legs which would have done credit to a woman half her age, and she picked up good tips. Seeing her come in, her Mother smiled, and beckoned her over. She went across smiling at two of the other customers she knew, and kissed her mother on the cheek. "Hi Mom!"

Her mother smiled back at her before turning back to the men in the booth who were watching them.

"Georgie, you know these gentlemen, don't you?"

Georgie knew what to do and gave them collectively a dazzling smile. "Sure. Aren't you the guys working on the Burnell Tower"

The men preened themselves under her attention.

"Raised the twenty-sixth floor this morning," one of them said proudly.

"I don't know how you have the nerve to walk around up there with nothing but girders," Christine said.

You get used to it," one of the others said, and they all nodded as if to do such a thing was like coming home for Christmas.

"Ain't nothin." a third added, in case the two women had missed the point.

Christine said: "Well, it would scare me to death. I guess men are just built differently. Don't you think so Georgie?"

"I hope so!" Georgie answered innocently, but with just enough twinkle in her eye to tickle the men's ego, and they all guffawed appreciatively.

"Now then, you know that's not what she meant" Christine said, playing up to them, and Georgie looked back at her eyes wide.

"How do you know, mother?"

This just about slayed them, but enough was enough, and when she could, Christine said "And now, if you'll excuse us, I just want a quick word with my daughter. Enjoy your food."

The men smiled and nodded in acquiesce, but watched them wistfully as they moved to the other side of the counter before resuming their own conversation.

"What is it?" Georgiana said, when they were out of earshot. Christine pulled a face.

"I want you to have a word with your father. He's in the kitchen."

"What about?"

"You know I have to go over and give Polly her supper and tidy up the place. She still can't manage without help."

"Pop knows that."

"But he read in the morning paper that some woman got her throat cut not far from our apartment," her mother went on. "He says he'll only let me if he comes with me. And you know he can't do that."

Georgiana shrugged. "You'll take a cab won't you," she said. But Christine pulled another face.

"They think the guy who did it was pretending to be a cab driver."

"Oh. "

"But I always ring the same company." Christine persisted. "I never go out in the street and just call one passing by." She paused for a moment, then said more intently: "Talk to him anyway. He'll feel better now you're here."

"When do you have to go?"

"Not 'til about five. I'll stay here 'til then. But if you could then cover for me?"

Georgiana glanced round. "You don't need me now.?"

Her Mother shook her head. "You go and do some study. Doris can stay on today."

"O.K. I'll come back at five then."

"Bless you." Her mother gave her a quick peck on the cheek and smiled. Already she looked relieved.

"Now go and talk to Pop".

"O.K." Georgiana gave her mother a conspiratorial smile before pushing open the door into the kitchen with her shoulder.

A young boy was washing dishes and her father was shaking a pan of fries over a burner. The heat hit her like a slap in the face. It was no wonder her father looked older than he was, having to live in this heat twelve hours a day. But as soon as he saw her he smiled and nodded, turning down the burner then walking over to kiss her, wiping his hands on a cloth.

"Georgie!"

"Hi Pop."

"I was not expecting you so soon."

They exchanged a kiss. Then Georgiana said "The Teacher was sick. I worked in the Square for a bit, now I'm on my way home. I just thought I'd look in."

"I'm glad you did." Her father lowered his voice in a manner that matched the secretive air her mother had used not a minute since." I want you to have a word with your mother about Aunt Polly."

"Now Pop"

"No," her father interrupted." Things aren't like they used to be any more. I worry about her. No one is safe."

"But she gets a cab right to the door," Georgiana protested. But her father made a gesture of dismissal.

"Maybe one night she will not be able to find one, and start walking. A beautiful woman like her, who know what could happen?"

"But she's got to look after Polly", Georgiana persisted, and after a moment she saw her Father's face fall. "I suppose so," he said miserably. Then he brightened momentarily: "Maybe we should close early until Polly is better?"

Georgiana said gently: "Pop...you know we can't afford to do that."

CHAPTER III

The Adams Gallery was founded by the father of John Adams who now ran it with his son Paul. It was typical of international dealers elsewhere having a modest, even slightly run down look about it from the street; also, nothing to indicate that the ownership had changed two years ago when both father and son had been caught out by a sudden, 'though temporary drop in the market, which had necessitated selling several important pictures at a considerable loss. Not so considerable that they were insolvent, but sufficient to deplete the liquid resources which any dealer needs to move swiftly enough to take advantage of opportunities as and when they presented themselves in an every changing and highly competitive market.

How George Lunas had learned of their predicament neither partner ever discovered, but the chances were that, long before such a humiliation became widely known, they would have decided to move into other fields - possibly using John Adams wish to retire as a cover. Then Lunas had come to see them.

At first, they had pretended that whatever the source of his information, he was mistaken. But he was not the kind of man you could play games with, and when he offered to refinance the Gallery on a limited partnership basis, and allow the Adams to continue to front the enterprise as if nothing had happened, they realised it was something they could scarcely refuse.

During the following hours the details were worked out. Lunas himself would take no hand in the day to day running of the business. Their name would remain on the sign over the front door, but it was agreed that, in addition to replenishing the trading cash, they would accept the advice he would give from time to time and take advantage of the intelligence his organisation would be able to provide. The division of profits was complicated, but after only six months both John and Paul were receiving salaries and commission considerably in excess of their previous earnings. Lunas was as good as his word in every respect, and far from resenting their partial loss of sovereignty, both wondered how they had ever managed before with just the two of them.

As Lunas turned the corner into the quiet street where the Gallery was situated, he saw John Adams and Maurice smoking cigarettes while waiting for him beside the car which was parked immediately outside. As soon as they saw him they threw their cigarettes away. Maurice got back into the car to await further instructions, and John Adams walked forward to meet him smiling, squinting slightly against the rays of the sun which slanted over the roofs of the buildings opposite.

The two men shook hands warmly, exchanging greetings. Then Adams shook his head. "Maurice said you only got in late last night. You look as if you were in bed by ten!"

Lunas chuckled at the complement. "You know, when I was young I often had nowhere to sleep, so I got used to cat napping in uncomfortable places -even airplanes." He took a deep breath and glanced round appreciatively. "There is nowhere quite like New York in the spring!"

Adams grinned. "From a Parisian, that is a compliment," he said."Coffee?"

"Please."

"And a little Armanac?"

"Comme d'habitude!"

"How I love your visits!" Adams sighed. "With anyone else, I would feel guilty drinking brandy so early!"

Lunas smiled. "Never feel guilty enjoying the simple pleasures of life, my friend," he said.

"Yes. But these days such pleasures are regarded as almost degenerate."

"Then let us drink to our imminent downfall!"

"Shall I lead the way?"

"Of course!"

The two men laughed easily and Lunas followed Adams through the front door of the gallery, but not before noting, with surprise, that the one picture on display in the window was a Braque he had flown over two months previously since it would achieve a better price in New York than Paris. Maybe there was a good reason. He would raise the matter before he left. But not now.

Even in the Gallery itself there were not many pictures on display but all were new to him. As he followed Adams through to the office at the rear of the Gallery he took his time to examine each one and Adams matched his pace to that of his visitor, conscious, even in the silence, that Lunas was impressed.

Finally they came to the last one which was by a young New Yorker they had both thought worth promoting.

"How is Stephen selling?" Lunas asked.

"Wonderfully..., after the exhibition you gave him."

"You gave him John."

Adams smiled. "Let's say we gave him, then. But it was your idea."

"And Paul's," Lunas corrected him gently.

"That's true."

They covered the remaining to the office.

"How is Paul?" Lunas inquired.

"Fine. He's in San Francisco, following up that lead you gave us."

Lunas grinned. "Ah yes, the Bay Gallery will be furious when they discover we bought the two Sisleys under their very noses!"

"Good morning, Mr Lunas." A pleasant faced black woman of middle age came through the door at the back of the office carrying a tray on which there was coffee, a bottle of Armanac and two glasses. She put it on a table then turned to him smiling.

Lunas held out his hand and shook hers warmly. "Anne. How nice to see you. How well you look."

"Thank you. I poured the coffee but I thought I would leave the rest to you.

"I'll do it." Adams came forward, uncorked the bottle and poured the brandy while the other two continued their conversation.

"And how is Joseph?" Lunas said, picking up one of the cups. He saw a cloud pass momentarily across her face.

"He has not been too well recently."

"I'm sorry to hear that."

"He stays in most of the time. But the Doctor says he is improving slowly."

"He had a stroke." Adams said quietly, passing him one of the glasses.

"Well then....please give him my very best wishes for a speedy recovery."

The woman looked pleased. "He will be touched you remembered him," she said.

"I've never known Mr Lunas forget a name," Adams put in.

Lunas turned to him and said seriously, "Ah yes; that, and the smile on my face, have often been the only things standing between me and disaster. Cheers!" He raised his glass and smiled again.

"Cheers." The two men toasted each other, then Adams remarked dryly, "That's hard to believe, by the way."

"Well, some things improve with age - like this excellent Almanac". Lunas drained his glass, then put it down on the tray and picked up his coffee.

"I must get back to the customs declaration. "Anne said. "If you will excuse me...."

"Of course." The women nodded and they watched her disappear into the inner office, closing the door behind her.

"You know, it has always been a mystery to me why you were interested in a small concern like ours." Adams ventured when he was sure his secretary was out of ear shot. "With all your other interests, we must be like a pimple on the elephant's trunk!"

"Not at all. The jewel in the crown." Lunas shrugged. "Certainly one of them."

"Your other Galleries.... yes, of course."

Lunas put his cup down, then he said seriously: "You know John, fine art is not just my business, it's my passion. Perhaps because I came from nothing, nothing gives me greater pleasure than to discover a spark of true genius." He smiled before continuing. "The excitement of never knowing where it is going to appear next. It is one of the things I anticipate each day when I wake up in the morning. "

Adams pulled a face. "Genius is hard to find these days," he said.

"I agree."

Adams saw the energy and heard the enthusiasm in his voice. He envied the Frenchman. He used to feel like that. He still enjoyed what he did, but somewhere down the line he had lost the fire.

"With so much mediocrity crowding in on all sides," Lunas continued; "so many fool critics - so called art lovers with more money than sense, no wonder people look back with longing to the great Masters where they feel sure of their ground. But we should not be discouraged. I am convinced that every age produces artists as great as any other. The trick is to recognise them while there is still time for us lesser mortals to be of some help. "

"Well, you've helped more than anyone else I know," Adams said, without flattery.

"I try. It is why I look forward so much to my visits here, and to our other friends, when I can get away." Lunas paused for a moment, then he went on. "Only half an hour ago I stopped on my walk here to look at the work of a young girl in Washington Square. There is no doubt she had some quality.... I couldn't put my finger on it with just one half finished picture to go on.I would have liked to have talked with her. Perhaps seen something she had completed." He smiled ruefully. "But she thought I was just trying to get 'fresh' I think you say. She was quite a little spitfire. Beautiful kid. Outstanding." He saw Adams looking at him thoughtfully.

"Dark.... blue eyes....about eighteen?" Lunas looked back at him in surprise. "Why yes. That sounds like her. How remarkable! Do you know her?!

Adams nodded. "Georgiana Montes." Then he smiled. "You're right. She is a little hell cat. She can certainly paint, but I've often wondered if she wouldn't make more of a living as a model. "

Lunas shook his head. "Not if she can really paint," he said. "Do you have anything of hers?"

Adams nodded. "As a matter of fact we do. As you suggested, we have been keeping our eyes open. I have the work of several young artists to show you in the store room."

"Excellent. But this Georgiana....?"

"Montes."

"Yes. You have something of hers?"

Adams glanced at his cup. "Have you finished your coffee?"

"Enough."

"Then follow me."

29

Adams opened the door to the inner office where Anne was working at a desk. She smiled at them briefly as they walked past and through another door which opened to a much larger room which was already lit by concealed lighting. All round the room Pictures leaned against the wall. In the center of the room was a display easel, currently unoccupied. Closing the door behind them, Adams flicked a wall switch which activated a spot light focused on the empty easel. He then went to the far side of the room, selected a canvas, then brought it to set on the easel. Lunas, meanwhile, moved into a good viewing position.

Adams said: "If you saw Georgie working in the Square, you may recognise this." He put the picture in position, then stood back, and Lunas saw at once it was of the same tree she had been painting earlier. Only this was finished.

"Yes, I recognise it," he said with a smile. "And her style."

Adams said: "I have to give credit to Paul for holding on to her when she called in here by chance." He paused for a moment, before continuing: "We've shown it to several collectors.... so far without success." He shrugged. "Still life is a bit out of fashion at the moment."

Lunas pulled a face. "Ah.... fashion!" he said, with distaste.

"Quite. It is, of course, much more than that. The way she has caught the spirit of the tree."

Lunas nodded in agreement. "My very words." he said. Then added wryly: "Before I was told to take a walk!"

Adams smiled sympathetically. "Paul says it has almost human qualities."

"Exactly. Wise.... tranquil. "

"And sad?"

Lunas looked at the picture in silence for a few moments before adding: "This comes out much more in this than the one she was working on. Of course, to be fair, the other wasn't finished." He paused for a moment. "Does she paint anything else?"

Adams nodded. "We have two others," he said. "I'll get them."

He took the tree off the easel and lent in carefully against the wall. Then he picked up two other slightly smaller canvas, put one on the easel then stood facing Lunas, holding the other up alongside it.

"We promised her we would always show these side by side," he explained. "Again, it was Paul who took them in. She said it was of her studio, where she lives with her parents I believe. "

Lunas saw that the first picture was of an attic bedroom, devoid of furniture except for an unmade bed. The second was of the same room, only this time, where there had been the bed, there was nothing but a grotesque shadow on the floor.

Lunas found his eyes being pulled into the shadow, which seemed to change shape as he looked at it, becoming even more threatening. He felt the hairs on the nape of his neck begin to tingle and practically had to tear his eyes away with an effort of will. He glanced at Adams and saw the other was looking at him keenly.

"It's chilling," Lunas said in a matter of fact tone he did not feel. "As if something quite horrible happened on the bed leaving its shadow printed on the floor where it stood. Did someone close to her die in that room? A parent perhaps, with suffering?"

Adams shook his head as he lowered the picture he was holding. "Her parents are both still alive as far as I know."

"Yes, of course. You said so just now."

Adams looked down at it in his hands. "Sometimes people like Georgie drag up things from their subconscious."

"Or sense something in the future perhaps." Lunas thought for a moment, then he said "You know, this really makes me think, despite my first encounter, I would like to meet this young woman again." He glanced at his watch. "Unfortunately I don't have much time. I must get on a plane for Rio tonight and we do have other things to discuss. "

"Another gallery?"

Lunas smiled and shook his head.

"Nothing so enjoyable this time, I am afraid." He paused for a moment, then came to a decision.

"Do you know where she lives?"

"Of course. It's not far from here."

"Good. Then let's see how we get on. If I can, I'll stop off on the way back to the Hotel.

CHAPTER IV

Apart from the sloping ceiling with its skylight, the window and the door, Georgiana's room bore little resemblance to her pictures. Half was devoted to her painting - the half under the skylight, and this was relatively organized. The other half, where she lived the rest of the time was a chaos of unmade bed, dressing table littered with make-up, and personal belongings of all kinds; clothes strewn everywhere.

When the buzzer went on the landing outside, indicating there was someone at the front door downstairs, she had just succeeded in mixing up the right tone of silver grey to touch on the clouds which raced overhead in her picture of the tree. At first she ignored it, but when it continued imperiously she swore loudly and threw open the sash window to peer down at the front step, four floors below.

Lunas was standing at the top of the flight of stone steps leading up to the front door of the Brownstone. Maurice waited in the car parked close by. On getting no response from the buzzer he stood back and gazed up to the top floor which was where the directory stated the Montes apartment was situated, just in time to see Georgiana stick her head out of the window.

"Are you ringing our bell?" She shouted crossly before he could say anything.

"Yes." He smiled up at her.

"Well there's no one in."

Lunas' smile broadened. "Aren't you in?" he called politely.

"No." The reply was emphatic.

Lunas frowned and decided on a different tack.

"Georgiana Montes?"

She paused, looking down at him suspiciously. "Who wants to know? Wait a minute, don't I know you?"

I'm a friend of John Adams," Lunas went on avoiding the question. "And of Paul, his son," he added as an afterthought.

"Oh.... Paul and John!"

Encouraged by her change of tone he went on: "May I speak with you?"

"What about?"

"About the Pictures you left at the Gallery."

"What about them?"

"I'd like to buy them."

"Talk to the Gallery."

She really was tiresome! But he took a breath and called back: "I've just come from there."

"So what's to talk about?"

"I want to give you the money."

There was a moment's silence before he heard her say uncertainly: "Money?"

"Yes." He paused then went on reassuringly "They said it was all right and they'd see you later about the commission."

Again there was a pause before he barely heard her say: "I thought they took that first, then gave you the rest."

"Look, do you want to be paid or not. I haven't got all day." He tried not to shout, but this was ridiculous!

Then he heard her say: "Come up," adding superfluously, "we're on the top floor." But before he could comment, a buzzer sounded and the front door sprang open.

She was waiting for him at the top of the stairs outside the apartment front door. By the time he reached her he had regained his humour and was pleased to note she was even prettier than he remembered from their brief encounter in the Square. Her smile, though brief, was ravishing. He was about to offer to shake hands when she turned on her heel and disappeared through the doorway into the apartment, assuming evidently that he would follow; which, of course, he did, but took the precaution of leaving the door open.

She led him through a sitting room to another flight of stairs opposite a bathroom and up into an attic Studio which he recognized at once from the paintings.

Georgiana walked to the still open window and turned to face him. For a few seconds he was aware of being given, what he believed the Americans called, 'the once over!'

"Well...." he began. But she interrupted him.

"The stairs don't seem to bother you, her tone was stark; frank, but not unfriendly. He shrugged.

"I keep taking the tablets."

"Really? What kind"

He held up his hand in protest.

"A joke!"

"Oh. right!"

"I deal in Art; amongst other things."

"And you want to buy the pictures I left at the gallery."

"Two of them. And to look at anything else you'd care to show me."

Georgiana stared at him again as if he was of a strange, if harmless species.

"You can sit down if you want.

He looked round and she pointed at the stool in front of the easel.

"Thanks." A stool was better than nothing.

"Look," she began, a little awkwardly, when he had sat down. "I guess I wasn't too polite just now."

"Or in the Park," he said nodding matter-of-factly.

"Yeah. That too." She planted herself on the edge of the bed, then added: "You can't be too careful. There are creeps everywhere." Lunas smiled.

"There is really no need to apologize." They looked at each other, and he was pleased to see her smile again. The fact of the matter was, the kid was nervous and he didn't suppose he could blame her. She really was gorgeous.

"So, how much do you want to pay me?" she said after a few seconds.

Lunas said: "For the pair of this room, I'm prepared to pay one thousand dollars."

"Holy shit! The smile disappeared and he saw her jaw drop in disbelief.

"Each."

Her mouth closed and he saw her swallow as she tried to get a grip on herself.

"Naturally," she managed after a moment. She looked at him with a straight face; then, quite suddenly, they both burst out laughing.

"You're sure you know what you're doing?" She said eventually. "No." She held up her hand. "Let me rephrase that. You sure know what you're doing!"

They laughed again.

"I think so." he said.

Georgiana paused for a moment; then she said simply "But what about the tree?"

"The tree," he repeated, then said quietly. "I think you should keep that. One day it will be worth a lot of money."

"Really?" She smiled again. Well.... with two thousand bucks I guess I can afford to wait."

"Good. Now then…" he reached into his jacket pocket and pulled out a wad of dollar bills. I take it you would prefer cash? Of course, I can give you a cheque if not?"

"No. No. Cash will be fine." She tried to keep her voice casual.

Lunas nodded. "By the way, we have still not introduced ourselves. My name is George Lunas."

She looked at him in surprise. "Really? That's almost the same as mine. I hope we don't get each other mixed up!"

He looked at her quickly, then saw she was teasing him. "I don't think that's likely, do you?." He smiled.

"I guess not. But you can call me Georgie."

"O.K. Then." He stood up quickly and moved over to where she was sitting. "Hold out your hand."

She did so and he slowly counted out twenty hundred dollar bills. Georgiana watched fascinated, but he was much more aware of the nearness of her. It was obvious she had no idea what effect she was having on him, and hoped, for her sake, she learned to use such power with discretion. In the past he had seen attractive young women allow themselves to become intoxicated by their own beauty, only to be destroyed by men unworthy to receive the love such creatures seemed to bestow so carelessly. Rarely had he met one as beautiful as this girl who was delightedly watching the pile of bills grow in her hands. In a few more years she would be sensational.

'How he would like to be around then! To protect her from herself, perhaps? To love even.' He heard himself count the last note and straightened up, dismissing such thoughts with an effort of will.

"There is just one thing," he said. "You did not sign either of the pictures. I would like you to go to the Gallery and do so. Mr. Adams will also have a bill of sale for you to sign."

"When?" she tore her eyes away from the money and looked up at him.

"In the next day or so. There is no sweat, I think you say."

"Fine." Georgiana got up off the bed and he stood back while she went to a bookshelf and tucked the notes inside one of the books.

"I take it this is your first sale?"

She turned to face him. "Yes, it is. I guess I'm a bit overawed. And sad," she added after a moment.

"Why sad?"

The girl shrugged. Then she said: "You can sell the right to a book or a piece of music, but you never really lose it. But once a picture has gone, you may never see it again."

He nodded understandingly. "But you're going to have to get use to that."

"Yes, I know." She looked at him full in the face, and he was startled that suddenly her blue eyes were glistening with unshed tears.

"But you will not lose the pair you have just sold me" he assured her. "Not in that sense."

"Why not?"

"Because I intend to keep them for myself so you will be able to see them whenever you like." He scarcely knew what he meant by that, but he was relieved to see her smile again.

"You'll never make any money like that!" She pulled a face. "But I guess you don't need me to tell you how to make money!"

He smiled back at her.

"We can all learn."

Georgiana looked around. "I can offer you a can of coke, if you'd like something to drink?"

Lunas shook his head. "I'd rather see some of your other work, if I may."

He saw her hesitate. Then she said :"I don't have much to show you. Canvas is so expensive. I often paint over something I did earlier. "

"So did many of the Masters."

"Well. O.K. Let me move the stool back a bit." She walked across the room and put the stool in a good viewing position in front of the easel. Lunas then dutifully sat at her invitation while she removed the unfinished painting and began to place a number of canvas on the easel in front of him which had been leaning against a cupboard.

She was right, there were not many; some obviously painted at different times of year. And there was a triple self-portrait which was quite outstanding. Then she put a larger canvas in front of him and stood back watching him.

He saw at once it was of the ice rink at Rockefeller Center. There were the usual crowds leaning on barriers looking at the action on the ice below. The angle of the heads and the expression on the faces of those close enough to be distinct indicated that there was something quite exceptional going on in the middle where the skaters were performing.

Again, Lunas felt himself being drawn into the picture, but this time the sensation was quite different. He felt the chill in the air. He heard the music of a waltz over the loud speaker system, and then, through the mist which clung to the ice he saw two dancers waltzing in each other's arms like two doves in flight. It was exquisite.

He watched as the dancers seem to disappear into the mist. Then he glanced away briefly to see Georgiana looking at him intently. And when he looked back, he saw that the center of the ice was empty. And the music had stopped.

He stood up, unable to help himself and took a deep breath. Then he looked back at her.

"It's in your imagination, she said in answer to his unspoken question. "I just nudge it a little." She took the canvas off the easel and was about to lean it back against the wall when he said hurriedly.

"I'd like to buy that one too."

Georgiana smiled and looked down at the canvas in her hands; then she said: "I'm sorry. This is not for sale."

"Another thousand dollars. No, two". But she shook her head and returned it to its place.

"Why not?" he demanded.

She turned to face him. "Because it's the best thing I've done so far."

"I agree."

"So it's my mark. When I've done one I think is better, then maybe I'll sell it to you."

Lunas took a breath, then he raised his hands in a gesture of resignation. "I understand," he said. "Keep it as long as you can. One day it will be worth much more. "

Georgiana suppressed a grin. "Oh. So you would cheat me, trying to get your hands on it now?"

But Lunas shook his head. "I would never cheat you, Georgie. I would like to help you."

"Oh?"

He saw her smile fade and said quickly: "Don't misunderstand. I want nothing from you personally. I would just like to help you towards the goal I can see you have set for yourself."

"How?"

"I will not lie to you.... nor flatter you. I think you are the most promising talent I have seen in years. But there are faults no, weaknesses in your technique and these can be eliminated. May I see that last picture again?"

"No."

He didn't even hear her as he strode to where she had put the canvas and picked it up.

"Now, just a minute...."

If he had been looking at her he would have stopped at that point, but he had the bit between his teeth and was holding up the canvas with one hand while reaching round to point at it with the other. "Take this quadrant here," he said confidently. "If it was cheated down a little it, would exaggerate the effect of the people standing here.... and here. Then over here...."

"Take your damn fingers off my painting." Georgiana said advancing on him angrily.

He looked at her in surprise. "I wasn't touchin' it" he said mildly.

But Georgiana snatched it from him. "I don't give a shit whether you were touching it or not."

Lunas swallowed. Then he said as calmly as he could: "Look kid, if you're going to be a professional artist, you've got to learn to take criticism."

"I didn't ask for your opinion," she threw back at him. "I didn't ask you here….and don't call me kid!"

"I thought you Americans used it as a term of affection."

"It sounds stupid with a French accent. And you can keep your affection. I don't need anyone telling me what to do."

"I'm not telling you what to do." Lunas protested. He was finding it increasingly difficult not to respond to her sudden hostility in kind. "I'm just suggesting…"

"Don't" she interrupted him "When I put the picture up for sale, then you can tell me what you think."

"I've already said I like it."

"That doesn't give you the right to preach."

"I'm not preaching, damn it." he shouted back at her. "Just shut up for a minute and let me finish."

"All right. Finish…. then get out."

Lunas took a deep breath trying to get a grip on himself. "The real reason I came here," he began, conscious of his voice wobbling with the effort of controlling his anger, "was not to tell you I wanted to buy the two pictures…. although that was true. It was to say I thought so much of your potential, on the strength of them…. and even more since I've seen some of the rest of your work, that I was prepared to pay for you to go to Paris to study under the greatest teachers in the world."

"Fuck the greatest teachers in the world." Georgiana said harshly. "I don't need them."

"Oh yes you do, Miss Bighead." Lunas smiled grimly. "We all need help to achieve the best that is in us. And in Paris…."

"Fuck Paris."

Lunas was about ready to hit her. "Have you no humility?" he raged.

"Fuck humility. The world steps on the humble. They don't inherit it."

Lunas drew himself up with a supreme effort to regain his composure. "You disappoint me," he said with as much dignity as he could muster.

"Then fuck you too!"

"That word comes easily to you, doesn't it?"

"O.K. Go screw yourself."

"You're being very stupid."

"Maybe."

"I think I'd better go."

Georgiana stuck her face closer to his, her face distorted with fury. "Well, Mister…you're slow….but you've got the message at last." She strode to the door, and tore it open. Lunas hesitated for a second, then he gave a snort of disgust and strode out.

Once he was gone, Georgiana felt the anger begin to drain out of her. By the time he emerged from the front door slamming it behind him, she was leaning out of the window to catch him.

"Hey, Mr. Lunas. " He looked up. "What?"

"What about the pictures?"

He pulled open the door of the waiting car and glanced up for the last time.

"Fuck the pictures!"

She saw him get in and slam the door.

"Does that mean you want your money back?"

She watched the car disappear into the distance, then she pulled her head back inside and thought for a minute. Then a grin started to develop.

"Gee, she murmured". I wonder if all my sales are going to be as exciting!"

CHAPTER V

Just before nine Georgiana's Father came out of the kitchen and glanced up at the clock; something he had done at ever diminishing intervals since the early evening rush had subsided. Ricki's wasn't the kind of place you went for dinner before the theatre, but the shift changed at six on the nearby building site and a fair number of the workers preferred to drop in for a bite rather than wait until they got home; particularly, those whose wives rarely bothered to cook.

He glanced round and saw only two tables were occupied, and that these had already been served. Georgiana was mopping the last of the vacant tables nearby. He said "You know, I think I'll go over to Polly's myself and see how she is. Maybe she thinks I never visit because I don't care!"

Georgiana smiled. "That sounds a swell idea Pop. We're through here."

Can you manage until ten?"

"Sure. Who's going to come in now?"

Ricki held up his hand smiling "I know but...." then they both said together "Don't forget the time Frank Sinatra came in for coffee!"

It was true. It had happened just before Ricki closed up about five years ago. What the Star had been doing in the neighbourhood no one ever knew, but suddenly the door opened and in he came with about four minders. It had since been a joke whenever they thought of closing early.

"See how it goes, anyway" he added, happy now the decision had been made.

"O.K. I'll see you. Go."

Ricki nodded and peeled off his overall, throwing it into a basket under the counter. He said "At least I won't worry about your Mother getting home safe!"

He paused to slip on his jacket which was hanging on a knob just inside the kitchen door. "Think I should call?" he asked, when he was set.

"No." Georgiana shook her head smiling. "Surprise them!"

"That's good. I'll be going then."

"Give Aunt Polly my love."

"I will." Ricki leant forward and gave his daughter a peck on the cheek before adding, "Don't forget. Just close."

Georgiana opened her mouth, but her father grinned and waved away what was coming: "Yeah, yeah, yeah." He gave her a last smile, then pushed open the door leading out into the street.

Once outside, he paused for a moment and took a deep breath. Up-Town the Empire State was lit in contrasting colours, which made it look like a tall wedding cake. From where he was standing it seemed it was just at the end of Thompson Street, but he knew that was because of its gigantic size. In fact, it was over two miles away.

Ricki took another breath, then he walked to the next intersection, and took a left, following Spring Street until he hit Sixth Avenue, where there was an up-town bus. He did not have long to wait, and after throwing his money into the can under the baleful gaze of the driver settled into a window seat just behind him.

The bus was warm, and Ricki was tired. Polly lived up on West 84th. street, so it was quite a ride. It was the first time he had sat down for three hours and soon his eyelids began to droop. He lent forward and tapped the Driver.

"Tell me when we get to eighty-fourth," he demanded. The Driver made a noise in his throat which could have been anything from agreement to a curse so Ricki decided he'd better try and stay awake. A moment later he fell asleep.

He was jerked awake by the Bus pulling up suddenly at a stop. He glanced out of the window and saw they were still in the low Thirties. An experienced New Yorker knows these things instinctively. He saw the stop was close to the entrance of a cheap hotel. The kind that serves the same Clientele as some Motels out in the sticks. He saw a man and a woman come out of the entrance; the man self-satisfied, the woman clinging to his arm and looking up at him adoringly. For a second, the woman's face was in shadow, but he recognised the man instantly as one of the construction workers who regularly came into the Diner. The Bus gave a jerk as it pulled away from the stop. At the same time the couple moved so the shadow no longer hid the woman's face. Ricki stared for a second, then craned his head to look back as the Bus accelerated. It had been his wife, Christine.

He could not have been mistaken! The implications of what he had seen gripped him so he could neither move, nor even breathe. Then, with a cry, he broke free and rose to his feet.

The bus screamed to a halt without pulling in. The Driver recognised a crazy person when he saw one and knew not to argue when Ricki demanded to be let off. The bus had covered more than a hundred yards, even so, and by the time Ricki had run back to the hotel entrance his wife and her lover.... for that was what he must be, had disappeared.

Anger and hurt rose in waves inside him, jostling for top billing. He looked round wildly, then he saw them on the other side of the street, just before they disappeared down the steps of the entrance to a subway station.

The traffic delayed him a few seconds, then it thinned enough to take a chance.

The entrance only served downtown so there could be no doubt which way they had gone. But he fumbled for the right money then grabbed the token and burst through the barrier without waiting for change. Already he could hear the rumble of an approaching train.

The platform was crowded and people started to move back from the edge in anticipation as the train approached. He saw them at the far end of the platform. His wife was looking up at her companion, her eyes shining. How long was it since she had looked at him like that. He saw the man whisper in her ear and she laughed and squeezed him with a lover's intimacy.

The thunder of the approaching train was drowned by the roar of blood pounding in his ears as he started towards them. People who saw him coming shrank out of the way, others got pushed, and the resultant commotion finally alerted them to his charge.

He saw their faces turn to fear as he rushed towards them with a howl of rage that even drowned out the train. His hands reached towards the throat of his wife's lover, but she suddenly stepped in front of him, an action as fatal as it was courageous.

Ricki tried to stop himself. His hands turned up at the last second to try and stop himself crashing into Christine, but it was too late and he collided with her just as the man behind her stepped to one side. In a second they had fallen onto the track and the train passed over them, killing them instantly.

The train was already breaking, hard. It transpired at the inquest that the driver, who had his eyes on the end of the platform, did not even see what happened - which spared him the nightmares suffered by most of those who did.

All was chaos as people reacted in different ways to what had happened. Some screamed, some turned away white faced to vomit, and some craned forward to see if they could see under the train

Christine's companion was forgotten, if he was ever noticed. He turned away with a frightened look on his face, then pushed his way through those who moved forward for a better look.

Once at the back of the crowd, he turned for a moment to look back. Then he hurried away before anyone started asking for witnesses.

At the inquest it was mentioned that there had been a man standing beside the woman who was pushed onto the tracks by her husband, but his identity was not thought worth spending police time establishing, and it never occurred to anyone who knew them, least of all their daughter Georgiana, that the dead couple had been anything but happy with each other.

No there was one exception. Polly, who had been covering for her sister for several months. She had her suspicions of course, but Christine had once done something similar for her while she and her husband Jack were still married, and as Christine had chosen to keep her reasons to herself, Polly had not probed.

She had no need to lie to Georgiana at the Funeral. And after it was all over, the two women never saw each other again.

Paul Adams favoured his petite Mother - the daughter of Old Money from Atlanta, who had never got used to living in New York, even 'though, until her premature death from influenza one particularly hard winter, there had been no hint of the financial difficulties that were to follow.

Paul himself was three inches shorter than his father. He was extremely handsome but with the looks of a good looking schoolgirl: dark, curly hair cut short; small hands and feet, saved by a strong jaw line, he looked almost, but not quite effeminate. He had fallen in love with Georgiana the first time they had met, but she looked younger than she was and it was not until after the funeral of her parents he discovered her true age.

He called at the Diner a few weeks later and was disturbed to see it boarded up. He then hurried round to where he knew she used to live. There was no response to the bell, and after trying unsuccessfully again, several times later, was forced to think she had gone to live somewhere else.

He tried writing, on the pretext of having someone interested in the remaining picture in their possession, intending to pay for it himself as a way of helping her without risk of rebuff. He hoped the letter would be forwarded to the new address, but there was no response. Nor, on the other hand, did he get it back 'return to sender'.

No one in the Brownstone knew where she had gone. The inhabitants seemed to keep themselves to themselves, and the Montes had been no exception. He finally gave up in despair.

In fact, Georgiana had gone to stay with Mary. She stayed with her for four months, then the little money her parents had left her ran out and she had to get a job. At the same time, she decided to move back into her old apartment until she could find something smaller, but it was another three weeks before the Vietnamese woman who lived on the first floor with her family thought to give her Paul's letter which had previously lain on the floor for a month with everyone stepping on it, before she had decided to rescue it and hold it until she saw Georgiana again.

Georgiana rang Paul and left a message with the Secretary. But the same day a letter had arrived from Paris which had turned his world upside down.

As soon as he returned to the Gallery and got her message he called and arranged to meet her within the hour at a coffee shop just around the corner from where she lived. They squeezed into a small booth next to the steamed up window through which they could see the snow still lying on the school playground opposite from a storm three weeks previously.

"So what took you so long?". Georgiana smiled at him as she broke a piece from the danish he had insisted on buying as well as the coffee. He saw she looked thinner, but even more beautiful.

Paul explained how he had tried to contact her and she nodded from time to time, listening carefully, and looking at him over the cup which she held in front of her, while resting her elbows on the table. "And you've really got a buyer for the Tree?" she said, when he paused for a moment.

Yesterday he would have lied. But now everything was different, so after a moment he pulled a face and shook his head slowly.

"I see."

He was relieved she did not look particularly disappointed, or angry.

"You thought I might be broke?"

"Partially. But we wanted to see you. We missed you." Paul paused again, then he added: "You were doing so well. We felt sure you would start painting again."

"I tried." Georgiana shook her head slightly. "I just seem to have lost it. I've heard of writer's block...."

"It can happen. "Paul paused for a moment, then he said: "What you need is a complete change of scenery."

"I've thought about that," Georgiana admitted. "But here, at least, I've got Mary, and one or two others."

Paul looked at her steadily, then he said: "Georgie, I think I'd better level with you."

"Oh!"

"I wanted to come round and see you so many times. But I was afraid you'd think I was sticking my nose in."

Georgiana smiled a little wistfully: "I wish you had," she said.

"I tried eventually. But you were never there."

"No."

"I want to be your friend. But...." he hesitated uncertainly, and Georgiana suddenly reached across the table and squeezed his hand.

"I really can use a friend like you."

"Which makes what I have to say now so hard," he went on miserably. "I got a letter only this morning. From Paris".

"Paris!" Georgiana sat up looking at him."

"I am to renew an offer. And if you accept, it means you will be going away." He hesitated then said quietly "I'm afraid of losing you.... just when I thought, maybe I soodd a chance."

He looked at her, almost pleading, but he saw she was only half listening.

"George Lunas," he heard her say softly. "What makes me still think about him?!"

CHAPTER VI
Paris - Three Months Later

The plane touched down just before four. The sun had already dipped beneath the horizon and it was starting to get dark.

Georgiana emerged from Customs into the arrivals hall at Charles de Gaulle Airport pushing a trolley on which were two bags: the larger, contained her paints, brushes, collapsible easel and stool: the other, all her clothes. She had no make-up and was wearing trainers, jeans, sweater and a woolly hat, which made her look sixteen years old. She looked around at the crowd waiting to greet their friends. She had worked out something cool to say to him in case he brought up the subject of their last meeting, but he was nowhere to be seen.

Georgiana waited with mounting impatience for ten minutes until a dark, rough looking man carrying a piece of cardboard on which the word "Mondes" was unevenly printed in chalk approached her.

"Are you Mondes?" he growled in English with a heavy accent.

Georgiana looked him up and down with surprise, then glanced at the card. "It's Montes," she said. "With a T."

"What is?"

"My name."

"Georgiana?"

"Yes."

Maurice shrugged. "O.K. Follow me. " He dumped the notice in a refuse bin and set off through the crowds without a second glance at such a pace she had to exert herself to keep up with him.

"Where's the fire?" she panted, but he took no further notice until they reached the automatic doors leading to one of the car parks, where he paused for a moment.

"Leave the trolley here," he ordered.

"Are you going to help me, then?" Georgiana demanded, making it clear it was as far as she went otherwise.

"Very well." After a moment's hesitation he picked up the small bag. "This way."

Georgiana opened. her mouth to say something but he had already walked through the doors and they were beginning to close behind him.

"Thanks a bundle!"

Georgiana grabbed the other bag and hurried after him, fearful of getting left behind; a development, she felt would not be too unwelcome as far as he was concerned.

The road between Charles de Gaulle and the centre of Paris has to be the most depressing in France; not made any more welcoming by the fact that all four lanes are so overloaded at the time when most transatlantic ""passengers arrive, the traffic barely moves. Many travellers would gladly turn back at this point and go somewhere more welcoming like Afghanistan or outer Mongolia but for the impossibility of doing so until reaching Paris itself, by which time things had usually started to improve.

Georgiana gazed out of the rear window of the car as it joined the beginning of the buchon, or cork as the french describe their traffic jams. "It looks like the Triboro bridge in the rush hour!" she said disgustedly.

She waited for a second, then glanced in front at the man who was driving. "You don 't talk much, do you?" she demanded.

Maurice shrugged, but glanced at her in the mirror."Vous n'parle francais du tout, Alors!"

Georgiana stifled a yawn. "What?"

"I said, don't you speak any French?"

"Oh." Georgiana brightened a little. "So that's what's wrong!" She paused, looking back at him in the mirror. "Um.... I guess not. But I expect to learn."

"Learn…Good!"

Maurice nodded; and encouraged, Georgiana said : "I speak Spanish 'though. I learned it off my father. Let's see.... Um... La ballena e animal mu' s grande del munda. Did you know that?"

Maurice shook his head, and Georgiana smiled: "No I guess not," he said. Then she saw he was smiling back at her for the first time and before she could speak again, he shot a volley of Moroccan Spanish at her. They laughed for a while as they tried to understand each other 's Spanish, her Puerto Rican being as far from Madrid as his Casablancan. Then he saw her yawn again and suggested she sat back and closed her eyes for a while. She must be tired after her journey. He was about to add that it would also help to pass the time when he saw she was already sound asleep.

Half an hour later Maurice pulled up outside a small hotel in a narrow street in the centre of Paris half onto the pavement so the traffic could still pass. He got out and opened the rear door as an elderly bellhop came out of the front entrance. They both glanced inside the car and saw Georgiana was still asleep.

"Le Jet Lag." Maurice explained and the old man nodded wisely.

"Mais oui. C'est souvent le meme chose!"

Maurice reached inside and shook Georgiana gently by the shoulder.

"Mam'selle. We have arrived!"

Before he could say anything else a portly, middle aged woman came bustling out of the hotel and more or less elbowed the two men to one side.

"Ah….la pauvre!" her face was all compassion as she reached in to wake Georgiana, but then she hesitated and looked over her shoulder.

"But this is only a child! We were expecting a young lady."

Maurice shrugged said defensively.

"I think she is older than she looks," he

"Well, I hope so. We were told she was going to the Conservatoire. We cannot have children staying here by themselves. Not even for Monsieur Lunas!"

The object of her concern suddenly opened her eyes and looked around.

The plump woman beamed. "There…. you are awake!"

"Where are we?"

"Welcome to the Hotel Croix Rouge M'amselle. I am the Housekeeper.

Georgiana sat up. "Oh right. I guess I must've dropped off."

The Housekeeper offered her arm. "Here. Let me help you out."

"No. I'm O.K. Honest. "Georgiana gave her a reassuring smile and climbed out nimbly enough. Meanwhile Maurice took the Bellhop round the back of the car and handed him the two cases from the trunk.

"I'm sure you will be very comfortable here," the housekeeper continued. "Please follow me.... I will take you to your room." But Georgiana hesitated, looking at Maurice who had slammed the truck shut then moved to join them.

"Is Mr Lunas here?" she asked.

Maurice shook his head. "Monsieur Lunas is not in Paris, Mam' selle."

"Oh!" Georgiana' s face dropped.

"I expect you will be contacted by someone from his office."

Georgiana nodded. "I suppose he's very busy," she said.

"Yes, he is." Maurice paused for a moment. The girl suddenly looked small and vulnerable. 'But she would have to get used to it:' he told himself. "Goodbye, then," he offered.

"You're leaving me?" Her blue eyes expanded as she looked at him.

"Of course." He tried not to sound too abrupt. "I have other duties."

Georgiana shrugged a bit helplessly; then held out her hand. "Oh well.... thank you for meeting me, anyway." They solemnly shook hands, then Maurice got into the car, slamming the door behind him.

"Take the young lady's bags to room eleven, Jean," the Housekeeper said in a business-like tone. She sensed the young American girl's disappointment and decided the best thing was to move things along. She turned back to Georgiana as the car drove away and the old man made for the entrance carrying her bags.

"My name is Madame Gilbert," she said with a smile. "You may call me Claudine. "

"Thank you," Georgiana returned her smile and the two women shook hands briefly.

"I'm Georgiana Montes."

The older woman nodded. "Yes, I know." Then she said: "I'm sorry there is no one else here to meet you." She gave a dismissive shrug." Well.... we'll do what we can! This way please."

Madame Gilbert led the way into the Hotel: Georgiana followed.

The Lobby was very small and most of this was filled by the cage of an old fashioned elevator where the bellhop was waiting, holding the iron grill door open.

"The dining room and lounge are on the first floor." the Housekeeper said, as if reading Georgiana's thoughts. She led the way into the elevator and the bellhop pulled the gates closed behind them with a crash. Even with so few of them, there was barely room. For a few seconds nothing happened, then the cage gave a slight shudder before beginning to rise at a pace which gave Georgiana ample time to study the lobby below before it finally passed from view.

No one said anything for a while, as two floors moved sedately by, then Georgiana ventured: "It seems a long way up!"

The Housekeeper smiled. "It only seems so because the elevator takes it's time" she said reassuringly. "The owners put in a faster one, but our regular guests complained it made them feel sick, so they brought back the old one!"

Suddenly the elevator gave a lurch and stopped. "Are we there?" Georgiana asked anxiously peering through the grill into a darkened corridor. In answer to her query the old man pushed the gate open and set off into the darkness carrying the two bags.

"Monsieur Gros thought you would prefer to be on the top floor", the Housekeeper explained as she stepped out of the elevator. Before she followed the bellhop, she pressed an illuminated button on the wall opposite and the corridor was lit by a low watt overhead light, by which it was possible to see the old man had reached a door at the end and was unlocking it, having placed her bags temporarily on the floor.

"Who is Monsieur Gros?" Georgiana asked, following the older woman, who had set off towards the door through which the bellhop and her bags had disappeared.

"Monsieur Gros is Monsieur Lunas' Lawyer. He looks after things when Monsieur Lunas is out of Town."

"It 's very dark" Georgiana said, looking round. "Why did he think I'd want to be up here "

"He thought it would be quieter for you."

"Quiet it is!" Georgiana agreed. They reached the door at the far end in silence. The Housekeeper then pointed to another illuminated wall switch before leading the way inside.

"There is another corridor switch here," she said. "But remember, the lights turn themselves off after thirty seconds."

"What for?"

"Economy, of course. One does not wish to waste electricity. "

"One doesn't?" Georgiana repeated frowning, then she said "I mean, doesn't one?"

"There is plenty of time to reach the elevator."

"Jeepers!"

But Mrs Gilbert was already going through the door.

Following her, Georgiana found herself in a room which seemed huge in comparison to the one she had left behind in New York.

"This is your room," the Housekeeper said, turning to her with a smile.

Georgiana looked round awe-struck. There was a large high double bed and much antique furniture which looked more valuable than comfortable.

"I'm to sleep here?' she said.

The Bellhop put her two bags on the bed, then nodded to Georgiana and left without any hint that he expected a tip. The Housekeeper walked to the far side of the room, opened a door and turned on the lights inside. "The Bathroom," she announced proudly, and glancing inside the brightly lit room, Georgiana could see it was much more modern; but before she could say anything the Housekeeper moved onto the full length shuttered windows, and after pulling the shutters back, flung the windows wide and stepped out onto a narrow balcony beyond. Georgiana followed and stood beside her.

Having slept through the last part of the journey it was her first view of central Paris, and whatever she had been about to say was immediately forgotten. Looking across the rooftops she saw the ground rose to a hill about a mile away on the top of which a floodlit white church presided over the lower buildings surrounding it. Lights also shone from many of the buildings which separated them from the bottom of the hill and from the shops in the streets below. It was not an overpowering view, like the blazing lights of Manhattan Georgiana was used to. Here the lights were more subdued, more secret, but at the same time, more exciting, as any make believe story has the advantage over reality.

As she looked down at the nearer buildings Georgiana could see right into some apartments. There was a woman feeding a child, both of them sitting at a plain, wooden kitchen table, while looking over her shoulder, trying to get some response from the husband who sat with his eyes glued to a television. In the alley immediately below two old women stood gossiping at the entrance to the building opposite. She supposed it was too cold for them to sit outside. And on the second floor of the same building a man in his underwear sat on a bed watching with lustful eyes a woman who was not his wife, and who was wearing a negligee the other would probably not be seen dead in, begin to close the shutters on what would be. Just before they closed the woman chanced to glance up and saw Georgiana looking at her. It was too dark to make out her expression, but for a second the two woman looked at each other in a moment of shared intimacy; sisters in a world where men still made most of the rules. There was no judgement or envy on either side. Just a sudden awareness that had circumstances been different, each could be standing in the place of the other. The woman lent back into the room as she closed the remaining shutter and the spell was broken.

Georgiana raised her eyes once more to the Church at the top of the hill and the Housekeeper, who had been watching her, smiling, said: "Le Sacre Coeur... the Church of the Sacred Heart. The hill is Montmartre, the artists' quarter." She lifted her hand in a gesture encompassing the view. "I think this is why Monsieur Gros wanted you to have this room. It is the only one with such a view. I am sure you will come to love it."

Georgiana turned to her, eyes sparkling, but suddenly the phone on the bedside table inside rang and the Housekeeper turned back into the room to answer it without waiting for the American girl's response. Georgiana let her eyes stray back to the view for a moment, then turned to follow.

"Oui. Yes, she is just her," she heard Madame Gilbert say, before holding the phone out to her. "It is for you," she said. "Monsieur Gros himself!"

Georgiana took the phone from her. For some extraordinary reason she suddenly felt nervous.

"Hello."

"Miss Montes, may I call you Georgiana? Welcome to Paris."

"Thank you."

Gros was a pleasant man in his early fifties with iron grey hair and a neat moustache. He was presently sitting on the end of a long conference table in his shirt sleeves with the remains of a meeting dissolving around him; several men and women packing up and leaving with silent waves so as not to interrupt his conversation.

"I am so sorry I was not able to be at the Airport to meet you." His voice was warm, and he sounded genuinely sorry so that Georgiana was immediately put at ease as he continued: "Unfortunately, my Meeting was scheduled some time ago and I simply could not get away."

"That's O.K." Georgiana smiled, and feeling more relaxed, sat on the edge of the bed.

"I hope Maurice looked after you."

"Yeah. Once we found a language we could both speak!" She heard him chuckle and warmed to him even more.

"I went to sleep in the car before we could say much," she said

"Yes, of course. Le jet lag as we say. Poor French, of course!"

"When will Mr Lunas be back?" Georgiana asked.

"Ah, yes. We are expecting him next month."

"Next month!"

"Yes, when he will most certainly make an appointment with you a top priority." Georgiana swallowed, but before she could say anything she heard him say "Now.... I hope you are not too tired to go out for dinner?"

"I guess not." Despite her disappointment she was reassured by the invitation.

"Splendid. Can you be ready in about an hour?"

"Yeah. I guess so."

"And we can do a little sightseeing?"

"Why not?" That didn't sound right, so she added: "I'd like that."

"Good. My Secretary has booked us a table for dinner on the first floor of the Eiffel Tower. "

"It's not swanky, is it? I don't have anything smart!"

"No, it's not swanky!" She could tell from his voice he was smiling as he added : "As a matter of fact, it will probably be full of tourists, but we will have a nice table and there is a wonderful view. I think you will like it."

"Sounds great!" Suddenly, she was really looking forward to being taken out for dinner to such a place by an elegant Frenchman. (She could tell by his voice he was elegant!")

"In an hour then. I will come to the Hotel. Goodbye until then." Georgiana put down the phone and turned to Madame Gilbert who had been waiting patiently during her conversation.

"I'm being taken out to dinner," she said, eyes shining.

The Housekeeper smiled. "Then I will help you unpack!"

As soon as Gros walked into the small lobby where Georgiana was waiting for him she knew immediately who he was and she had been right. He was elegant!

It was her escort for the evening who got the surprise. The girl had sounded pleasant enough on the phone; but no one had told him anything about her, apart from the fact she was another young artist George had decided to promote and had left him to deal with. Nothing had prepared him for the sensationally beautiful young woman waiting for him, with such blue eyes and thick dark hair piled on top of her head.

He stepped forward to take her hand, realising he was grinning like a complete fool, and as he bent down to brush it with his lips his eyes travelled down the simple scarlet dress she was wearing, which did nothing to hide the youthful proportions of her body. He was prepared to bet - and elegant Frenchman are experts in such matters - that she had fantastic legs; but the length of the dress prevented confirmation of all but a pair of deliciously slim ankles and medium high heels the same colour as her dress. He raised his head to look her in the face and as calmly as he could introduced himself.

Georgiana said: "Hi!" And her smile made him forget for a moment he was still holding her hand. He let it go gracefully and pulled himself together. Whatever the relationship, she was his employer's protégé and one did not take liberties with a man like George Lunas.

"It is very nice to meet you, Georgiana, " he said with as much warmth as he dared.

"And you, Mr…"

"Please…. call me Charles."

Georgiana nodded happily. "It's nice to meet you too, Charles."

"I have the car outside." He glanced round. "But where is your coat? It is a fine evening but it is cold."

"I don't need a coat."

"But I insist. You will catch your death."

He waited while she went up to her room, and eventually reappeared carrying a thick short jacket she had bought in Odd-Jobs on 36th Street at the beginning of the winter. He saw why she had not wanted to bring it, but he stepped forward smiling and took it so that he could help her into it.

"There, that's better," he assured her, when she had slipped into it and was doing up the toggles.

"It's not really suitable to go out in the evening though, she sighed. But Gros would have none of it.

"You look fine," he insisted. "You will take it off when we get there." He turned to open the entrance door for her and soon they were sitting side by side as he drove down to the River Seine and over the Pont au Change before turning right into the Express way which took them down the left bank of the river.

Gros pointed to places of interest on the way. It was obvious few of the things he mentioned meant anything to her, but he saw her eyes wide with interest as she took in the cafes and bars, the shop windows and the passers-by, so he fell silent, and let her absorb it all undisturbed.

He glanced at her from time to time. She needn't have worried about the coat. He knew many women who could afford to be dressed by Yves St. Laurent, or any of the top fashion houses, would have given their eye teeth to look like the girl beside him. Unconsciously echoing a thought expressed by John Adams over a year ago he wondered what she was doing as a struggling artist when she could so obviously earn a fortune as a model.

The floodlit Eiffel Tower rose up before them from the Field of Mars like a gigantic rocket on its pad waiting for lift-off. Gros took a left and eventually parked close to one of the feet where the ticket office was located.

Although, seen from a distance, the first floor of the Tower seems no height at all, it is sufficient to give a bird 's eye view of the City, and once they had been settled in the Restaurant at a table next to one of the windows Gros was able to entertain her by pointing out the main Boulevards; Notre Dame Cathedral and The Arc de Triomphe, which she had heard of, as well as Montmartre, with the Sacre Coeur on the top which Madame Gilbert had pointed out to her earlier.

The Restaurant was full. The waiters moved between the tables, and in one corner a small combo played cool Gershwin. Eventually, Georgiana sighed contentedly and put down her fork.

"Well.... even if the food is lousy the view is wonderful!"

Gros smiled. "I didn't say it was lousy," he protested mildly. "I just said it wasn't swanky!"

"Whatever. I guess I'm just not into eating things I used to feed in Central Park."

Gros nodded. "The Duck a l'orange was a little dry. More wine?" He nodded at a waiter who hurried forward to fill their glasses.

"Sure. Why not?" Georgiana watched the waiter for a second. Then she said: "I don't suppose I'll be eating like this when I'm on my own." She picked up the refilled glass and took a healthy swig.

Gros said. "I don't think you'll starve on the allowance Monsieur Lunas has arranged for you." He paused for a moment to take a sip from his own glass, before adding frankly. "Besides, with looks like yours Georgiana, I'm sure you 'll be getting plenty of invitations."

Georgiana grinned. "Are you being what the French call 'gallant'" she demanded, but Gros shook his head.

"Certainly not. I'm simply stating the obvious. You are an extremely beautiful young woman, and there is nothing French men of any age enjoy more than the company of someone like you."

Georgiana looked at him coolly. "Does that apply to you?" she asked.

"I did say, of any age Georgiana."

"But not the exalted Mr. Lunas, it would seem. By the way, did I tell you, the only time we met we ended up shouting at each other?"

But Gros was not listening. "Why should you say that?" he demanded.

Georgiana shrugged "Well.... I did think he would be here when I arrived," she said.

Gros paused for a moment, looking at her. "Why do you think Monsieur Lunas offered to pay for you?" he said eventually.

"Well …. I know what he said" Georgiana said, suddenly defensive. "Or rather, what he told Paul. "

Gros said: "There is nothing George Lunas loves more than great painting. He has helped many young artists over the years. It just so happens you are the first female he has found with what he considers to be sufficient potential."

Georgiana digested this for a moment in silence. Then she said: "Has he paid for anyone to come from America before?"

Gros shook his head. "I don't know," he admitted. "I've only been with him five years."

Georgiana nodded. Then she said: "Tell me more about him?"

Gros thought for a moment. "He loves art for art's sake," He said. "But because of an extraordinary ability to spot gold amongst the rubbish he has also made a great deal of money."

Georgiana thought about this. Then she said: "Does he hope to make money out of me?"

"I'm sure that is not his present concern." Gros smiled in spite of himself.

"Then what is his main concern?" Georgiana asked sweetly, "Getting into my pants?"

If she expected to shock her companion she was disappointed. "You'll have to wait and find out, won't you," Gros said calmly.

"Some interest would be better than none!"

Gros paused, looking at her. Then he said: "You are quite upset because he was not here to meet you."

"Yeah. I guess I was kind of expecting it."

"He will be sorry to hear that."

"No, please. Don't say anything," Georgiana said quickly.

Gros smiled. "You may rely on me," he said.

But Georgiana looked at him, suddenly serious. "May I Charles?" She paused for a moment, then went on: "I've got a feeling, one day I might need a friend."

Gros looked at her frowning: "Why should you say something like that?" he said. "I would love to be in your shoes." He grinned suddenly. "In the sense that you are young, talented and about to be discovered by the most exciting city in the world."

He saw her relax again.

"Yeah that's true!" They looked at each other, and once more he got the feeling that if he wasn't careful he would forget he was only a stand-in for the evening. He glanced round the room, then back at their table.

"Would you like some desert?" he suggested. But Georgiana shook her head.

"I don't think so." I guess I'm not as hungry as I thought. "

Gros nodded. "Then let's get out of here. Perhaps a little sight-seeing if you're not too tired?"

They drove back across the river to the Place Trocadero where Gros parked the car for a moment at the top of the steps so she could look back across the Field of Mars for the best view of the Tower. He pointed to the lights twinkling on the first stage from the Restaurant they had just left. Then they got back into the car and he drove up the Avenue Kieber and round the Arc de Triomphe before cruising down the Champs Elysees to the Place de la Concorde and along the Rue de Rivoli beside the Tuileries Gardens to the Palais Royal, which he explained to her were respectively the front garden and town house of the French Kings, before Madame Guillotine collected their heads in a basket and they installed the World' s most famous art collection instead - since which it has been known as the Louvre!

His style was light, and Gros could see that she was interested. But once or twice he caught her eye lids drooping and decided to cut the tour short.... stopping only at one last place - she had already told him she was determined to visit.

He parked the car as close as possible to the white floodlit Church at the top of the hill. Georgiana tucked her arm in his as they walked up the path to the front entrance. He opened the side door for her, then they stood in silence just inside.

The interior of the Church was dimly lit except by the Altar where two enormous candles burned, and a rack of smaller candles offered by petitioners illuminated an alcove. Music from a hidden source played softly.

Suddenly Georgiana stepped towards the rack of candles, and after putting some money in the box took a new candle and lit it from one of the others. Gros watched with some surprise as after standing still for a moment, she placed the candle in a holder to join the others, then crossed herself and knelt on one of the nearby prayer stools.

After a while she rose to her feet, then came back to him smiling shyly and said softly. "Thank you for bringing me here."

Outside, Gros steered her past the waiting car to a stone balustrade at the edge of a terrace on the side of the hill from which a long flight of steps led down from Montmartre to Pigale at the bottom. From here they could see in the distance all the places they had driven past and, not so far away, he pointed out to her the Hotel where she was staying.

Georgiana leant against the balustrade, then she took a deep breath and turned to the man beside her. "It's quite beautiful," she breathed. "It's how I imagined Paris would be. You can 't imagine how disappointed I was when we drove in from the airport!"

Gros nodded. "There is very little new here that one can admire, he said. Perhaps, the rebuilt quarter of the Clock Makers, not far from your hotel."

"They said that about the Eiffel Tower."

"That is ugly. It's just that we've got used to it." He paused for a moment before continuing, "That is the trouble with bad taste: if you aren't careful, you do get used to it; then, suddenly, you 're surrounded! " He glanced back at the view. "Fortunately, the old City Centre is heavily protected. But not even that is sacrosanct. They put a pyramid of glass right in the middle of the Louvre. If they can do that, they can do anything!"

"But you should be glad that so much has been preserved. In New York, nothing lasts more than a few years!"

They smiled at each other, then he saw her suppress another yawn.

"Come on," he put his hand on her arm. "I should take you back. Don't forget, tomorrow you start your French language lessons."

Georgiana pulled a face. "He thought of everything!"

"No. As a matter of fact the lessons were my idea."

"I see. Well, I'll wait to see how I get on before I thank you!" They turned and started to walk back to the car.

"Maurice says you speak Spanish?"

"My father was Puerto Rican."

"Was?"

"He was killed."

Gros glanced at her. Her face was impassive but he decided not to pursue the matter and reverted to their previous topic of conversation. "You'll find it a help. You have five months until the Conservatoire begins the new Academic Year. You should have all the time in the world.

CHAPTER VII

The following morning Georgiana woke up in the huge bed and found herself staring at the ceiling, wondering where she was. Then it all came back to her and for a few moments she felt a pang of homesickness.

But what was there now for her at 'home'? Mary, it was true. She missed her already. But not much else. She had to learn to live within herself, and for her work. That was what mattered now.

So....they thought they were going to teach her how to paint! Well, we will see. But at least she would be free to paint without having to worry about earning her living, and there was no doubt Paris was a beautiful place to see if she really could begin again.

By association Georgiana found herself thinking about George Lunas again. So, she wasn't that important to him. One of many he had helped in the past; certainly not worth putting himself out enough to be there when she arrived! Suddenly Georgiana almost hated him. What made him think he could patronise her! That she would come running if he gave her another chance!

But that was exactly what she had done.

She wondered how much he knew about what had happened back in New York. Paul had never said anything. Was it coincidence he renewed his offer when he did? Did he simply feel sorry for her? Either way, she knew she had grabbed the chance with both hands.... like someone drowning.

Well there was one way she could assert her independence and that was to show him : that she was one in a million, and far from having to feel grateful to him, he would be grateful for the reflected glory of having been lucky enough to have given a hand for a short time to the greatest artist ever to have come out of the United States of America!

Feeling a lot better, Georgiana jumped out of bed, and having dressed she ventured down-stairs in search of breakfast.

Madame Gilbert had offered to show her the way to where the Language Professor lived. As they walked the maze of narrow streets together Georgiana realised it was just as well as she would never have found the house by herself.

Eventually, Madame Gilbert stopped in front of a door beside an antique shop, and knocked, using the old iron knocker that looked as if it was about to fall off the door. She then pointed to a small plaque which read 11 Francois Vlamertynge Etudes Anglais.

The door was opened by a severe looking young woman. Madame Gilbert spoke to her in French and the woman nodded then stood back so that Georgiana could enter - still without the trace of a smile.

Georgiana thanked her guide, then stepped inside. The woman closed the door behind her, then led Georgiana down a narrow, poorly lit corridor which smelt vaguely of urine; past several rooms, one of which was a kitchen from which two half dressed young children - probably the source of the smell - stared at her with saucer eyes from the wooden table where they were eating large hunks of bread.

She eventually stopped at a door at the back of the house and knocked, but she opened it without waiting and ushered Georgiana inside, barely giving her time to do so before shutting the door firmly behind her.

Georgiana found herself facing a tall pale man in his late twenties who had obviously tried to make himself look older by growing a beard. He walked around his desk smiling, and held out his hand. "Miss Montes.... welcome to Paris, and to our little establishment. I am Professor Vlamertynge. "

He spoke with an English Accent, and after she said: "Hi," and they had shaken hands a little formally, he invited her to sit on one of several plain upright wooden chairs which were dotted around the room.

Georgiana did so, and while he was perching on a similar chair facing her, she glanced round curiously. This was a much lighter room. The window overlooked a small courtyard at the back of the house which was bathed in sunshine. Apart from the desk and the chairs there was no other furniture, but the walls were lined with books, except to the left of the desk where there was a large blackboard.

Once seated, they looked at each other smiling in silence for a few moments. During this Georgiana noted that his efforts to acquire some maturity had left him looking a bit seedy due to the uneven quality of his beard.

The Professor cleared his throat and began with studied cheerfulness. "Well, I must admit that I normally teach adult French students English, so it is going to be a novelty for me to teach an American young lady French."

"Not as much as for me to be taught" Georgiana said smiling, trying to put him at ease.

"Ah, yes. Quite!"

"And you can start by calling me Georgie."

"Well, thank you." Obviously he did not understand she expected him to respond in kind and continued: "Now, I understand we have until September to prepare you for the Conservatoire?"

Georgiana nodded: "I don 't know if anything is going to do that Prof, but you can teach me French anyway!"

He looked at her for a second with a vague frown before realising this was a joke.

"Ah.... yes! Well, I will do my best."

And he did.

As the Spring turned to early summer, Georgiana divided her spare time between rediscovering her painting which she soon realised had somehow acquired a greater intensity; possibly, for having been left fallow for so long - and exploring Paris.

She browsed the book-shops and bird sellers alongside the Seine, and discovered the very bridge under which Gene Kelly was supposed to have danced with Leslie Caron and sang 'It's very clear, our love is here to stay!' She learned to dodge the traffic like a native; gazed at Notre Dame and walked in the Tuillerie Gardens returning the open smiles of girls her own age as they caught her looking at them between their lovers' kisses.

She discovered the delight of the pavement cafes frequented by students and other young artists, and as her French improved started to join in their conversations.

Charles Gros took her to the Bank where an Account had been opened for her and introduced her to the assistant manager. He took her out to dinner from time to time and noticed, after a while, she ceased to ask him about her still absent Patron - which saved him having to tell lies, because Lunas had returned to Paris a month after Georgiana arrived and had made several trips and returned again since. But whenever Gros suggested that his Employer really should take the trouble to go and see his young protégé, there always seemed some perfectly good reason why he could not yet spare the time.

Gros also noticed that as the summer progressed, and Georgiana 's skin turned the colour of light honey with her being outside so much, she not only became even more beautiful, if that was possible, but looked more and more like a young French girl and less like an American. He decided he had definitely fallen in love with her, although it was a love he was quite happy to enjoy at a distance. But he was certainly glad Lunas' neglect gave him an excuse to see her more frequently.

Setting up her easel in any number of places, Georgiana soon found that here, more than at home, people stopped to admire or comment on what she was doing, and she gradually learned to relax, and even enjoy these interludes in a way she had found difficult before.

As the French lessons continued, she became more confident' the Professor, more longing, and the Professor's wife, more suspicious.

Eventually, unable to resist any longer, he reached forward one day and grasped her hand passionately to declare his love. Georgiana retrieved her hand firmly, but gently and turned to leave. She realised lessons were over. But it was already September.

Joining the throng of students, Georgiana walked up the steps and through the grand entrance of the Conservatoire looking more confident than she felt. Immediately inside was a vast lobby which reminded her of Grand Central Station, complete with wide marble staircase, except that those who hurried up and down with tense expressions weren't rushing to catch trains but find the right lecture hall in this Labyrinth.

She stopped for a moment, looking round. Then she took a breath and was about to ask a girl the way to Registration when a tall young man came up to her with a smile and offered to guide her to the appropriate desk at the end of the corridor which stretched the entire length of the building and from which seemingly endless doors opened into any number of lecture halls and studios. He bade her farewell as soon as he was sure she was all right, but the pleasant faced middle-aged woman who confirmed her enrolment and gave her an identification badge and locker key insisted on conducting her upstairs to the first year lecture hall, which this morning, according to the notice on an easel outside, was to be presided over by a Professor Albert.

Georgiana found herself in a large room with chairs arranged in concentric semi circles facing a raised dais on which was a large easel, currently empty. The chairs were spaced sufficiently far apart to make room for an easel and working space in front of each student, but these presently pushed to one side so that the students, most of whom had already taken their places, had a clear view of the dais. The room seemed to have filled up from the back, so the remaining seats were in the front three rows, and Georgiana was compelled to take one of these.

There was barely time to look around when Toulouse-Lautec entered from the side - evidently having grown normal sized legs since he last frequented the Moulin Rouge. Georgiana concluded this could only be the Professor and had to suppress a sudden urge to giggle - which was as well as he stood not ten feet from her, looking round quizzically.

Ordinary conversation faded, to be replaced by a buzz of excitement to Georgiana's left and she saw the Professor glance in that direction and his smile widen in recognition before nodding and turning back to the rest of his audience. He cleared his throat and began to speak in a surprisingly high voice

"Good morning, Ladies and Gentlemen. I thought I recognised some of you." He pointed at a young woman sitting on a seat in the second row. "You were at my Summer School in Barbizon if I am not mistaken," he said pleasantly.

"Yes, Professor." The girl simpered and Georgiana looked away in disgust.

"Madamoiselle Milau, if I am not mistaken. "

"Yes, Professor."

Georgiana glanced back at her then saw Albert bearing down upon her out of the corner of her eye. "Well, well," he said stopping opposite her and adopting an expression of mock surprise. "A foreign visitor, if I am not mistaken!"

Georgiana forced a smile.

"I see" the Professor continued. "And to what do we owe this pleasure?"

Georgiana took a breath, then she answered as pleasantly as she could. "I'm not sure if it's going to be a pleasure, Professor, for either of us."

"Ah!."

She could see he was offended, so not wishing to make an enemy this early continued sweetly: "I'm here to learn, best I can. Same as everyone else, I guess."

He nodded solemnly, then straightened up. "Well.... let us hope your expectations will not be disappointed."

"Right!" Georgiana nodded and smiled as if he had made a really witty remark and this enabled Albert to make good his escape to the centre of the room."

"Now then," he began again, addressing the room in general, "all of you have been sent here because someone thought you talented enough to benefit from this, the greatest Conservatoire of Art in the World. Here, we will assume you are proficient in perspective, the use of light and shade, and so on. But before we start to build on those qualities we shall look back at the past to try and see what it is that makes a promising artist a great one. And in the course of this you may well want to re examine the basis of some of your own work". He paused for a moment, looking around. "Are there any questions?"

His audience looked at each other for a moment, but only one spoke.

"I don't want to paint like other people.... no matter how good they were," Georgiana said. But Albert only half heard and turned to her.

"What was that?"

Georgiana shrugged. "Nothing, I guess." The Professor took a few steps to stand again in front of her.

"No.... what was your question? Don't be afraid. We are all friends here!" He beamed round and one or two chuckled. "Please...?"

"Well.... I was hoping to learn to do what I want to do better. I thought that was the idea."

"Of course." Albert nodded. "But first we must make sure we are building on sure foundations."

Georgiana looked at him, but decided she'd said enough and after a moment he nodded as if the matter was settled and turned back to the others. "We are so fortunate that, within two kilometres of here are the most comprehensive collections of art and painting in the World. And it will be my privilege, and of my colleagues, to introduce you to the greatest Masters who ever lived. Some of whom will be familiar to you; particularly, those who attended my summer school." Albert allowed himself a modest smile before continuing: "But some you may not know... perhaps, because their output was small for one reason or another, or in some instances, because most of their work was destroyed leaving only a few brilliant masterpieces to remind us just what the world has lost."

It was nearly five o'clock in the afternoon before Georgiana joined the throng of students as they poured out of the main entrance of the Conservatoire and crossed the Courtyard before disbursing into the narrow streets and alleys surrounding the building. She was lost in thought until she became aware that someone had fallen into step beside her, and glanced up to see the tall young man who had helped her earlier. She gave him a smile.

"You don't look very happy!" he said gently.

Georgiana pulled a face. "Well…so far we have been told they are going to try and make us paint like everyone else. We've had one lecture on anatomy and even longer one on the art of the thirteenth Century! "

The young man shrugged. "Well, I don't know about the last, but you know Leonardo used to sneak into mortuaries when he was a young man to watch the medical students dissecting corpses. He felt it was only if he knew exactly how the body was constructed he could draw it properly."

Georgiana saw they had reached the gateway which led out into the street. "Well, thank you for that. I have to go now." She began to turn away but the young man put out his hand.

"Wait.... please. We haven't introduced ourselves."

She turned back and took the hand he held out to her. "My name is Jules," he said. Jules Lavosin."

"Georgiana Montes," Georgiana responded, and they shook hands until he let go of her hand and smiled broadly.

"Now we have met, come and have some coffee or tea if you prefer. Meet some of the other students."

Georgiana looked doubtful, but his smile was dazzling. "Come on, We' re all in the same boat!"

She looked at him again, then chuckled. "All right, then."

"Splendid". He took her arm confidently, and began to steer her down the street which led away to the right of where they were standing. "I am from Belgium," he told her. "And you are from New York."

"How do you know that?" Georgiana said, loosening her arm.

"I asked the Registrar if I could look at your form."

Georgiana frowned. "You 've got a nerve telling me something like that!" But her companion shrugged, unabashed.

"You can look at mine if you want to. Or ask me. I'll tell you everything."

"I don't know I want to know you now." Georgiana complained with more severity than she felt and she saw his face fall.

"But I had to find out about you before everyone else." he said simply.

"Why?"

"You know why. Because you are by far the most beautiful girl I have ever seen in my life!"

"Nonsense!"

But he saw she had forgiven him and started to tell her about their fellow students until they reached the corner of a small square on the opposite side of which was a cafe with tables outside already crammed with a chattering crowd of their contemporaries.

"How come you know so much about everyone if you come from Belgium?" Georgiana asked as they crossed the Square.

"I went to Professor Albert's Summer School."

"Did you learn anything?"

"I improved my French!" I come from the Flemish region.

When they reached the tables, further conversation was suspended while he introduced her to three girls sitting at one of the nearer tables. They greeted her warmly enough, but then turned back to their friends, her presence forgotten. 'Which is 0.K.' Georgiana consoled herself. 'She couldn 't remember their names anyway a second or so later, and she wasn' t at all sure her French was good enough yet to join in their fragmented conversations which seemed to be conducted at amazing speed.'

Jules guided her to a small table further on, and after a waiter had banged down two coffees on the table in front of them without waiting to be asked, she turned to him and said: "That's what I was doing."

"You were at summer school? Not in Barbizon. I would have noticed you!"

Georgiana smiled. "No. Learning French. My teacher was very good. Of course, it helped living here all summer."

"Did you speak any French before?" Georgiana shook her head, so he continued: "That's amazing! Of course, you have a bit of an accent, but it's charming!"

Georgiana picked up her coffee and took a sip, but it was black and so hot it burned her lips so she put it down again quickly, aware Jules was watching her.

"How was Barbizon?" she asked. "Now, that's somewhere I have heard of!".

"It's in the middle of Fontainbleau forest; about fifty miles from here."

"I'd love to go there."

"You can get a bus" Jules said, then brightened, "We could go together. "

Georgiana avoided the question by risking her lips once again to the coffee. "Tell me about you," she said a moment later, before he could pursue the matter. "Why did you come here?"

Jules grinned. "You don't want the story of my life?"

"The short version. "

"Well.... you know I come from Belgium." Georgiana nodded.

"My father died when I was quite young. But my mother was a good portrait painter, and her commissions, plus the salary she received from the college at Bruges as a teacher enabled her to feed us all until we were old enough to look after ourselves. "

"You say all?"

Jules nodded. "I am the youngest. I have an elder sister and two brothers. When my mother retired from teaching recently they offered me the position."

"So why aren't you teaching?" Georgiana asked.

"There was an exhibition to which I contributed which was visited by the wife of the Minister of Education. She liked my work and spoke to her husband. So one day, through the post, came a letter from the Ministry offering me a bursary to come here."

"What about the College?"

Jules grinned. "I think they were so flattered that one of their junior staff had caught some attention they agreed to give me a year off on full pay. "

"That's wonderful" Georgiana said sincerely. "So that's your real interest is it, portraiture?

Jules nodded. "Very much so." He hesitated, then said seriously: "I would consider it a great honour if you would allow me to paint you one day."

"We'll see," Georgiana said noncommittally. Meanwhile we have our education to attend to."

Jules looked at her, surprised. "You don't sound very keen," he said

Georgiana pulled a face. "I don't know. Until today I was really looking forward to being here. I loved my summer in Paris, but now I'm not so sure.

Chapter VIII

The weeks which followed confirmed Georgiana 's worst fears. She attended numerous lectures which seemed to have no bearing on her own work. She traipsed round dark galleries in a column with her fellow students while Professor Albert held forth, principally on artists of the classical period and only very occasionally on the Impressionists, he r real interest - never on anyone later. The rest of the time was spent in various studios in the Conservatoire sketching innumerable naked and unattractive old models.

She confided her frustration to Charles Gros during one of their lunches together, but he advised her to stick it out. Things could only get better! And under the influence of the two bottles of wine he had ordered, anything seemed possible. But a few days later she decided it was make or break time, and went to work.

Two weeks later, after most of the students had already gone inside Georgiana walked through the front entrance of the Conservatoire carrying a canvas picture holder. She found Jules waiting anxiously for her.

"There you are Georgiana," he said moving towards her. "I was wondering what had happened."

"You shouldn't have waited," she remonstrated.

"What's that you're carrying?" he asked, as they fell in step on their way to the lecture hall.

"This?" Georgiana glanced down briefly. "This is the fourth of July!"

"Fourth of July! What is this fourth of July?"

"Independence Day!"

He looked at her and saw an expression on her face he had never seen before. He was suddenly filled with foreboding. "What are you going to do?" He slowed for a moment, but Georgiana marched on, pushing open the double swing doors at the back of the lecture hall with such energy Jules, just behind her, had to hold out both hands to prevent himself being felled by the return swing.

In the middle of the room was the usual naked male model and round him were clustered the easels of the students who were just beginning to sketch while Albert moved from one to the other, breathing suggestions. After exchanging a brief glance with him, Georgiana walked to a vacant easel a little removed from the rest and began to take a picture out of the holder while Jules slipped unobtrusively into a vacant place on the other side of the room, but with his eyes still on her.

Albert walked across just as she was putting the picture on the easel. "You are late, mam'selle! What is this?"

"I'm just about to show you, Professor." Geogiana's tone was controlled. She did not want to spoil the point she was about to make by antagonising him unnecessarily.

The picture she placed on the easel was a pastel on cardboard - a view of the Pont Neuf and Right Bank from the perspective of the Isle de la Cite and Notre Dame Cathedral in the middle of the river. She had done the original sketch a month previously and had spent the past two weeks working it up into the form now presented for his inspection.

In the picture there was no traffic or pedestrians in sight. It was not dawn the only time one might expect to see it so deserted, but that moment which occurs in the Cinema sometimes when a frozen frame is just about to burst into motion and the empty streets flood with life. Looking at it under Albert's scrutiny, Georgiana knew it was good or she would not have brought it in the first place. The one thing she had absolute confidence in was her judgement of her own work.

Everyone joined Jules in craning their necks to see Georgiana's picture, and even the old model slipped on his robe to take a look. "You see Monsieur," Georgiana said after a few seconds while they looked at it in silence, "this is the kind of work I want to do - the work I know how to do," she corrected herself. "And I would like you to teach me how to express my ideas better... but in my own style." She looked at him directly now. "I thought that was why I had been sent here. Not to go back and relearn some of the things I left behind when I was fifteen."

Albert tore his eyes away from the easel to look at her. For some reason he felt suddenly uncomfortable. But after taking a breath he recovered his composure. "Yes.... I see. Very well. " Suddenly he reached forward and picked up the picture. "If you would permit me...." Before Georgiana could say anything he had made his way to the low dais and put the picture on the empty easel which was standing there. He then turned to the class.

"Ladies and Gentlemen.... I apologise for this interruption, but Mademoiselle Montes has given us all the opportunity to learn something. I hope you can all see?" Georgiana looked round and saw she was blocking the view of some of those at the back, so she sank into a vacant chair.

Albert cleared his throat, then continued : "The famous Chef, Escoffier would never allow his pupils to try anything else until they mastered the art of making perfect mashed potatoes."

"What the shit's he on about now?" Georgiana muttered to herself not so loud Albert could here, but enough to draw the disapproving glances of those close to her.

"The reason is simple," the Professor continued. "To make really good mash potatoes you must try, and try again. You will possibly have many failures, and may become discouraged. And only those will succeed in the end who have the patience and subtlety to learn that to prepare the simplest dish takes as much skill and care as the most complicated. "

He glanced briefly at Georgiana. "And so it is that we at the Conservatoire require our pupils to learn that most basic skill in art - drawing, and to do it really well, for the same reason.

He looked at Georgiana again and continued not unkindly. "It is not to humiliate you that we need to satisfy ourselves that you are masters of that most basic skill, but, as with great cooking, to make sure that what follows is built on a sure foundation."

He turned to the rest of the class and Georgiana noticed that one or two were grinning as if they knew what was coming next. "Let us consider what happens when this is not the case," Albert moved closer to the picture so he could point.

"Consider the whole composition: first, it is true that its constituent parts are not badly drawn, although this area ", he reached forward, "shows signs of carelessness. But their relationship to each other is unrealistic and fails to communicate the reality of the subject.... with which most of us here are familiar, and can therefore judge with some authority."

Several members of his audience nodded as he pointed again "Take this building here, for example on the opposite bank river. I know for a fact it is smaller than the one next to it, and they certainly do not have these contrasting colours."

Georgiana opened her mouth to say something, but thought better of it and hugged herself to try and stay calm.

"But most particularly, " Albert went on in the raised voice, that she had always found irritating, "the Artist" he deliberately put the words in quotes for sarcasm, "has forgotten the most basic rule of any picture in that it has no focus. The eye wonders all over the frame looking for somewhere to rest; and, finding none, turns away with lack of interest". He allowed himself a brief chuckle. "Rather like those holiday snaps you see of a distant view… so breath-taking in reality, so lacking in reproduction!"

Again, one or two students sniggered in appreciation. "No, Ladies & Gentlemen," Albert continued becoming serious again and drawing himself to his full height. "Like lumpy mashed potatoes there is only one thing to do.... " he suddenly reached forward, and removing the pastel from the easel, tore it in half before finishing his,sentence " and start again." He turned and dropped the two halves of Georgiana's picture into the nearest waste paper basket.

This time no one was laughing, because while his back was turned they all saw Georgiana rising to her feet, her face a mask of fury.

"You fucking bastard!" she screamed at him. And by the time he turned back quickly in surprise she was upon him. Albert 's mouth sagged as he saw her lash out at him catching his cheek solidly with the palm of her hand, before bending down quickly to retrieve the two halves of her picture. Catching him off balance, the Professor staggered backwards knocking easels right and left before finally falling onto the couch recently occupied by the model.

Most of the onlookers were paralysed with shock. Only Jules moved forward to her side, but she took no notice of him, and having picked up her canvas bag, marched to the door by the most direct route, scattering students and their easels indiscriminately until she reached the door, where she paused for a final shot.

"And you can all go and screw yourselves!"

Back at the Hotel, Georgiana was so preoccupied with flinging her clothes furiously into the two suitcases on the bed she did not hear the knock on the door. But when she saw it open out of the corner of her eye, she swung round to face whoever it was, then froze, her eyes wide with surprise.

"What are you doing?" Lunas asked, glancing round the room.

Georgiana straightened up and stared back at him. "I was wondering when you'd show up!" she said bitterly.

"I apologise. " He took two paces into the room. "I meant to come before. I hope Charles explained?"

"Oh sure... he explained", Georgiana said throwing the socks still in her hands into a case. "Every month!"

"May I come in?"

"Why not. You're paying for it."

Lunas turned and closed the door behind him.

"Look, there's nothing you can do or say," Georgiana said as he turned back to face her "It's too late."

"Too late for what?" he asked mildly.

"Anything." There was a note of desperation in her voice. "I hate this place and I want to go home." She picked up a bra and flung it in after the socks.

"Aren't you being a little childish?"

Georgiana swung round to face him again. "I don't want to fight with you again."

Lunas smiled for the first time. "Me neither. May I sit down?"

Georgiana shrugged and he sat on the arm of one of the easy chairs. " I understood," he continued, "that until recently you were happy and enjoying yourself?"

She looked at him again then suddenly flopped miserably on the edge of the bed. "It's true," she said staring at the floor. Then she looked back at him. "I'm only sorry I haven't seen you before to thank you."

"I think we've already agreed, that was my fault."

Georgiana took a deep breath, then she said. "Everything was great until I started school." After a moment, she stood up and went to the open window to look out across the roof tops for before turning to face him. "It's no use," she said as calmly as she could. "I don't understand what they're trying to do. I only know it's no good for me. " She shrugged helplessly."The guy who's supposed to be teaching is a weirdo! All he does is talk about mashed potatoes and tear up people 's pictures!"

She looked so forlorn he ached to comfort her, but unable to help himself he threw back his head and laughed.

Georgiana' s expression changed at once and she stamped her foot in anger. "It's all right for you. It wasn't your frigging picture he tore up!"

Lunas took a handkerchief out of his pocket and wiped his eyes, trying to contain himself. "I'm sorry!" he gasped.

"Stop it, you bastard! Stop laughing at me." Despite her words, he saw her mouth had twisted into a half smile, but a moment later her face contorted and she flung up her hands to cover her face as she burst into tears.

Lunas was on his feet in an instant. He moved to her and put his hand on her arm. "Georgie, I'm sorry. Please forgive me. I was not laughing at you. It was just the image your words conjured up."

He paused for a moment, then he said: "Look, I've been to the School. I know what happened. "

She shook her head without removing her hands from in her face. "It was horrible," she mumbled. "They all hate me there."

"But it's not true."

"Yes, it is."

"Here " he took her gently into his arms and she rested her head on his shoulder while he stroked her hair.

"Don't say any more," he soothed. "I promise." It will be all right.

He felt her tears wet against his cheek as she shook her head slightly. "It's no use," she mumbled. "I've blown it. They wouldn't take me back now. Not even you could not make them."

Lunas held her away so they could look at each other. "Possibly" he said with a smile. "But it was not necessary."

"What?"

He held up the handkerchief he was still holding. "Here. It is your turn."

"Thank you." She took it and dabbed her eyes. He thought she looked about fourteen... but so perfect his heart gave a lurch.

"What do you mean, it wasn't necessary?" she said, pausing to look at him.

Lunas shrugged. "By the time I got there it was all over. The students thought you would be asked to leave, so they sent a delegation to the Principal to say that if you left, they would all go with you!"

He saw her eyes widen with amazement, and he took her hand and made her sit beside him on the bed.

"What happened?" Georgiana asked.

"They told him exactly what happened. How the Professor had gone out of his way to humiliate you, and had then torn up your work."

Georgiana shook her head in wonder. "But I thought they all disliked me," she said.

Lunas' smile broadened: "Evidently not. Don't forget, these things take longer here. Anyway, being France, there was a lengthy discussion.... negotiations, and it was eventually agreed that in class tomorrow the Professor would apologise to you for his behaviour.... we all like giving a performance, but he got carried away!"

"He certainly did that," Georgiana nodded and Lunas was pleased to see her begin to smile.

"... and you will apologise for hitting him," he concluded.

Georgiana accepted this with a shrug. Then she said: "Then what?"

"Then everything will be as it was before. He is, I understand, an excellent teacher."

"Oh no." Georgiana let go of his hand and stood up to face him. "I'm not going back to something I left behind four years ago. I want to go forward."

"And you will." Lunas held out his hand again. "Here, please, sit down again." After a moment 's hesitation, Georgiana did so, only slightly further away.

"Thank you." Lunas paused for a moment, then he said "Look.... I spoke to both the Principal and Professor Albert. They both think highly of you."

"Sez you!" Georgiana responded quickly, but he persisted:

"Then I will tell you something you must not repeat. The students in your class represent the most promising in the whole of France. Academies and Schools in the Provinces vie with each other to get their best pupils admitted. But of the thirty in your class, it is felt evidently that only you, and possibly two others have it in you to go on to become really great artists."

"They said that?!"

"On my word of honour."

"Then why do they treat us like children?" Georgiana protested.

"It's still early days." Lunas got up and stood looking down at her. "The course lasts one year. So, the first two months they start making sure there are no fundamental flaws in your technique. Of course, no amount of technique will make you a great artist. For that you have to be born with that rare something that lifts the merely talented to greatness. But no matter which direction your talent takes you, a really sound technique can only help you reach whatever goal you have set for yourself more effectively." He suddenly smiled. "But enough of this. The sun is still shining, and I have been cooped up in the office all day. I would like to walk for a while. Will you come with me?"

While he had been talking Georgiana had felt a weight lifting from her shoulders. With such a smile, his invitation was irresistible and she stood up quickly.

"I'd like that," she said eagerly.

"Good. Then we can have supper together."

"Then I must change," Georgiana insisted, and Lunas inclined his head.

"In that case, I will go downstairs and tell Maurice I will not be needing him for a while. "

"I'll try not to be long."

"Take as much time as you like. I 'm sure it will be. worth it."

He moved quietly to the door and out into the corridor, closing the door behind him. For a moment she realised the way he walked reminded her of a cat. A moment later she up ended the contents of the suitcases on the bed and started rummaging for a dress Charles had admired and which she knew would knock his eyes out. How was it possible, when she was so miserable not a quarter of an hour since, to be so happy!

When she joined him in the lobby, she could tell from his expression she had chosen well. She had put her hair up quickly and applied just a touch of make-up. For his part, he saw that in such a short space of time, the fourteen year old had become a sensationally beautiful young woman.

They strolled along the sidewalk overlooking the Seine in the shade of the lime trees and sat at a table outside a cafe. He drank a Bacardi and she sucked lemonade through a straw. They discussed art: The primitives - Rousseau and Lowry.

"And Grandma Moses" don't forget." Georgiana reminded him.

It was hard to keep his mind on their conversation. He was aware of the envious glances male passers-by gave him, sitting opposite such a creature. He wanted to reach out and touch her. To see if her cheek was really as soft and fragrant as he remembered from the brief moment when it had brushed against his own back at the hotel. To put his arms around her again, perhaps to kiss her this time full on the lips. To share her breath with his, perhaps as he drew her into an even more passionate embrace.

With an effort he dragged his mind back to what she was saying. "Grandma Moses," he repeated. "Is that how you see yourself?"

Georgiana looked at him to see if he was teasing her and decided it was difficult to tell. "Not exactly," she said carefully.

Lunas sat forward in his chair. "Because the Primitives are a curiosity - a miracle, if you like; flowers, pushing up through the concrete. And don't forget, for every one that sees the light of day, a thousand perish. They have their place, but can anyone honestly put such people on the same level as Rembrant, or Monet.... or Cezanne?

He saw her open her mouth to retort. But instead she threw back her head in a peal of laughter.

Lunas smiled. "I'm glad you're feeling better."

Georgiana nodded. Then she took a breath and said. "I wish you had come sooner."

"I told you," he answered gently. "I came as soon as I could."

She sighed. "And now, I suppose, I have to go back and hang up all my clothes again!"

"I'll help you. Then we will go for supper."

Georgiana looked at him a little anxiously. "Will I need to change again?"

Lunas shook his head. "We're only going to eat at my home. "

"In that case, I would like to look my best."

He could not imagine how she could possibly look any better than she did already. He told her the dress she had on was ravishing; but true to his promise they returned to the Hotel first and he helped her put away her clothes. Then she showed him the pastel Albert had torn in half, holding up the two halves together while he gazed at it in silence for a while before letting out a deep breath.

"This is good, Georgie. As good as your Rockerfeller Ice Rink But different somehow. It has more maturity. "

"You see the idea.... the freeze frame?"

"Of course. Put it away carefully now. I have someone who will put it back together so you would never know what happened."

Maurice was waiting with the car. They drove alongside the river to the Place Trocadero, where Charles Gros had stopped so she could look back at the Eiffel Tower that first evening.... which seemed so long ago now, before turning into the Avenue George Mandel, and so to the Boulevard Suchet bordering the Bois de Boulogne.

Lunas could see she was lost in thought and kept silent so as not to disturb her reverie; happy just to sit beside her - glancing at her from time to time, always conscious of her proximity and the subtle perfume of her body.

At last the car slowed at two large wrought iron gates through which Georgiana could see a tree lined drive-way leading up to a substantial town house surrounded by lawns and formal gardens. Georgiana turned to Lunas her eyes wide with surprise. She didn't know what she had been expecting, but nothing quite so grand right in the middle of Paris. She was about to say something, but her eyes were caught by the gates opening slowly and they simply exchanged a smile while the car passed through. Eventually it pulled up in front of a wide flight of stone steps leading up to the front door.

Lunas turned to her and said : "Welcome to Poussin le Bas!" He spoke with the pride he found impossible to disguise when referring to the house which he had first seen as a penniless urchin peering through the gates so many years ago. He had determined then that one day he would own it, or one like it, and it had been the crowning achievement of his life, in his own estimation, when he was able to buy the very same house. At the time, it had been almost derelict and nothing compared to its present state after he had spent so much time and money restoring it to its former glory.

"Thank you." Georgiana smiled back. "Quite a pad! "

Lunas nodded. If anyone else had referred to it as a 'pad ' he would have been annoyed, but he knew she was making sure their relationship stayed on an equal footing, and he was more than willing.

Maurice opened the car door on her side, and Lunas got out the other. By the time he joined her at the foot of the steps, the front door had opened and a man servant had come out smiling to meet them, quickly followed by a pleasant looking woman in her mid-fifties.

But before either could say anything, a Border Collie dog tore past them and down the stairs to greet Lunas with an ecstasy of yelps. Lunas bent down to stroke him and was rewarded with frenzied licking and tail wagging.

"Welsh it's good to see you too!" He glanced up at Georgiana who was watching them with an amused look on her face. "But you must say hello to Miss Montes as well. Georgiana, this is Welsh.

"Hello Welsh," she bent down to pat him and was rewarded by the dog transferring his greetings to her.

Lunas straightened up smiling, Be careful" he said "He will love you to death. Down Welsh, that's enough. Calm down...enough I say. Sit!"

The last word was said more forcibly, and the dog sat obediently between them looking expectantly from one to the other. "You must forgive him, "Lunas went on. "With a dog like this, when you go away, it's as if you had died. So, when you come back: a Miracle! "

"He's adorable" Georgiana said. "But you speak to him in English. "

Lunas nodded. "I thought it appropriate. He comes after all from the Border Country between England and Wales. But it also affords some protection. Some burglars have an amazing way with dogs.... but not if they can 't make them understand. But, I am neglecting my manners. Come." He took her arm and led her up the steps to where the couple who had come out to greet them were waiting. Then he said "Georgie, this is Madame Lummanec... otherwise known as Sylvie; an old friend, who also happens to be my housekeeper." He turned to the older woman. "Sylvie, this is Miss Montes, of whom you have heard me speak."

"Often!" The woman returned Georgiana 's smile as they shook hands.

"Often?" Georgiana glanced at Lunas with surprise, but Sylvie nodded vigorously. "Mais oui. Souvent. Often!"

Lunas smiled: "So you see, out of sight, not necessarily out of mind!"

He turned to the man-servant. "And this is Paul."

"Paul?". Georgiana spoke with surprise.

The man bowed, but did not offer to shake hands. Lunas said: "There is nothing to bring in." Then he glanced back down the steps to where Maurice was waiting. "We may need you after supper, Maurice. "

"Very well."

Lunas then turned to take Georgiana's arm to guide her through the open doorway into the house.

"You sounded surprised just now when I introduced you to Paul?"

"It was just that I've only ever met one Paul before. "

"Of course." His face cleared. "Paul Adams. John's son."

"Yes."

"Of course. No relation, I believe."

Once inside, he let go of her arm and paused so she could look around. To Georgiana the room which greeted her seemed huge; serving as both living room and library. Books lined the walls. The furnishings were of impeccable taste, if seeming, to her eyes, rather old fashioned. To the left of them a wide, curved staircase led up to a Gallery which in turn opened onto a number of corridors and, presumably, the rest of the house. She saw there was a log fire burning in a large grate opposite where they were standing and round which were gathered more comfortable looking chairs and a large sofa. After a moment, Lunas guided her towards this while Paul closed the door behind them. "I like to have a fire," he said, "unless it is unusually warm. With such a high ceiling, it can get easily quite chilly."

The dog padded past them and went to spread himself on the hearth.

"You see... Welsh agrees with me."

Georgiana was still looking round, her eyes wide with interest. "It's amazing," she began, but Sylvie stepped forward.

"If you will excuse me," she said. "I must put the final touches to your supper. We are almost ready."

"Of course." Lunas nodded and the woman went out through a door the other side of the staircase. Paul moved to the fire and threw on another log. Then he followed Sylvie out of the room.

"Are you hungry." Lunas asked, turning back to her.

"I'm famished!" Georgiana admitted with a rueful smile. "It must be all the excitement!"

"Excellent! But let me get you a drink first. I take it you do drink, besides lemonade?"

"Whatever."

"Perhaps a little champagne, then?"

Georgiana shrugged happily, and followed as he moved to a trolley on which there was already an opened bottle in an ice bucket and two glasses.

Lunas half filled the two glasses then picked them up and turned to hold one out to her.

"You must have been a boy-scout," Georgiana remarked, as she took it from him.

"How's that?"

"Be prepared. Isn't that their motto?"

Lunas inclined his head. "I always have a glass of champagne when I return home. Paul opens a bottle as soon as they know I have activated the front gates. "

"A secret signal. Why didn't I think of that?"

Lunas smiled and lifted his glass. "Here's to you, Georgie. And a new beginning." After they touched glasses they drank looking at each other, suddenly serious.

Georgiana wondered what was going on in his mind, and she eventually forced herself to look away and back round the room. "Poussan le Bas," she murmured. "That means the little chicken, doesn't it?" She turned back to him. "Why did they give such a large house a name like that?"

Lunas moved to the fire, careful not to tread on Wel sh and turned his back to it. "Ah well, you see it belonged to the younger son of a wealthy family. They had a country estate which was known as "Poussan en haut. "

"The high chicken!". Georgiana moved closer.

"Something like that. Perhaps even, 'the exalted chicken'! Who knows, perhaps the family fortune began by selling eggs!"

He paused while Georgiana chuckled appreciatively.

"Anyway," he continued, "the elder son inherited the Estate, and the younger one came to seek his fortune in Paris. And he eventually built this house. "

"And called it the little chicken. "

"Or lower chicken." Sylvie entered the room from the door by the stairs. " speaking of which, I think our supper's ready."

Sylvie nodded. "Whenever you are, Monsieur." Lunas glanced at Georgiana.

"Are you ready?" he demanded.

"I could eat a horse!"

Lunas turned to Sylvie.

"Is horse on the menu this evening, Sylvie?"

Sylvie smiled. "No, Monsieur."

Lunas turned back to Georgiana. "No, horse, I 'm afraid. Ah well, we shall have to make do! Shall we take our glasses through into the dining room?" Georgiana nodded as Sylvie turned and preceded them out through the door. Welsh, who knew what all this meant followed her eagerly.

"Let me escort you." Lunas offered his arm. They smiled at each other for a moment then Georgiana lightly rested her free hand on it, and together they walked out of the room into the dining room next door.

For Georgiana what followed had a dream like quality. The room was lit by candles burning in two holders on the table itself and another on the side board. He seated her beside him at one end of a long refectory table. In front of them silver and glass glinted in the candle glow. A large vase of old fashioned yellow roses, which he said were from the garden, was set a few feet down the table cutting off their view of the rest and adding intimacy as well as perfume.

Sylvie waited on them while Paul poured the wine and cleared away the dishes.

Welsh sat under the table at Lunas 's side for a while, but on getting nothing moved to Georgiana who secretly passed him a few tid-bits when she thought her host was not looking. As a matter of fact, he knew very well what she was doing, and although he did not approve of Welsh begging, he was so happy to have her sitting beside him he would allow her to do anything that made her happy or feel more welcome.

After the meal was over he showed her some of the rest of the house including a huge Orangerie, an organ room and second library, and finally several galleries displaying his private art collection.

Georgiana was dazzled by what she saw, particularly by the pictures, and she was flattered to see he had mounted the two pictures he had bought off her in New Y - was it really less than two years ago? - between a painting of the Sacre-Coeur by Utrillo, who had died virtually unknown some thirty years ago but whose reputation, she knew from Charles Gros, Lunas himself had done much to establish since, and a picture of the Seine by Vlaminck.

He watched her in silence as she stood in front of the two pictures. It must seem like meeting old friends or children, after a long separation. He wondered what she thought of his choice of company for her work, then he looked back at the second picture and remembered his conversation with John Adams when he first saw it: The shadow on the floor. He had thought at the time it represented something in the past - some terrible event in her life. He knew of course that later that same day both her Mother and Father had been killed. But she had never mentioned it during the time they had spent together since he went to her hotel, and he certainly had no intention of doing so. But was it possible the dark shadow she had painted was a premonition of the future.

Georgiana turned away at last from the pictures and he saw, with relief, she was at peace.

"Thank you," she said softly. "I'm glad you have them."

"I promised they would always be there for you, any time you wanted to see them again."

"Yes, you did." She reached out and took his hand, and so they remained as they walked slowly along the Gallery admiring the rest of his Collection.

Eventually he led her back to the big living room and settled her in a comfortable chair beside the fire. Welsh came to lean against her knees so she could fondle his ears.

Paul came in and poured generous brandies into huge balloon glasses. He made up the fire, then left them alone.

Georgiana closed her eyes. She did not think she had ever felt so content.

She woke up to find Sylvie bending over her smiling as she shook her gently.

"Mam'selle.... Mam'selle!

Georgiana looked round sleepily at first, then her eyes opened wide and she sat up.

"Good grief, I must have dozed off. What time is it?"

"Almost midnight. "

Georgiana saw that both Lunas and Welsh had gone, and she got to her feet. "I must go." she said apologetically. "Where is Mr Lunas? I don't know what he must think!"

"He was glad you were comfortable. He told me you had had a very tiring day." -.

"Oh." Georgiana stifled a yawn.

Sylvie said : "He asked me to apologise to you, but he had to go out. He left with Maurice in the car."

"That's O.K. I'll get a cab."

"But Monsieur Lunas suggested you might like to stay with us tonight as it is so late. I have made up one of the Guest Rooms. I'm sure you will find everything you need."

"But I really think...." Georgiana began but Sylvie interrupted her.

"Monsieur Lunas would be so pleased if you stayed." The two women looked at each other, then Georgiana nodded.

"O.K. Then."

"You will be able to talk some more over breakfast. Then Maurice will drop you off at your Hotel in plenty of time."

Sylvie led her up the stairs. Georgiana paused for a moment looking back at the room below, then she smiled softly and turned to see Sylvie looking at her. Had the older woman some way of helping her sort out the confusion of emotions that were coursing through her mind? One day, they would be friends, she felt sure. But she couldn't reveal to her things she could barely admit to herself. Yet it didn't seem to bother her that much, even so. What was the line the girl had said in that old film she had seen on T.V. just before she left?

".... fiddle-de-dee. I 'll think about that tomorrow! ". Georgiana smiled and Sylvie turned to continue leading the way.

She had a bath and put on the lovely warm full length night-gown Sylvie had put out for her. She climbed into the huge comfortable bed, turned out the lights and was sound asleep within a minute of her head touching the pillow.

Sometime later; Lunas returned to the house. Sylvie told him Georgiana had accepted his invitation and, on impulse, before he went to bed himself, he walked quietly along the corridor followed by Welsh and softly opened the door of the guest room. He saw she was sound asleep but stood looking at her for a while. There was no parallel confusion in his mind. He knew already he was in love with her... this young American spitfire genius. He would love her as long as he lived, but he had seen how quickly she could change. How would she feel if she knew that someone so much older was entertaining such thoughts? If he were to stand any chance at all he would have to have the patience of a saint. The trouble was, he felt anything but a saint as far as she was concerned. Perhaps it would be his punishment for all the women whose hearts he had handled so carelessly over the years.

If the best he could expect, now he had found someone who in so short a time and so unwittingly had taken possession of the space where he lived, was to love her from a distance as benefactor and friend - like a rich uncle, he thought to himself ruefully! Whatever, it would better than never seeing her again. That was no longer possible as long as there was breath in his body.

While he was thinking all this, Welsh suddenly padded past him and he watched anxiously as the dog went up alongside the bed on the side the girl was facing and stood for several seconds with his nose not two feet from her face, staring at her. Lunas held his breath. He dared not call him for fear of waking her. What would she think then, to find him standing at the doorway, staring at her?

The dog gave a low whine, but then, to his relief, came back and Lunas was able to close the door quietly behind them. Georgiana stirred. But she did not wake up.

CHAPTER IX

Mutual apologies said, life returned to normal at the Conservatoire and Georgiana realised she had crossed an invisible line of acceptance. Before, it seemed she only had one friend in Jules, now she had many. It was, therefore, with a twinge of guilt she found him waiting for her one afternoon as she was leaving with a group of companions and realised she had not really spoken to him for more than a month; not to sit down and have coffee together like they used to. But new friends were not the only answer.

She had come to like Professor Albert, who had not only been big enough to apologise but to offer the kind of support afterwards she had longed for. Instead of being forced into an artistic straight-jacket, she was now encouraged to pursue her own style, and after this new beginning, Georgiana also learned that the Professor was not the hide bound traditionalist she had thought originally but, particularly after he had shown her some of his own work, an artist who understood what she was trying to do; and such advice as he did offer, she found, carried her forward like a swimmer who suddenly finds the current moving in the same direction.

Lunas was still away from Paris most of the time, but from the point of view of her studies it was just as well. When he invited her she found she could think of little else than the prospect of spending a few precious hours in his company. Sometimes they went out together, and he opened for her a world of music, theatre and ballet that, had she had not already been so devoted to painting, she might have been seduced by one or the other.

As their relationship developed, he confided some of his past life to her and she was amazed that having had far less formal education than she herself, he knew so much, not only about the subject they shared above all the others but could open so many doors to worlds she had scarcely dreamt of before they met. Despite this, the evenings she enjoyed more than any other were those when he took her back to the house in the Bois-de-Boulogne for a supper prepared by Sylvie while they looked at his pictures, or walked in the Gardens surrounding the house talking endlessly, while Welsh, who now greeted her rapturously examined the bushes close by for items of interest, which he brought to her from time to time.

Lunas always made sure Maurice was available to take her home so that she was not too tired for class in the morning. She never stayed the night at the house, and if there was any shadow over the time they spent together, it was her sense that he was always careful to keep her at arm's length. He never asked her what she did in her free time while they were apart and never volunteered such information about himself, or where his travels took him. His behaviour towards her was like that of an elder brother and she wondered if that was really how he wanted her to see him.

"Georgie, have you got a minute?". Jules stepped into her path. "Sure." she turned to the others with a smile. "See you later, then."

Her companions nodded and took their leave, one or two of the young women looking curiously at Jules, then back at Georgiana with knowing smiles before finally waving goodbye.

Jules said : "I hope you don't mind. I've been waiting for you."

"Of course I don't mind." Then she remembered, she had noticed he had not been in class. "So what happened to you this morning?" She asked.

"I had to go and see the Principal," he told her unhappily as they started to stroll in the direction of her hotel.

"What for?

"Apparently, they are not very happy with my work."

"Gee!" Georgiana shot him a worried glance. "Why not?"

Jules shrugged miserably. "They say I'm not producing enough," he said. "But I find it difficult to work with a lot of people around me."

Georgiana nodded. "I know what you mean. I do most of my serious stuff in the evening or at week-ends.

"But it's more difficult for me. You seem to find inspiration where ever you are. But I really need models. They're expensive, and I do not have much money."

"But I'm sure some of the students would be willing."

"Not many. Besides, they have their own work to do."

Georgiana glanced at him again; then she said casually: "You can draw me, if you like; if it would help." They had reached the street corner where their paths separated and Jules stopped, facing her.

"Would you be willing?" he said, trying to disguise his excitement.

"Sure, why not? And I'll have a word with some of the others. I'm sure they would agree if they knew you were in trouble." But Jules looked alarmed.

"No.... Please. Don't say anything to anyone else. I don't want them to know."

"I wouldn't say anything about your interview," she assured him. "Just that you could do with some fresh faces."

"If you would help me, that's all I need," Jules said with surprising firmness. So Georgiana shrugged and grinned.

"Well.... O.K. But I might be a lousy model; fidgeting all the time!

"Let me worry about that."

"O.K. When do you want to start?"

Jules thought for a moment, then he said: "Perhaps you would come and have tea with me tomorrow?"

"Saturday? Sure, why not? She was sure Lunas was still away. "I'm not doing anything special." Jules hesitated, suddenly awkward. Then he said: "I'm afraid I cannot afford to pay".

Georgiana smiled. "Don't be silly," she told him. "I don't need your money.

"No.... of course."

What did he mean by that?, she wondered. But before she could say anything he went on humbly: "May I walk with you to your rooms?"

Georgiana shook her head. "No.... that 's O.K. I'm going to meet some of the others at the Cafe. Why don't you come?", she added as an after-thought.

"No.... thank you. I would prefer to go home and prepare."

"O.K. Tomorrow afternoon then."

"The afternoon. Yes."

"About four o'clock?"

"Yes. That will be perfect. Thank you Georgie."

"Goodbye, Jules."

They exchanged quick, student type kisses on each cheek, then Georgiana turned and walked away up the street which joined the one they were on at right angles. After she had gone a few steps she turned and gave him a final wave.

"See ya!"

He stood looking after her, his expression a mixture of excitement and longing.

The following afternoon found Georgiana walking along the narrow side street where she knew Jules had a small apartment, carrying a paper bag and looking at the door numbers. She eventually stopped outside one, and after reading the cards which said who occupied which apartment, rang one of the bells.

She did not have long to wait before the door opened. Either he had been waiting just inside or had run down the stairs. Probably the latter as his face was quite flushed.

"Georgiana!"

"Hi!"

He stood back opening the door wide. "Come in please. Welcome."

"Thank you."

When she walked inside she turned and waited for him to close the door. Glancing round she saw they were in a minute lobby at the end of a narrow passage which led to two ground floor apartments and the foot of a narrow staircase. Having shut the door firmly he turned to face her. She held out the paper bag she had been carrying.

"I brought you some cookies."

"Cookies?"

"Sorry.... biscuits, I guess you call them."

"Ah.... biscuits!" He took them and peeped inside.

"Claudine, at the hotel, is always making them." Georgiana said: "They're delicious.... but fattening!"

Jules pulled a face. "I don't think I will worry about that."

"That's right." She looked him up and down. "You should eat more."

Jules smiled; then he said: "Please, follow me. I'm afraid it is all the way to the top. But the view is good!"

Georgiana smiled to cover her embarrassment, realising her last remark might not have been the most tactful! "Lead on," she said, and Jules started up the narrow stairway.

"Also it has a sky light which is a big advantage," he called over his shoulder.

Each of the three small landings they passed on the way up were the same as the lobby, below with a short passageway leading to two apartments. But when they reached the top floor the lay out was different. Here the front doors of two apartments faced each other.

Jules stood to one side of an already opened door to the right of the top of the stairs. "Here we are. Please.... go in." Georgiana did so and paused looking round while he closed the door behind them.

It was just one room, with a bed in a corner; a desk, a china wash basin with water jug underneath, some drawers, and a rail for hanging clothes. Most of the room, the area under the sky light, was given over to his painting activities. The whole reflected both his interests and his financial circumstances, but it was immaculately neat. There was a small fire grate, currently empty, and on the far side another door, presently standing ajar, and through which she could see a small balcony not unlike the one outside her room back at the hotel.

She turned to him with a smile. "It reminds me of my room back at the Village," she said.

"Which village is that?" Jules moved a few paces towards her.

"Greenwich village. One of the older parts of Manhattan. Is it always this neat? Mine never was!"

"I tried to make it better," he confessed. "I did not want you to think I lived in a pig sty." Georgiana shrugged. "You needn't have bothered," she said. Then she walked to the open doorway and out onto the balcony. A moment later, he stood beside her.

"Mm.... I love the old part of Paris!" Georgiana sighed as she gazed across the uneven roof tops. "I know it's corny. I just can't help it!"

Jules said : "One day I would like to show you Bruges. Some people think it is the most beautiful city in Europe!"

"It can't be as beautiful as this, surely," Georgiana challenged, her eyes twinkling.

"You must judge for yourself " Jules said seriously.

They looked at each other for a moment then she said : "Well.... we are not going to get any work done out here."

"Unfortunately, that is true!"

Once inside, Georgiana walked to the centre of the room and stood under the sky light where there was a chair in front of an easel on which a canvas was already mounted. Beside the easel was another chair and a small table on which were boxes of paints, pencils and crayons.

Georgiana walked round to look at the canvas and saw it was a full length painting of a woman in her early fifties; handsome rather than beautiful, but with a face full of character as she gazed appraisingly at the painter. She was herself standing in working clothes beside an easel and with paint brushes and a palette in her hands.

"My mother," Jules explained coming to stand beside her. "We sometimes paint each other at the same time."

"It' s very good." Georgiana said sincerely. "I wondered for a moment why she seemed familiar. Of course, you look alike." She turned to face him. "I would love to see her painting of you."

Jules smiled. "She insisted on keeping that!" He half turned. "But that is one of hers on the wall above the bed." He invited her to examine it, and she saw it was of a young man holding a tennis racquet who was wearing old fashioned tennis clothes with long pants. Jules said : "She painted this just after she and my father were married."

Georgiana looked at it carefully. "They were very much in love," she said after a while. Jules looked at her with surprise. "Can you tell that by looking at it? " he asked.

"Of course. All good pictures say as much about the artist as the subject. "She looked back at the picture on the easel. "It's the same with your portrait of your Mother. I can see how much you admire her."

Jules sighed. "I don't think I will ever be as good." He said.

"But you must not be afraid of her."

"Afraid?"

"Of her reputation." Georgiana explained.

Jules thought for a moment, then he said : "If that is true, it is history repeating itself My father loved tennis, but his father was Champion of Belgium before the War. He played in Paris and at Wimbledon in England." He shrugged. "Everyone expected my father to be as good, but all he wanted was to enjoy playing for its own sake. He gave it up not long after that was painted."

Georgiana said: "That's sad. I hope you never think of giving up!"

"Well, I have to admit, sometimes I have felt like it. Like after the meeting yesterday with the Principal!"

Georgiana looked at him, then she said firmly. "Which is why I am here." She indicated the chair in front of the easel. "Do you want me to sit here?"

After a moment, Jules nodded. "Yes, please," he said, and Georgiana seated herself while he sat on the chair opposite and picked up a pad of paper and a pencil.

"How do you want me to sit?" Georgiana asked him.

Jules smiled. "Anyway that is comfortable," he said. "I'm just going to do some rough sketches to begin with."

"Fine," She composed herself on the chair and Jules began to work quietly. "Will it put you off if we talk," she asked after a while.

Jules shook his head. "Not at all," he said. "I'd like that. I really know so little about you."

Georgiana paused for a moment, then she said: "Do you know, I was all packed and ready to go back to New York the day I socked the Professor.

"No!" He looked up at her shocked. "What stopped you?"

"My Benefactor."

"Monsieur Lunas."

"Yeah. It would have been a big mistake. He stopped me."

Jules forced himself to start again before saying casually: "How?. I mean, how did he stop you?"

"I don't know." Georgiana gave a wry grin. "He seems to have a way of making me do things".

Jules felt a surge of jealousy, but forced himself to comment as calmly as he could : "Like coming to Paris?"

Seeing his expression, Georgiana gave him a dazzling smile and said: "Just think Jules.... he brought us together!"

November gave way to December, and suddenly it was Christmas Eve. Georgiana swallowed her disappointment at not having heard from Him. She really thought they would spend Christmas together; perhaps just the two of them with Sylvie, Paul and Welsh at the house in the Bois-de-Bologne. But when she called Charles he said he had no idea where he was.

Jules invited her to come and see the completion of his latest portrait of her.

There was a small band playing carols in the street as she walked through the snow to his apartment carrying a small present for him: a bottle of brandy she knew he loved, but could rarely afford. Most of the tunes were unfamiliar to her, but the music moved her and she suddenly wanted to turn and go back to her room and howl her eyes out into her pillow. But she remembered that Jules was probably looking forward to seeing her as much, and she could not bring herself to disappoint him.

When she got there, she found there was a coal fire burning in the grate. He had made some sandwiches and there was an opened bottle of red wine on the table with two glasses. But as soon as he saw the brandy he insisted on opening it so they could wish each other a Merry Christmas more suitably.

She ate a sandwich to please him, although she did not feel like it, and drank some brandy. But Jules was in an expansive mood, and when he had poured himself a second glass, he led her over to the easel on which the finished portrait stood covered with a cloth. He made her stand in front of the easel in the best viewing position, then dramatically pulled off the cloth and stood back.

To be truthful, Georgiana was getting a bit tired of looking at portraits of herself; this was the fifth. But she had to admit, as she looked at it, it was probably the best. She knew he was waiting expectantly so she turned to him and nodded.

"Yes.... I like it very much."

"You think it's good?"

"Yes, I do."

"Really?"

"Yes.... really, really!

"I think it is the best so far."

"Yes. It probably is, " she agreed truthfully.

"Then keep it." Jules said suddenly.

"But you might be able to sell it," she protested.

"You have given me so much, Georgiana," he said passionately.

"What, sitting around while you work!"

"So much of your time. You've really encouraged me to go on."

Georgiana looked back at the portrait. "You've certainly grown as an artist. I can see that."

"That's exactly what my mother said," Jules said, triumphantly draining his glass and moving to the table where he had left the bottle and refilling it. "I sent her the last portrait I did of you, and she wrote to me immediately to say how much she liked it. She also wanted to know all about you."

"Oh dear.... I hope she doesn't get the wrong idea!" Georgiana took a few steps towards the fireplace, then suddenly made up her mind and turned to face him. "Look, Jules.... I hope you are not going to be upset by what I am going to say."

"Please.... " Jules held up his hand, but she insisted.

"I really think you should work with some other people now."

"Georgie!" He looked at her aghast.

"No.... it would help you to continue to progress. You can't go on painting the same person all the time!"

"But there is so much more I want to say.... to express," he protested.

"I know," Georgiana said firmly. "That's what I'm saying. Look, I've got some money.... if it would help...." But he wasn't listening.

"But with you," he interrupted. "You are the most wonderful model. I would never to able to reach the same standard with anyone else!"

"But you're going to have to, aren't you, if you're going to be a professional portrait painter?"

"Some day, yes."

"As I was saying...."

"No. I don't want to know," he interrupted again.

She was shocked to see he was close to tears, and suddenly felt bad. She put out her hand to touch his cheek.

"Don't look like that," she said softly.

Jules swallowed, then took a deep breath and forced a smile. "All right. I know I could not keep you for ever. I'm sure Monsieur Lunas thinks you are wasting your time!"

"Jules, this has nothing to do with him. I have not even told him."

He looked at her for a moment like a drowning man. Then he said tensely: "Then let me paint you....one last time."

"Just once more?" Georgiana looked at him. She could normally tell what he was thinking, but not now.

Jules nodded, then seemed to get a grip on himself. When he spoke again his voice had almost returned to normal: "Yes. Just once more, and I will always keep it."

He turned and took the picture off the easel and held it out to her. "So.... this is for you. Let it be a Christmas present."

"Thank you." She took the picture from him, and while she was looking round for somewhere to put it Jules drained his glass, then bent down and put a blank canvas in its place.

"And I will keep this."

Georgiana rested the picture he had given her against the chair she normally sat on in front of the easel.

"You want to start now? " She said pointedly, but with a smile to soften her words. With what he had drunk, she did not imagine he was in any state to start drawing.

"Why not?" Jules turned to face her, his face flushed. "Who knows how long I have before I never see you again?!"

'I'm not going anywhere," Georgiana protested mildly.

"Never mind." He looked away, then swung back to face her. "But as this is for the last time, would you pose for me.... like a professional?"

Georgiana looked at him, awkward at first, but then gave a wry smile. "Like a professional," she repeated.

"Please."

"Like.... with no clothes?"

"Yes."

Georgiana paused for a moment, then she smiled. "I thought that's what you meant. I just wanted to make sure!"

"You are so beautiful, Georgie," he said, in a voice from which all the aggression had vanished.

Georgiana took a deep breath then she came to a decision. "O.K. I'll do it."

"You will?" Jules said eagerly.

"Yes. But not now."

Jules face fell. "Why not now," he demanded, a note of petulance returning.

"Because we've both been drinking," she told him calmly.

He looked at her frowning for a moment, then his eyes widened in comprehension. "Georgie....you can trust me."

"But can I trust myself?"

Jules shook his head. "But I would never harm you, or take advantage. You know that."

"I believe you. But now I'm going home. I won't take the picture now, I think it's still snowing."

"But it's Christmas Eve!". Jules looked round wildly. "Look.... we still have some brandy." Seeing it was useless arguing with him she turned, saw her coat on the bed and went to pick it up.

"No Georgie, please." Jules took a step after her and put out a hand to restrain her, but he was too slow and she managed to pick up the coat and get halfway to the door before he caught up with her and tried to take the coat off her.

"Jules, stop it," she warned sharply, but he persisted and she suddenly turned on him. "Take your hands off me!" She gave him a push and he staggered back a few feet with the unexpected strength of her. Somehow his feet got mixed up and he suddenly tripped over backwards knocking the easel and paints flying and hitting his head on the bare wooden floor where he lay inert for a few seconds.

Georgiana looked down at him, eyes wide with shock. Then, suddenly contrite, she dropped her coat and rushed to kneel beside him.

"Jules.... I'm so sorry!" She bent down to hear if he was still breathing, which he was; and when she straightened up, she was relieved to see his eyes suddenly open.

He smiled up at her vaguely. "Georgie?"

"I'm sorry, Jules. I didn't mean to hurt you."

"No?" He tried to raise his head and she bent forward to help him sit up. "You frightened me for a minute."

But he was not listening. "I don't feel well!" Jules confessed.

Georgiana smiled with relief "I don't suppose you do," she said with mock severity. "You've had a lot to drink and now you've fallen over and banged your head."

"Oh."

"Here, let me help you to the bed." She tried to lift him but he was a ton weight. "Come on," she demanded.

"I'm dizzy."

"Jules.... you've got to stand up. I can't lift you, you're too heavy!"

"Oh." He smiled at her sympathetically, but made an effort and together they managed to get him onto the bed. Once there, she was able to remove his shoes and make him comfortable.

"I love you," he said simply, looking up at her.

Georgiana paused for a moment, then she stroked the side of his face. "Yes, I know," she said simply. "But now you must get some rest. You'll feel better in the morning."

"You will see me again?"

"Of course. And thank you for the lovely picture."

She looked down and saw he had passed out. So she smiled, feeling suddenly motherly, and pulled a cover over him. She checked the fire to see it was safe, then picked up the easel and replaced the canvas. The floor was still a mess of paints and brushes. She decided to leave these for him to sort out in the morning, but she bent down and picked up the pallet knife and put it next to the brandy bottle in case he should get up in the night and tread on it in his stocking feet.

Georgiana picked up her coat again, and slipped it on. Then she made for the door and opened it, turning back for one last look round to see that everything was O.K.

As a result, she did not see the figure of a man who had been standing at the top of the stairs immediately outside shrink back into the doorway of the apartment opposite; then, surprised to find the door open, slipped inside and closed it, leaving just a gap so he could watch Georgiana switch out the light and close the door behind her before starting down the stairs.

It would not have mattered to him if he had killed her too, but he was a professional with no brief but to eliminate the owner of the apartment she had just left. And what, by the greatest of good fortune as far as she was concerned, she had not seen, there was no need to worry about.

He waited until he heard her open and close the front door below as she left the house. Then he moved silently back onto the landing, closing the door behind him and opening the one by which she had just left.

It was a matter of a minute to assess the situation: with his 'hit' lying out cold on the bed,. nothing could be simpler. In a moment of inspiration he put away the silenced automatic and picked up the palette knife in his gloved hand. He had heard the commotion before the girl had left. Why spoil a perfect set up with a bullet?

CHAPTER X

The Chief of Police for the 3rd Arrondissement did not appreciate being dragged away from his Christmas Lunch by the Inspector whose lot it had been to make preliminary inquiries into the violent death of an art student the previous evening. He saw no reason for his junior to disturb him over such a routine matter, but when told that the victim was Belgian and the prime suspect a young American girl protege of George Lunas, head of Lunas International, he asked the Inspector to start from the beginning once more and tell him what he knew in greater detail.

The Inspector smiled with grim satisfaction. He had never cared for his superior, whom he regarded as a pompous ass, and it pleased him to be able to spoil his festivities, seeing that his own were already in ruins.

"It appears the Victim and Suspect were close friends", he reported "possibly lovers. At least, they had spent a great deal of time together recently. The girl has admitted they had been drinking together, and an autopsy has already shown that the victim had consumed a considerable amount of Brandy before being hit on the back of his head, then stabbed to death, apparently with a pallet knife. The girl, one Georgiana Montes, insists that she left the Victim's apartment after he had passed out on the bed, having banged his head on the floor when he had slipped, and that he had definitely been alive when she left. Her finger prints on the murder weapon she accounted for after having given the matter some thought - by her picking it up off the floor where it had fallen, and it was true that examination has revealed no trace of blood on the suspect nor, having turned the room at the Hotel where she was staying inside out, on any item of her clothing. But there could, of course, be a number of explanations for that. It had to be admitted that all the evidence they had so far was circumstantial. What had to be decided was did they release the girl for the moment or hold her until the Preliminary Inquiry?"

Georgiana was allowed to telephone Charles Gros, who waited just long enough to put a call through to Lunas International asking them to contact Monsieur Lunas, wherever he was. He then drove to the Police Station where Georgiana was being held and did his best to persuade the Inspector that he had no real evidence on which to hold his Client. But when the other came back from speaking again to his Superior he was told that his orders were to hold Miss Montes in custody, pending a preliminary examination, which would be arranged as soon as possible. He was sorry, but the matter was out of his hands.

Georgiana had to spend the weekend in Jail. Gros told her he was trying to contact Monsieur Lunas but, in any event, he was sure she would be released by the Magistrate once the facts were laid before him; and although feeling as helpless as a bird in a trap when she was brought in to stand beside Gros facing the Magistrate on the Monday morning, the sight of Lunas, who had flown back from Hong Kong as soon as he had been informed what had happened and had arrived straight from the airport, sitting across the Court as close to her as he could, lifted her spirits like nothing Gros had been able to say to her.

For his part, despite the encouraging smile he gave her, he was distressed to see how drawn she was, which confirmed what Gros had already told him when they met briefly in the corridor outside the Court just before the Hearing. He glanced up at the Public Gallery and saw it was full. Word must have got out over the weekend, because in addition to the youngsters he took to be Georgiana's fellow students, he recognised several reporters and guessed that many of the others present were the same.

After banging for silence, the Magistrate explained that as this was not a trial the proceedings would be informal. All that was necessary was for Georgiana to explain what she knew of the case under consideration and he allowed her to do this, almost without interruption, simply making notes, and prompting her from time to time when the meaning of what she was saying was not clear.

He continued to nod for some time after she had finished. Then he glanced at her and said: "You returned to your Hotel on foot? You met no one; no one saw you at the Hotel when you returned, and you went straight to bed?"

Georgiana nodded. "Yes, sir."

"I see." The Magistrate continued to nod, glancing down at his notes. Then he looked up suddenly and spoke in a sharper tone than he had used previously: "So....the gist of your story is that you went to Monsieur Lavosin's Studio to pose for him...."

"Not that evening," Georgiana insisted. "He simply asked me in for a drink, being Christmas Eve."

"Ah yes. But this was a favour you had done for him on other occasions?"

"Yes."

"But on this occasion, after you had eaten with him and drunk some brandy, he asked you to take off your clothes?"

"So he could paint me in the nude."

"Which you were unwilling to do."

Georgiana paused for a moment. Then she said: "Which I was unwilling to do then."

"But you had done so before?"

"Never."

"Oh. Why not?"

"Because he never asked me before."

"But you were willing to do so later?"

"I wanted to help Jules. But I needed to think about it. We had both been drinking."

The Magistrate looked at her unblinking. "Were you in love with him?" He asked flatly.

"No." Georgiana shook her head firmly, and glanced for a moment at Lunas, but his face was impassive.

"But you seem to have spent a great deal of time with him," the Magistrate persisted.

Again Georgiana rested her eyes on Lunas before turning back to answer. "I sometimes had time on my hands, and Jules needed a model. He didn't have any money to pay anyone else."

"He didn't pay you."

"I said. He didn't have any money."

"But enough to buy a bottle of Brandy."

"I bought that."

"I see."

"As a Christmas present."

Her inquisitor nodded again. Then he said: "Was he in love with you?"

"He thought he was."

"Very well." The Magistrate organised his notes for a moment. Then he looked up again and said: "What did he do when you refused to pose for him that night....in the nude, I think you said?"

"He was disappointed."

"I said.... what did he do?"

Georgiana hesitated, then she said : "He tried to stop me leaving."

"How?"

"He.... tried to stop me putting on my coat."

"By force?"

"Well.... he kinda grabbed it."

"The coat or you?"

"Both.... I guess."

"So a struggle ensued.?"

"Not really."

"But I understood he was considerably bigger than you?"

"He was. But he'd been drinking like I said. I just gave him a shove and he lost his balance and fell on the floor, banging his head."

"Ah yes."

"He tripped over and just sort of fell,." She shrugged helplessly and glanced at Gros who was standing beside her.

"Your Honour," Gros ventured, but the Magistrate held up his hand.

"One moment," He turned back to Georgiana. "The Police have suggested that after you had been drinking, you possibly quarrelled. And when he tried to force himself upon you, you lashed out with a palette knife....the first implement that came to hand."

"No." Georgiana shook her head again fiercely. "We did not quarrel. It was all over in seconds."

"Your Honour...." Gros insisted. "None of the neighbours heard anything. He held up a sheaf of papers. "I have their sworn statements if you would care to examine them."

But the Magistrate shook his head. "Later...."

"The walls are thin." Gros continued. "Surely such a quarrel would have been heard?"

The Magistrate looked at him with a touch of impatience. "Your client is asking us to believe that after the deceased tried to rape her...."

"He didn't try to rape me." Georgiana said angrily.

"But by your own admission he forcibly tried to detain you when you refused to get undressed!"

"I've told you, it was all over in seconds."

"After which," the Magistrate persisted, "you would have us believe you helped him to the bed.... then left, as if nothing had happened! Yet the following morning, he was found by the Concierge of the building lying on the bed having been stabbed to death by repeated blows from a pallet knife which had your finger prints all over it.... and no one elses! How do you explain this?"

Georgiana stared back at him, but before she could make any rejoinder Gros said : "Someone else must have come in after my Client had left."

"With the express purpose of murdering the deceased? Which he managed to do without any sound of a struggle.... which would surely have been heard if the walls were as thin as you say!"

"But by the time Miss Montes left, Monsieur Lavosin had passed out. Clearly he was murdered while still in a stupor.

The Magistrate paused, then nodded. "That is possible," he admitted. "But by whom?" The two men looked at each other, then the Magistrate turned back to Georgiana.

"Did Monsieur Lavosin have enemies?" Georgiana opened her mouth, but before she could say anything he continued: " Other admirers of yours who were jealous of your friendship with him?"

Georgiana was about to glance at Lunas, a knee jerk reaction she managed to control by forcing herself to look at the floor instead. Besides, he was thousands of miles away at the time it all happened. But Jules himself had hinted that her Patron would not have approved of their friendship if he had known about it. After a moment, she looked up and said : "Everyone liked Jules. He was...." But the Magistrate was not interested and prevented her from continuing.

"Which brings us back to the more logical explanation," he insisted.

Georgiana shook her head again. "I didn't kill him," she repeated doggedly, then looked round the Court addressing anyone who would listen. "He was alive when I left!"

The Magistrate banged his gavel to quieten the ensuing noise. When all was silent he asked in a more kindly voice: "Is it possible you are telling the truth as far as you can remember? But you yourself had been drinking." Georgiana opened her mouth, but he held up his hand. "Perhaps you genuinely do not remember what happened towards the end of the evening?"

"No!.... I didn't kill him!" Georgiana could restrain herself no longer. "I was fond of him," she sobbed. "Why won't you believe me?" She covered her face with her hands and began to weep uncontrollably."

Lunas sprang to his feet, and sweeping a protesting Court Attendant to one side hurried to Georgiana's side to put his hand on her arm and speak comfortingly to her.

The Magistrate watched this development sympathetically, but when Georgiana was calmer he said. "Well.... as I have already explained, this is not a trial but a preliminary hearing to decide if, in fact, there appears to be a case to answer as far as Miss Montes is concerned." He glanced around the Court before looking again at Georgiana. "In my opinion, there can be no doubt about this." He saw her grit her teeth as he continued: "I hereby rule, therefore, that you Georgiana Montes be sent for trial to answer to the charge of the murder of Jules Lavosin on Christmas Eve by stabbing him to death. Do either you, or your Attorney wish to add anything to what you have already said at this point?"

Gros raised a hand. "Yes, your Honour. I ask bail for my Client."

"Bail!" The Magistrate looked back at him, eyebrows raised. "It is not customary with such a serious charge."

"I agree." Gros said equably. "But my Client is an American citizen. It will be possible for the Court to retain her passport so she cannot return home, or go anywhere else, for that matter. I am also authorised to say that Monsieur George Lunas here, of Lunas International, who sponsored Madame Montes' attendance at the Conservatoire of Art is prepared to stand security for her."

The Magistrate nodded and smiled briefly. "Monsieur Lunas. Of course, I thought I recognised you. You may recall we met briefly at the Annual Dinner of the Legion d'Honneur?"

Lunas bowed gravely. "With pleasure, your Honour," he lied.

The Magistrate nodded again. "And are you prepared to stand bail for this young woman? He asked.

"I am", Lunas assured him. "She is a talented young artist, and having brought her over from New York, I feel responsible for her."

"In Loco parentis, as it were?"

"Precisely."

But the Magistrate still looked doubtful. "Even so, it is as grave responsibility," he said. "You do realise that if, for any reason, the Accused should fail to surrender herself to the Authorities on the date set for her trial it would be a most serious matter?"

"I do understand that, your Honour."

The Magistrate hesitated a moment longer, then he banged the gavel on the desk in front of him.

"Very well.... I order that Miss Montes be released into the custody of Monsieur Lunas, to deliver her up for trial at a date to be notified. And I post bail at....one million francs?" He glanced at Lunas, who nodded in acquiescence. Gros also bowed.

"Thank you, your Honour."

Lunas waited downstairs with Maurice in the car while Claudine went upstairs with Georgiana to help her pack. He tried to make conversation with her on their subsequent drive to Poussin-le-Bas but Georgiana seemed to have shrunk into herself, to some place he could not reach and he too fell silent for the rest of the journey. There was so much he wanted to say; to take upon himself some of the hurt she was suffering, and the anger at the injustice done to her - which might only just be beginning. But for the moment, it was hopeless. Perhaps in a few days, she would be able to talk about it. For now, all he could do was offer her sanctuary and the peace of knowing she was with those who believed in her innocence and would do anything to protect her.

Sylvie greeted her at the front door and gave her a motherly hug, and while Maurice was getting her things out of the car, led her upstairs without another word to the room she had slept in the first and only night she had spent beneath their roof; a happy association, the woman hoped, that would help her fill less strange.

It was very different from that last time. Now the tall windows were wide open and sun-light flooded into the room. Sylvie moved straight to the window and invited Georgiana to join her.

"There is a wonderful view of the gardens," she said encouragingly. Georgiana came to stand beside her and looked out for a moment before nodding and turning away.

Sylvie looked after her. "I expect you would rather have remained at the Hotel?" She said gently.

"It doesn't matter." Georgiana turned to face her. "I've been suspended by the Conservatoire anyway."

The older woman could not resist coming and resting her hand on Georgiana's arm for a moment. "Try not to worry" she said softly. "I'm sure everything will be all right."

"Perhaps for me," Georgiana said. "But Jules is dead. Perhaps I really am responsible in some way."

"Nonsense," Sylvie said firmly. "You must not think like that. You are no more responsible than if he had been hit by a truck. Nobody knew him well. Who knows who might have wanted him out of the way.... or for what reason?"

Georgiana looked at her, and Sylvie realised how badly she had taken it. Perhaps the young man's death had stirred memories of her parents' tragic accident, which had not occurred that long ago. "Monsieur Lunas has many friends," she said quietly. "I am sure they will find the true murderer before the trial. And Monsieur Gros is one of the finest lawyers in France." She gave the girl's arm a gentle squeeze, then let go and glanced round the room. "Please let me know if I've forgotten something."

Georgiana managed a smile. "I don't think you ever forget anything, Sylvie," she said.

The older woman looked pleased. "Well, I hope not. Anyway, Maurice will be up in a moment with your things. When you are ready, please come down. But take your time." She made for the door.

"George? I mean... Monsieur Lunas," Georgiana called after her, and Sylvie turned in the doorway.

"He will stay and take tea with you in the Orangerie," she said, then smiled mysteriously, "I think he has something he would like to show you." She closed the door quietly, leaving Georgiana wondering just what she meant.

Maurice appeared a few moments later having knocked on the door and pushed it open without waiting for an invitation. He put the two cases on her bed without a word then turned to leave but paused momentarily before closing the door. "Welcome home," he said quietly. Then grinned suddenly, his teeth brilliant white against his dark complexion. But before she could respond, he was gone. She heard him whistling tunelessly as he walked away down the corridor.

Georgiana started to put away her clothes. Then, tiring of the task, she walked to the window and looked down at the garden at the rear of the house. She saw Lunas standing by a flower bed talking to one of the gardeners. Welsh appeared from undergrowth carrying something in his mouth, which proved to be a ball. He dropped it at the feet of the two men, then stood back wagging his tail. When neither of them took any notice, he barked impatiently so Lunas had to break off his conversation to throw it and Welsh set off in hot pursuit. She saw it bounce once on the lawn then disappear into some trees, the dog after it.

Georgiana transferred her gaze back to the two men. After a few seconds she saw Lunas, who had his back to her, stop what he was saying, and turn to stare up at her. She met his gaze without moving for a few seconds, then she raised her hand to wave. But before she could do so he turned back again to resume his conversation without giving any sign he had seen her.

It was after dark when he invited her to follow him through to the back of the house to the second staircase which led to the top of the house and a floor he had never shown her before. On the top landing there was only one door facing them. He opened it and reached inside to touch a light switch, then before stood back to let her go in first.

The room was a huge studio that must have extended over at least half the area of the house. Round the walls were a number of paintings which she recognised as coming from his collection downstairs - those he knew she particularly admired, as well as the pastel which she had given to him when it had been repaired and the two pictures he had bought when they first met; all skilfully lit by concealed spot lights. Glancing up she saw that large skylights reached over the centre of the room and realised the light they would give in the day time would be ideal. There were a number of easels, including a large one directly beneath the sky light, and an artist's chest which probably contained paints and brushes. There was a book case - presently empty, two easy chairs and a table; in fact, everything any young artist could possible dream of.

Georgiana glanced at him and answered his inquiring look with a smile of appreciation. She knew how much he had tried to please her. If only she could feel more enthusiastic. If only she could feel anything but the numbness that had replaced the shock of Jules' death and her arrest, and which had stayed with her ever since.

"This is yours during the time you are with us," he said, after a moment.

"You did this for me". It was a statement, not a question.

Lunas took a few steps into the centre of the room looking round, then turned to face her. "When I bought this house, I knew what a wonderful studio it would make." He glanced up. "With those great north sky lights." She moved a few steps towards him, forcing herself to look round again with apparent interest. He looked back at her and shrugged. "But it is one of Nature's ironies.... or cruelties, that so often she bestows a great love for something.... music, literature....art, while depriving that person of the slightest gift for the very thing they yearn for. And so this room has remained empty.... until now." He smiled and moved back towards her. "Now, the long wait is over."

Georgiana held his gaze, the her eyes slid away. "It's wonderful," she heard herself say.

"I hoped you would think so," he said warmly. "Now you must look around properly. Take it all in. It is all yours."

Obediently, Georgiana started to walk around, stopping from time to time in evident satisfaction, conscious he was watching her the whole time, his expression changing swiftly from concern to delight whenever she looked back at him and nodded in appreciation at some new revelation. Eventually, she stopped in front of the pastel. She stared at it for a long time, then turned and he saw her eyes were glistening with tears.

In a moment he was at her side. "Georgie?" He rested his hand on her arm and she looked down at it.

"I'm sorry."

"Sorry for what?"

She looked up at him, then wiped her eyes with the back of her hand and glanced back at the picture. "I can scarcely remember the girl who did this. I don't know if I'll ever be able to do justice...." She glanced around the studio before turning back to face him.

He pressed her arm reassuringly. "You only feel like that now because of everything that has happened," he said gently.

"But you expect me to start work again."

He let go of her arm and said quietly: "I don't expect anything Georgie."

"Then why all this?"

"It is for you. But only if and when you want it. I cannot tell you how much pleasure it has given me to prepare it for you. As it gives me pleasure to have you staying under my roof. So that I can see you.... often". He pulled a face. "But I can see now I was only thinking of myself. The last thing I want is to put more pressure on you. I started it after you first came here. Then, when all this happened, I thought it could be somewhere you could escape; back to a world where I hoped you would feel safe."

Georgiana impulsively rested her hands on his shoulders for a moment, then she let go awkwardly, and took a step back, "Why are you being so kind to me?" she said; then swallowed: "I don't want to disappoint you again."

Lunas frowned and shook his head. "You will never do that," he said.

They looked at each other in silence for a few seconds before she glanced away. "Don't envy people like me, George." She looked back at him and was surprised to see him smiling.

"What?"

"You've never called me George before.

"Not to your face!" She gave a half smile.

"I was hoping you would want to some day."

Georgiana looked at him quizzically, then she said: "You know, you have a far greater talent."

"As a critic?"

Georgiana shook her head. "No, as a wonderful audience."

"Audience?!"

"Don't you know everybody longs for one. To be loved for what they are, or what they can do. You give love more selflessly than anyone I have ever met."

"But to be worthy of that love...." his voice trailed away as he saw her smile fade.

"I don't feel worthy of anything at the moment." She spoke, so quietly he could barely hear her. "I just feel like a talentless little bitch who got someone killed somehow."

He was about to answer her when she turned back to face him and again forced a smile. "But I will try. Thank you for my wonderful studio."

CHAPTER XI

The following day and for days that followed Georgiana watched the car, with Maurice at the wheel; Welsh beside him and George Lunas in the back, already on the phone organising his day, glide down the drive, then pause as the automatic gates opened before turning into the rush hour traffic on Boulevard Suchet and disappearing.

When they had gone she made her way up to the studio, now illuminated by the great sky lights, and after walking round looking at everything, she found a pad of drawing paper and some pencils in one of the drawers of the cabinet and sat on the stool in the centre of the room. She looked at the pad on her lap for a long time, then put it on the floor beside her and moved to the window to gaze outside.

That night, and for the nights that followed, when he was sure she was asleep, Lunas made his way up to the Studio and looked round. He picked the pad of paper off the floor, saw it was blank, and was about to put it on the stool, but replaced it carefully on the floor instead, where he had found it. He then went out, turning off the lights and closing the door quietly behind him.

Unless he went to the office particularly early, they had breakfast together, and he would tell her a little about the kind of things he was dealing with. He never asked her how she planned to spend her own day. She was not a prisoner in the house and could come and go as she pleased as long as she returned by night fall, but they discovered that going out in the evening to the theatre or concerts as they used to was spoiled by the attention such visits attracted so they were bound to find pictures of themselves in the papers the following morning with wildly speculative comment on their relationship. To begin with, some reporters hung around outside the gates of the house, and on one occasion two got into the grounds. But Maurice discussed the likely outcome of this behaviour with those concerned, who all proved to be interested in preserving their limbs in one piece, and so, apart from the occasional newcomer - until they too got the message - this ceased.

Most evenings they ate dinner together. Sometimes they watched television, but more often Georgiana would be left by herself while he retired to his study to continue work until long after she had gone to bed. He never asked her what she had been doing, unless she volunteered the information, and she avoided the subject of her use or otherwise of the studio so painstakingly he knew his evening visit would prove fruitless before he had even made it.

Sylvie became increasingly concerned, until one day she had an inspiration and spoke urgently to her employer before he left for work. Intrigued, he readily agreed to her suggestion, and so, after he had left and she had watched Georgiana traipse up the stairs to the Studio, she went down into the kitchen and opened the door.

Upstairs, Georgiana was staring at one of the pictures when there was a scrapping sound at the door, and when she went to open it, Welsh marched into the room.

"What are you doing here?" She bent down to pet him. "Didn't he take you to the office?" The dog whined softly looking at her with his liquid brown eyes and Georgiana sighed.

"I know how you feel. But it's lovely you've come to see me!"

The dog allowed himself a few more pats, then he began to examine the room in detail before finally settling in a pool of sunlight in the middle of the floor.

Georgiana, who had been watching him with an amused expression suddenly froze. "Stay right there," she told him, and moved quickly to pick up the sketch pad and pencil.

That evening, while Lunas was warming himself by the fire with his customary glass of champagne and wondering where Georgiana had got to - she usually made a point of being there to meet him - he saw Welsh bounding down the staircase followed by the girl who seemed to be carrying a sketch pad cover. She looked very different from the aimless young woman he had left after breakfast, and when the dog had been sufficiently greeted, he looked up at her smiling.

"Georgie....you looked pleased with yourself Would you like a drink?"

"No....thank you. But I've got something to show you."

"Oh?" He looked at her keenly and felt a sudden surge of hope, but he tried to sound casual.

Georgiana pulled the sketch pad out of the cover, and after dropping the cover on the floor she turned to hold up the pad for his inspection.

It was not her usual style: just a pen and ink sketch of a very contented Collie dog lying in a pool of sunlight looking up at the artist with an expression of loving trust Lunas knew the dog had reserved for no one but himself....until today. After a moment, he glanced at Georgiana and saw she was looking at him with an almost wicked grin. "Well....what do you think?" She asked.

Lunas sighed. "If it was anyone else, I would be jealous!"

"You think I have stolen him from you?"

"I suppose I could not blame him."

Georgiana chuckled. "Don't worry," she told him. "He's still yours. He doesn't look at anyone else like that. But as I was going to give it to you, if you want it, I thought I would....you know!" She finished the sentence with a smile, and held it out to him.

Lunas took it from her and turned with his back to the nearest light, holding it with both hands so he could study it properly. He was not aware she had ever had a dog herself. That she had observed, then been able to capture in one moment in time, the depth of the relationship between the dog and himself he found as extraordinary as any aspect of her work he had been aware of so far. Eventually, he tore his eyes away and looked back at her nodding seriously.

"You know, this really is excellent!"

"I know!" Her eyes were twinkling and a smile spread across his face.

"I thought you might."

"Otherwise, I wouldn't give it to you." She paused for a moment, then she said softly: "Perhaps it's another new beginning."

"Yes, it is."

"Thanks again to you."

They looked at each other, then Georgiana took a breath and said more lightly: "There's just one condition."

"For me to keep the picture?"

"Yes. Let me keep Welsh home for a few more days. I want to try him in oils!"

Welsh adjusted easily to his new responsibilities. Lunas had tried leaving him occasionally in the past but the dog had made it clear from the beginning that he hated the idea. But now, everyone was happy. Without having to think about Welsh, Lunas found his day easier to manage. Welsh had a new and interesting job of his own, and Georgiana had a loving companion who, as the days turned into weeks, helped her to put out of her mind for most of the day the looming trial and establish a routine of work which she realised, after a only a short time, had set her feet back on the path of discovery which the shock of Jules death and her arrest had seemingly brought to an end.

When the weather was poor she worked in the Studio, but as the early spring warmed the earth of the sheltered garden at the rear of the house, encouraging all kinds of bulbs to rediscover the half-forgotten world above, Georgiana spent progressively more of her time outside. At first, she was content to walk the grounds and play with Welsh in between sketching and painting, but as the days lengthened, and the date of the Trial had still not been fixed, she lost patience and declared her intention to go further afield. At first this alarmed Lunas, but seeing the look on her face when she announced it over supper, he realised there was no stopping her. After all, he could not keep her prisoner, but he did insist that Maurice went with her. In fact, this too proved unnecessary. Time had passed, and public interest in their situation had been replaced for the moment by other sensations. Few, if any, reporters ever bothered to even pause outside Poussan le-Bas these days.

Georgiana had grown to like Maurice, but she found his supervision tiresome and protested to Lunas after a few days that with Welsh by her side she was perfectly safe. Even so, Lunas insisted at first on a halfway stage, with Maurice shadowing her from a distance, but the Moroccan reported after a while that, in his opinion, Georgiana was no more likely to be bothered than any young woman of equivalent looks, a situation no different from that which had existed when she was attending the Conservatoire, and which she had learned to handle from her early teens. So, from then on, when the weather was fine, Georgiana would set out with Welsh on his lead into the Bois-du-Bolougne carrying her paints, stool and easel to set up for the day in various places.

The beautiful young American girl with her dog soon became well known to the other users of the Bois: young mothers with children, joggers, people with other dogs and a few vagrants. But once Georgiana managed to put the superimposed fears of Lunas and Sylvie out of her mind, she relaxed and was able to concentrate on the countless subjects demanding her attention, from the amazing variety of buildings lining the Bois to the Bois itself; trees, lakes, bridges, and the life both human and animal which coursed through it each day.

Few bothered her. She was struck again by the reserve with which most Parisians treated each other and which she had taken at first to show how basically unfriendly they were - in contrast to New York, where a perfect stranger was likely to confide the most intimate details of their lives within half a minute. But she had come to realise that this was because one of the strongest characteristics of those around her now was respect for the privacy of others. The vast majority of the ones who did attempt to strike up a conversation were those who stopped to take an interest in her work - many more, and usually far better informed than those who might have done so at home.

Georgiana had adjusted to this during her first summer in Paris, and often enjoyed the exchanges which could develop into quite long conversations. But, then, of course, there were those who, while professing interest were simply trying to pick her up, and Georgiana was amused to see how accurately Welsh distinguished one from the other and growled discouragingly and even showed his teeth when required.

She often sketched him in various situations and was interested to see that although he looked at her lovingly too, it was different from the adoration reserved exclusively for Lunas; an almost closer love in her case - as if between equals, she guessed. But she was no dog psychologist. She only knew there was a bond between them now that was unique, yet expressed in some indefinable way the relationship between she and George, which now seemed suspended in Limbo. She was happy; not as happy as she knew she could be, but she was afraid to reach out further for fear of upsetting what they had. Life had taught her how transitory such things could be, and there was, after all, the Trial which had to be faced sooner or later. It was like being in a waiting room with two doors. Beyond one, was a state of bliss denied to all but a few. Beyond the other, a world of uncertainty she dared not think about. Better to enjoy what life had given her as long as possible. They would not keep her waiting for ever.

The wait came to an end as quickly as it was unexpected. On her return to the House not long after these thoughts first formed in her mind, Paul opened the door for her, and Welsh, having been let off the lead for their walk up the drive, galloped past him and rushed over to Lunas, who was evidently back early. Paul took the paints, easel and stool but Georgiana kept hold of her sketch pad and went over to where he was waiting for her, smiling and with his customary glass of champagne already half empty.

"Why are you home early?" She asked him.

"I'll tell you in a minute. Would you like a glass?"

Georgiana shook her head and was about to repeat the question when he looked at the sketch pad and said : "May I see?"

She did not always show him her day's work, but he guessed from the pad in her hand she had something she wanted to show him now.

Georgiana suppressed the butterflies in her stomach, knowing that any departure from their routine might be the signal she dreaded, but she nodded and forced a smile while pulling the pad out of its cover and holding it up for his inspection. She did not often do single portraits, but the sketch was of a very old woman feeding pigeons.

"She told me her name was Marguerite," Georgiana murmured while he was studying it. "She lives in the Bois all summer, unless the police catch her and take her in."

"What then?" Lunas glanced at her. Georgiana shrugged.

"They put her in a hostel for the night, but they can't lock her up!"

Lunas nodded and looked back at the sketch.

"She must be nearly a hundred years old, the things she remembers," Georgiana went on. "What things?"

"The first World War....things like that." Georgiana paused for a moment, then she said: "Now tell me why you are home so early? Has something happened?"

Lunas nodded, and turned to her. "Yes, it has." He handed her back to the sketch pad. "You should try working this up in oils, by the way.... when we get back."

Georgiana caught her breath. "The Trial! You've got a date for the Trial!" Lunas looked at her frowning, then his brow cleared.

"No, no. I meant, when we get back from vacation."

"Vacation?" Georgiana looked at him bewildered. "Vacation?" She repeated, stupidly. "What Vacation?"

Lunas smiled broadly. "I've decided I need one."

"But you said when we get back."

"That's right. We're going together. You can paint, and I can relax." Georgiana still stared at him.

"But I can't go anywhere," she said. "You know that."

"You can go anywhere you like," Lunas insisted with a grin. "As long as it's in France....and as long as I am there to keep an eye on you." He looked at her. "Stop looking at me like that, Georgiana, and for heaven's sake close your mouth. It's not very charming!" Georgiana shut her mouth hurriedly as he went on. "It's time you got to know the most beautiful country in the world." He smiled broadly and turned to the side-board. "Now then, you really ought to have that glass of champagne!"

"I think I need it!"

"Good." He poured the glass and topped up his own before turning back to hand it to her, by which time she had more or less recovered her composure.

"Here's to us then....and to a wonderful trip." They clinked glasses.

"Where are we going?" Georgiana asked when she had taken a sip.

Lunas beamed. "It's not so much where we are going....it's how we are going," he told her. "How then?"

"You are going on a 'Grand Tour' of France, sitting beside me in the most wonderful car on the road."

"What's that?"

He suddenly looked serious. "It's a 1950 drop head Rolls Royce Phantom. They only made fifty. As far as I know this is the only one in France!"

"I'll bet you've given it a name," she teased.

"But of course."

"Go on then?"

"Belinda." He looked at her still trying to keep a straight face.

"Belinda! I thought it was only the British who did crazy things like driving around in old cars with girl's names."

"Certainly not!" Lunas drew" himself up with mock indignation. "Anything worthwhile, the British learned from us!"

Georgiana laughed happily and Lunas allowed himself to smile. "You would like to come then?" he asked.

"What about Welsh?"

Lunas glanced down at the dog who had sat between them looking up eagerly as he usually did when they were together and who now wagged his tail at the mention of his name.

"Welsh will come, of course."

Georgiana nodded. "In that case, I would love to come," she said, then lowered her glass and looked at him. "You cruel bastard!" She said, softly.

"Me!....why?" He looked at her with feigned innocence.

"You know why. You do anything like that to me again and I'll kill you!"

CHAPTER XII

The following day there was not a cloud in the sky. Lunas decided it was warm enough to have the drop head and wind shield down from the beginning of their journey. The trunk was loaded with their suitcases; Welsh shared the back seat with Georgina's painting equipment and a picnic basket for lunch.

Lunas drove, looking casually elegant, except for the old fashioned goggles he insisted were necessary to be properly in tune with the car and Georgiana sat beside him wearing jeans and a light sweater over her T Shirt. She also had wrap round sunglasses and had jammed a baseball cap, worn back to front, over her hair to stop it blowing into her eyes as they went along. They planned to spend the first night in Fontainebleau in the heart of a forest some sixty miles south of Paris and site of the immense Chateau once so favoured by Napoleon. But, after stopping for a picnic at the edge of the forest, Lunas took a diversion to the village of Barbizon.

On either side of the narrow street were low, thatched roofed cottages, most of which had been turned into souvenir shops or little art galleries. It was early in the season. Despite this, they found it already crammed with tourists. Lunas looked round, then glanced at Georgiana apologetically while they were waiting for a large coach to navigate the restricted space left after they had pulled out of its way as far as they could to let it pass.

"Like ourselves, people find Barbizon a convenient place to grab a little culture after a picnic in the forest" he said. "Perhaps we can find a space in the car park at the end of the village and walk back?"

Georgiana nodded without answering.

"It was the home of a group of nineteenth century landscape painters." Lunas continued, "forbears of the more famous Impressionists. So, in a way, they were your artistic grandparents: Millet....Theodore

Rousseau, Daubigny.... Diazz.... they all lived here. The cottages are genuine enough. If you can imagine it without the traffic, it's very much as it was a hundred years ago. " He looked at her more closely. "What's the matter? I thought you would be interested. Don't you like tourists?"

Georgiana looked at him then she shook her head slightly. "I'm sorry," she said. "I keep thinking about Jules."

"Jules Lavosin"

"Yes. He spent last summer here."

Lunas frowned. The bus was almost past and he put the car into gear. "You should have said," he told her.

"But I know you love to come here."

"Not if it upsets you." He guided the car out into the traffic and they began to move slowly up the village street. "But it's true," he admitted. "I do find it fascinating. I don't suppose anywhere in the world saw such a gathering of genius at any one time."

"When does an art lover become a tourist?" Georgiana said after they had navigated almost to the end of the street.

Lunas shrugged. "I suppose, when there are so many they cannot help but destroy the thing they have come to admire!"

Georgiana turned to him. "That includes us then," she said. "We are no different!"

Lunas nodded. "That's true." They had reached the car park and he could see a space, but instead of pulling in he suddenly put his foot down and they accelerated past the entrance.

Georgiana looked at him with surprise and he glanced at her with a grin as they reached the end of the village and he changed into a higher gear.

"We'll leave your artistic forebears in peace. I think there's more space where we're headed!

The entrance to the town of Fontainebleau took them up the straight, mile long carriage way which used to be the southern approach to the Chateau, an enormous structure now rising up in front of them like something out of a story by the Brothers Grimm. Georgiana would not have been surprised if he had told her a giant lived there, so heroic were its proportions, and these were matched by the formal park which used to be just part of the private grounds of the Royal residence, and which extended on either side in lawns, artificial lakes and fountains surrounded by steps leading up to marble terraces, which in turn were decorated with statues of stags, hounds, gods, goddess's and long forgotten warriors. Only one name was recalled however: Napoleon Bonaparte. His initials, entwined with those of the Empress Josephine could be seen repeated in a long frieze which ran along the side of the Chateau facing them just below roof level, and his presence hung in the air, a challenge and a rebuke to those lessor mortals who had conspired to bring him down.

"Not for nothing did admirers after his death raise so many statues of a noble stag surrounded by baying hounds," Lunas remarked as they passed one.

The road passed through a gate and they left the park to enter the town itself with its narrow streets in the shadow of the Chateau. Lunas followed one of these until it opened out into the main square of the town on the north side, and on the opposite side of which was the Hotel Aigle Noir....the Black Eagle, Napoleon's emblem.

As they pulled into the small Courtyard in front of the Hotel, two bell-hops came hurrying out to take their bags, and while they were doing this Georgiana helped Lunas to put up the canvas roof. They had no sooner done so when one of the bell-hops came back outside with two keys in his hand. "You are in rooms six and seven as you requested, Monsieur." He held out the keys, but Lunas turned to Georgiana who was putting Welsh on his lead.

"Do you want to go to your room before we walk round the Chateau?" he asked.

Georgiana shook her head and straightened up holding onto the lead. "Not really," she said. "I'd much rather stretch my legs. So would Welsh, I'm sure!" She glanced down at the dog, who wagged his agreement.

Lunas nodded approvingly. "Good. The gates of the Chateau close at six." He glanced at the clock in the centre of the square and narrowed his eyes momentarily against the sun: "Which gives us time for a look round before dinner." He turned and threw the car keys to the bell hop. "Put the car in the garage," he instructed. "We will not be needing it again this evening.

"Oui Monsieur." The man nodded dutifully but glanced anxiously at the Rolls - something missed by Lunas who had turned immediately to Georgiana to take her arm.

He led her out of the Hotel Entrance then round the square retracing the way they had come in the car. "We'll just walk around the outside today," he explained. "Then we'll come back to the Main Entrance and look at the front of the house. It will give Welsh a chance to have a run in the park first."

It was an hour before they had walked right round the Chateau and examined as much of the sculpture as could be seen without heading off into the far reaches of the park. Welsh was then content to wait after they put him in the car while they made their way back to the gate leading into the vast courtyard in front of the main entrance to the Chateau.

This was enclosed by iron railings, ten feet high, painted black and tipped with gold. The main gates were closed, and they entered by a gate at the side to find themselves facing the huge main building across the gravelled and stone slabbed expanse at a distance of two hundred yards, making the Courtyard itself a perfect square. On either side of the main building, lower buildings extended towards them down either side to make three sides of the square. Exactly opposite, in the centre of the main building, a double horse shoe stone staircase led up to the great doors.

They walked half way towards this, then stopped and Georgiana took a deep breath. "Now that's what I call an entrance," she said, turning to him. "Tell, me about it."

"The house was built originally as a country retreat for the Kings of France," Lunas began. "A sort of lodge where they could hold hunting parties for their cronies. The forest was full of game in those days."

"Some pad!"

"Napoleon greatly preferred it to Versailles. Whenever he could get away from affairs of State..."

"Or laying waste the rest of Europe!"

"Or from his campaigns," Lunas persisted, "he would come here." He paused for a moment, and looking at him quickly Georgiana saw he was deadly serious.

"It was here, with his loyal troops paraded before him, he came down that staircase to review them for the last time," he went on quietly, "and to say goodbye, before being sent off into exile." He glanced at her with a wry smile. "Not that they held him for long; within six months he escaped and nearly beat the lot of them at Waterloo. Would have done too if that stupid Prussian Bluthner had only arrived with his reinforcements half an hour later. They were almost too late to save Wellington as it was!" He put his hand on her arm again and they began to walk forwards.

Georgiana said: "How often life turns on chance!."

Lunas nodded. "That's true." He paused for a moment, then he said: "Think, if I hadn't asked Maurice to drop me off at the comer of Washington Square two years ago so I could take a walk, we wouldn't be here now. They stopped to face each other.

"And I wouldn't be facing a murder rap," Georgiana said softly.

Lunas paused, then he said: "Do you blame me for that?"

"Of course not." She looked at him; and suddenly it was so easy. "I love you," she said simply, then smiled as if she had told him something so obvious it was scarcely worth mentioning.

"Georgie!" He could scarcely breathe.

"No matter what happens," she said. "I'll always be glad you came into my life."

Lunas felt himself drowning in the eyes that were looking up at him - he suddenly realised - no differently from the way she had looked at him as long as he could remember. What a blind fool he had been! Impulsively, he took both her hands in his. 'Dear God, let him not make a fool of himself '. Even now, he feared to assume she meant what he longed for. There was more than one kind of love.

"I have come to love you too, Georgie," he heard himself saying. It was like listening to someone else. "At first, I just admired you as an artist.... but now it is so much more." (But did she really love him in the same way he asked himself even as he spoke. Was that what she had meant?)

"I would do anything for you."(It was true....and to anyone who tried to take her from him!) "I knew you were grateful....but I never imagined you could love anyone like me." He waited. There could be no more ambiguities surely? It was elation or despair!

"You are the most wonderful thing that ever happened to me," Georgiana said softly. "I always thought, as long as I had Welsh, I had part of you."

"And I always thought he had a part of your heart you would never give to me yourself!". His heart flooded with relief.

Georgiana moved into his arms, and as he held her she thought. 'Now she was safe. Nothing could touch her anymore. For the rest of her life she would rest in his love and approval. She would become the woman she had dreamed she could be for him alone, and an artist whose horizons he alone understood and shared.

For Lunas, it seemed like the end of a long journey. He knew a moment of peace and happiness he would remember as long as he lived.

"Let's go back to the hotel," he heard her whisper.

"Don't you want to walk round?"

"Tomorrow. Take me back now."

She pulled her head back, then suddenly kissed him with an urgency that set him ablaze.

* * *

Lunas opened his eyes. Then he sat up and glanced at the empty bed beside him. The bedside clock showed six - ten. He smiled to himself, then slid out of the bed and went to open the shutters. The first rays of the sun were just striking the highest chimney of the Chateau opposite.

He glanced down to the railings on the opposite side of the square and into the still darkened courtyard beyond. Was it his imagination, or could he see a figure sitting on a stool of some kind right out there in the middle? He frowned, then stared again; probably some trick of the early light...or perhaps a statue he had not noticed before. He turned from the window and slipped on a robe which he had dropped on the floor, then moved to the door, opening it silently before stepping out into the corridor.

Georgiana's room was next door. He found the key still in the lock and half opened the door to glance inside. One look told him she was not there. There were some clothes on the bed beside the opened suitcase but the bed itself had not been slept in. She must have gone back to her room, dressed, then gone straight out again; perhaps to take Welsh for a walk.

Lunas went back to his own room. He showered quickly, then threw on some clothes and went down the stairs to the entrance lobby of the Hotel. The night porter told him that the young lady had gone out with her dog on a lead, but $he had first asked him to unlock the garage so she could get her paints. Lunas nodded his thanks, then strode out of the Hotel and across the square to the side entrance gate leading into the Chateau Courtyard. His eyes had not been playing tricks on him after all!

The Sun was up, but there were few people and vehicles about. He remembered it was Sunday. The gate was open and he could see Georgiana sitting on her stool in the middle of the Courtyard facing the Chateau, busily at work on a canvas set up in front of her. The black lump on the ground beside her must be Welsh catching up on his sleep. He made to walk through, but a uniformed attendant stepped into his path with hand upraised.

"The Chateau is not open until ten o'clock on Sunday Monsieur." Lunas looked over the man's shoulder and nodded in Georgiana's direction. "Then what is my young friend doing there?" he demanded.

The Guard turned to follow his glance for a moment before turning back to face him, and gave an embarrassed smile. "The American girl," he conceded. "She was so anxious to start work on her painting. She asked so prettily, and in such nice French.... I had not the heart to refuse."

"Well, I am responsible for her," Lunas said reasonably. "So I am asking you in my nice French to allow me to join her."

This presented the guard with a dilemma. But after wrestling with himself for a moment he said: "You must stay where I can see you."

"I am not going to disturb her," Lunas assured him respectfully. "I just want to see she is all right. I am her guardian, you see."

The guard brightened considerably at this. Clearly the newcomer did not present any competition. A guardian, after all, was almost the same as a parent, and so his plan to invite the stunning young woman for a coffee when he came off duty at midday might not be frustrated after all.

"Very well, Monsieur," he said generously. "On this occasion also I will make an exception." Lunas nodded and said dryly: "It takes a big man to override the rules when the need arises." Taking this at face value, the guard's face flushed with pleasure and he waved Lunas through.

Georgiana had her back to him and was not aware of his approach until Welsh suddenly sat up wagging his tail and whining with pleasure. She turned around, brush in hand and gave a dazzling smile as soon as she saw him.

"Good morning!"

"Good morning." He reached her side and bent down to kiss her upturned face. Watching this from a distance, the Guard stirred uncomfortably. What kind of a guardian was this that kissed his protege full on the lips?!

"Couldn't you sleep?" He asked as he straightened up, smiling.

Georgiana pulled a face. "You've got to be kidding! I slept like a log after we made love the last time. Then I woke up with too much energy I had to get up. I thought I'd let you sleep on. You looked so cute!"

"Cute!"

"Yeah.... Cute!" She grinned up at him. "Does that demean your masculinity?

"I'm not sure!"

"Well.... Don't worry about it. I still love you!"

"Hmm!" Lunas looked doubtful, then he said. "Are you ready for breakfast?"

"Oh no!" Georgiana shook her head.

"I couldn't eat. Look, you haven't looked at my painting."

It was true, his eyes had not strayed from her face since those blue eyes of hers had locked onto his, but now he turned at her invitation to the canvas in front of her. What he saw gave him quite a shock and within a moment he was riveted: He saw that she had recreated that moment in the history of the Chateau he had described to her the previous day.... when the Emperor Napoleon had come out of the main entrance at the top of the huge double stone staircase and walked slowly down to review his elite troops for the last time before going off into exile.

The atmosphere was of sadness; of memories and never to be repeated glories; of pride, defiance.... resignation, but this last with a hint it might not be the end after all. Lunas found his eyes being pulled first this way then that across the scene depicted in front of him in an explosion of impressions: the bearing of the Emperor; the set of his shoulders, and of course, his smouldering eyes; then his body-guard drawn up at the front of the steps, those who had followed him from the triumph of Austerlitz to the hell of Moscow and back, and were still willing to risk death for him, no matter how hopeless the odds. The face of the young drummer who had joined too late for all of this, but who looked up at his Emperor with an expression that begged for a chance to prove that he too could be like the rest. And finally, the Tricolour, fluttering in the breeze like the trumpet call to battle Lunas swore he could hear. He tore his eyes away for a moment to glance momentarily at Georgiana, who, was watching him closely, before returning to the picture. But now it was different, and he realised that what he had thought he had seen in such detail was only there in outlines which had somehow tricked his imagination into filling in the rest. He shook his head slowly, then looked back at her.

"How do you do that?" He asked humbly.

"How do I do what?" She was grinning at him and he realised she knew perfectly well what he meant.

"How do you make people see so much more than you've actually drawn". He looked back at the picture. "I've noticed it with your other work....but never so strongly as this."

Georgiana stared at the canvas, then took a breath and looked back at him. "Perhaps I've never been anywhere that moved me as much," she said softly. "Or at a time when I felt so completely happy."

Lunas made a decision. "You must not go back to the Conservatoire, Georgie," he said firmly.

"No?"

Lunas shook his head. "No matter what happens. This is the path you must follow now. Nothing must interfere."

Georgiana looked at him, impressed by the strength of his feelings. "Can I stay with you, then?" She asked.

"Of course; as long as you want. But on the understanding that if you ever want to leave, you will feel completely at liberty to do so."

"I'll never want to leave you," Georgiana said looking up at him calmly. "Not as long as you want me."

It was mid afternoon before she was satisfied and agreed to be taken back to the hotel for something to eat. It was a busy day for tourists and Georgiana, her painting and her dog were an added attraction. The guard who had let them in went off in disgust at midday with a final remonstrative glance in their direction, and when Lunas came back after taking Welsh for another run in the park he found Georgiana scarcely able to continue for people crowding her and, he stayed close by for the rest of the time to keep the curious at a distance. Irritating though this was, it set his mind racing: If one picture could stimulate such interest!

They left Fontainbleau in the late afternoon. Lunas drove due west, passing under the main Paris to Marseilles a.0utoroute to Chartres where he showed her the monument to Jean Moulin, the great hero of the French Resistance in the Second World War, who had been betrayed to the Vichy collaborators but who had died under torture without giving anything away.

Having checked into the Hotel de la Poste, they took Welsh for a final walk after dinner to find all the lights on in the great Gothic Cathedral which he had intended to show her the following morning, as it normally closed by 6p.m. But on making inquiries they found a performance of Mozart's Requiem in progress and slipped into one of the back pews in time for most of the second half. If anyone noticed Welsh sitting in the far comer by the wall next to Georgiana they did not say anything, and Lunas noted, not for the first time, how a beautiful woman in France was able to write her own rules....as long as she smiled and spoke nice French! But he was soon caught up in the performance, and his imagination soared with the music to the high vaulted roof, doubly mysterious in the shadows and he was carried to the imagined fulfilment of a new ambition which had taken possession of him only that afternoon, as he had stood watching the crowds as they stared at Georgiana's painting and Georgiana herself He knew then she needed neither his help, nor anyone else to become a truly great artist....one who would be remembered long after the bodies which they had held and shared so passionately were dust. But perhaps he would be remembered, not just as someone who had loved and protected her, but who forced the world to acknowledge her genius while she was still young enough to enjoy it.

After Chartres he showed her the Chateaux of the Loire and the French Kings' other great hunting lodge in the forest of Chambord. They also stopped further down the river at a smaller, simpler house in the town of Amboise where Leonardo da Vinci spent his last years flattering his Royal Patron with his genius. There were few paintings of any merit there, but there was an exhibition of his designs - of everything from helicopters to machine guns three hundred years before their time.

They turned South. The Rolls took its time and they stopped often. Once they spent an afternoon watching millions of sunflowers which stretched to the horizon, slowly tum to keep their faces to the sun. Further on, were the snow brushed mountains of the Massif Central, and the rolling uplands of the Auvergne, which were still carpeted with endless fields of wild daffodils and narcissus.

They spoke little during the day. Lunas let the beauty of the countryside speak for itself. In the evening they stopped at small inns where the food was usually delicious and the owner and his wife happy to receive visitors so early in the season and who went out of their way to make them comfortable and to point out local items of interest.

"It's amazing how the Devil got around in the old days," Lunas remarked during one such stop. Every time there's a large rock standing alone, a hole in the ground or a narrow gorge, the poor fellow is accused of having either thrown it, dug it or jumped it!"

Georgiana smiled at him across the plain wooden table on which they were sharing supper and surreptitiously passed a piece of spiced rabbit to Welsh under the table who was leaning affectionately against her knees and who was rapidly acquiring the status of canine gourmet from such attention. "I expect he's retired," she remarked. It all seems to have happened a long time ago."

But Lunas shook his head. "No. I think he's moved with the times," he said. "Nowadays, he runs large corporations and fast food restaurants!"

"I like junk food," Georgiana confessed. "There was a report in the New York Post just before I left; it's just as good for you as any other."

Lunas snorted disbelievingly. Then he said: 'Speaking of the Devil, I sometimes think you're in league with him!"

Georgiana shot him a glance and saw he was half serious. "Don't say things like that," she said. "It scares me!"

Lunas was immediately contrite. "I'm sorry," he said. "I only meant the way, in your paintings you create an effect without any obvious explanation."

"It's all in your mind," she told him. "If it's not in you, it doesn't work."

"Maybe!" There was a pause, and he saw her hand disappear under the table again. "You're ruining that dog," he said with mock severity. "You shouldn't feed him at the table."

"Oh....but he's a friend, Georgiana insisted. "Besides, he told me his hobby was rabbit! That was in confidence, by the way, so don't let it go any further!"

"And chicken, and steak, and any other thing that happens to be on the menu!"

"No." Georgiana thought for a moment, frowning. "He doesn't like fruit....except for bananas....which he needs for potassium, I think he said. And he doesn't like red wine!"

"But he does like the cheese that goes with it!"

"Of course. " Georgiana reached down and fondled the dog's silky ears, smiling across the table. "Everyone adores cheese!"

Lunas smiled back with a serenity he suddenly did not feel. Was it possible she had become even more beautiful since they had begun this trip together? She seemed to be lit by some magic from within. He had never believed such happiness was possible. How could he face life now without her? They never mentioned the Trial. But ever since leaving Paris it had been necessary for him to report by telephone every few days to the Court and he always tried to do this when she was unable to overhear. He was also in touch with Charles Gros, but so far the team of private detectives they had employed had not been able to come up with anything that might point to the real killer of Jules Lavosin. Time was running out. Against this, was the satisfaction of the knowledge of the growing number of completed canvasses in the big trunk of the Rolls which evidenced her growing power. He was sure he would have been able to arrange them in chronological order, even if witnessing the birth of each had not been burned into his memory. Often he sat with her while she was working. At first, he had made a point of leaving her alone for fear of cramping her style. That was when he took Welsh for walks and made phone calls, but she told him she liked him watching if he wanted to.

He was glad she could not read his mind sometimes when he had dark thoughts. In the past, he had sprung accomplices from under the noses of the police and he would stop at nothing to save her. French justice took a more lenient view of what they described as 'crimes of passion'. But in order to obtain such leniency it was necessary to plead guilty and throw oneself in the mercy of the Court; and being innocent, this was something he would never ask her to do. So it was all or nothing. The guillotine was reserved now for treason and acts of terrorism. But if she was found guilty, having pleaded innocent, she could, in theory, be sentenced to years in jail. Gros had told him that only a few weeks before a French national had been condemned to death in Texas. It should have nothing to do with Georgiana's case, Gros had assured him. In which case, why did he mention it?!

They returned to Paris with still no firm news concerning a date for the Trial, but Gros had told him when they spoke that morning, just before leaving, that the police had asked for a postponement, 'so they could sift further evidence'. "It might mean they are not so sure they have a case after all," he had said comfortingly, and when Lunas told Georgiana this as they were approaching Paris they both agreed it did look hopeful.

"I hope you do not mind if we do not go out tonight?" he said, sometime later.

Georgiana shook her head. "On our first night back home? I just want there to be the two of us."

"I hoped you would say that. One of the things I asked Charles to do this morning was phone Sylvie and ask her to prepare a cold supper we can serve ourselves. "

Georgiana closed her eyes and nodded happily.

The front door opened as soon as the Rolls pulled up outside the house and Paul, Sylvie and Maurice came down the steps to greet them. "Did you have a nice trip?" Sylvie asked when the two women had hugged each other. She looked at Georgiana and realised at once how much she had changed. "Tell me later," she whispered.

Lunas was giving orders to Paul, and Georgiana nodded quickly before turning away and saying to the world at large. "I can't tell you how much we've seen. It'll take for ever!"

"You'll find the trunk is almost full of canvasses," Lunas said to Maurice. "Take them up to the studio the back way....and be very careful, please."

Maurice nodded, but as he was turning away Lunas called after him. "I shall need to go to the office tomorrow. Be ready at eight o'clock."

"D'accord."

We shall not be going out again tonight, so when you have taken the canvas upstairs...."

Maurice glanced back and grinned. "I understand. Make myself scarce!"

Lunas returned his smile, and watched the Moroccan let himself out of the front door before turning to face Sylvie who was standing waiting.

"Yes, Sylvie?"

"Monsieur Lunas....I am sorry to trouble you as soon as you get back, but there is someone here to see you."

Lunas looked at her impatiently. "I don't want to see anyone tonight. Tell them to come to my office tomorrow."

"It's Marie."

"Marie?" He looked at her frowning "who....?"

"Marie Gerard." Sylvie interrupted. "Who used to work for you."

Georgiana glanced at Lunas and saw at once the name meant more to him than simply that of an old employee. "Marie Gerard," Lunas repeated after a moment.

" What does she want?"

Sylvie shrugged. "I don't know. She will only speak to you. I knew you would not want to see her."

"She betrayed me"....this to Georgiana who was looking from one to the other curiously.

"She has just come out of prison," Sylvie put in.

"Prison!?"

Again Sylvie shrugged. " I would have sent her away, but she looked exhausted. She had not eaten anything today, so I gave her some food and let her rest for a while."

"Where is she?"

"I put her in the small study. If you like I will get rid of her, but I was not sure. She said she had something important to tell you."

"What can she possibly know of interest to me?" Lunas demanded, impatiently. Sylvie looked at him, then she said flatly: "Perhaps, something she heard in Prison."

Before he could answer, Georgiana said: "Who is this Marie?"

Lunas turned to her. "She used to by my Secretary," he told her. "She gave the security codes of one of the strong rooms to her boyfriend and his brother so they managed to get away with some valuable pictures."

"She should have known better at her age!" Sylvie growled.

"That's what I assumed," Lunas agreed, before turning back to Georgiana and adding, "fortunately, Maurice caught up with them."

"What happened?" Georgiana asked, eyes wide.

"He had to kill the boyfriend in self-defence," Lunas said quietly. "Marie was arrested. But we did not pursue the matter."

Suddenly, Georgiana felt the hairs on the nape of her neck tingle with apprehension. "Be careful, George," she begged. "That woman could be dangerous. She probably holds you responsible for her boyfriend's death!"

Lunas smiled and squeezed her arm gently. "There is no need to worry," he assured her. "She has undoubtedly come to ask for money." Georgiana glanced at Sylvie, who nodded in agreement and Lunas went on: "You go upstairs, and get ready for the marvellous supper I know Sylvie will lay out for us. I'll see her meanwhile and find out what she wants."

Sylvie nodded again. "Very well, Monsieur. " She turned and made her way back to the kitchen. "Go on, Cherie," Lunas said to Georgiana, who still hesitated. "I will not be long."

"Will you give her something?"

"I will see."

"People do things for love they would never do otherwise."

"That's true. But betrayal is betrayal."

Georgiana looked at him. She was on the point of saying something - perhaps in mitigation; to tell him what she would feel like doing to anyone who harmed him. But, seeing his expression, she thought better of it, and after giving him a quick peck on the cheek, turned and ran up the stair-case after Paul.

By the time she reached her bedroom he had laid her old suitcase on the bed as well as the new one she had to get in Montpellier to accommodate all the things he had insisted on buying for her.

"Do you need any help unpacking, Miss Georgie?" He asked with a smile. "Shall I call Sylvie?"

"Gee no!" Georgiana pulled a face. "Don't stop her doing supper, I'm starved!" Then she glanced at him a little shyly: "And why Miss Georgie, all of a sudden? What happened to plain Georgie?"

Paul shrugged, then he said without rancour: " I think your position here has changed."

The two of them looked at each other before Georgiana said simply: "I guess it has, Paul. And I couldn't be happier."

"I am glad too."

"But I haven't forgotten that soon I have to stand Trial. I may not be here for long."

Paul looked at her, then he said softly. "Monsieur Lunas would never let anything happen to you. I know him."

She was on the point of asking him what he meant when there was a loud bang from somewhere in the depths of the house.

"Stay here!" Georgiana looked at Paul in alarm, but he flew to the door without another word and she heard him running down the passageway to the head of the stairs. Shock, suddenly turned to fear.

Georgiana ran after Paul, half tripping over the coat that had fallen off the bed onto the floor where she had thrown it on entering the room. As she reached the corridor she heard two more shots, and a woman scream.

As she hurtled down the stairs Georgiana's first thought was that George had shot his visitor, but then she heard the same voice screaming for help and realised it was Sylvie.

Georgiana reached the bottom of the stairs and ran in the direction the sound was coming from. The door of the study was open. She saw Sylvie standing just inside the room staring at a middle aged woman who was holding a small Automatic, and looking down at the floor behind the desk. Lunas was nowhere to be seen.

Paul snatched the gun from the woman while Sylvie flung herself down on her knees beside the desk and Georgiana's brain finally accepted what her eyes were telling her. In a moment she was beside the desk herself and saw Lunas lying on the floor on his back with his eyes closed and With a trickle of blood coming from the side of his mouth. Sylvie had taken a grip on herself and was examining him with evident professionalism. She glanced up quickly. "He's still alive," she said. "Quick, call an ambulance. The phone's on the desk."

Georgiana snatched up the instrument to dial the emergency number. She heard Paul ask: "Can you stop the bleeding?"

Sylvie shook her head briefly. "I don't think so."

Paul turned as the woman who had not moved since he took the gun from her. "What have you done?" he shouted at her.

Georgiana heard the woman say calmly : "I've shot the bastard!"

Paul hit her backhanded in the side of the face with the gun and she collapsed in tears into the chair behind the desk.

While Georgiana was giving the address of the house to the ambulance service Maurice appeared in the doorway. He took in what had happened in a moment and, strode across to pull the women's head up by her hair so he could look at her.

"You!" he said harshly. "I should have killed you as well!"

Georgiana put down the phone and sank to her knees beside Sylvie who was now pressing hard on the unconscious man's chest with her left hand.

"The bullets must have just missed his heart or he would be dead already," she said.

Georgiana looked dumbly at where she was pointing, then her eyes moved to his face. She had never felt so helpless. "They said the Ambulance should be here in ten minutes," she heard herself say. "Will they be able to save him?"

"I don't know." Sylvie then reached across to squeeze her arm with her free hand. "He is very strong."

Paul handed the gun to Maurice then left the room to open the gates for the ambulance. Maurice sat on the edge of the desk.

"Can I do anything to help?" Georgiana asked, but Sylvie shook her head. "They will be here soon," she said.

"Yes."

Georgiana nodded. Then she stood up leaning on the edge of the desk. She looked down at the two of them, then turned her head and stared at the woman who was sitting in the chair behind the desk nursing her injured face. Seeing her looking, the woman returned her stare, then she said. "Are you his lordship's bit of stuff?"

"Shut up!" Maurice snapped, unless you want the other side of your face decorated!"

But the woman continued to look at her. "Now you know how I felt!" she said matter of factly.

"I warn you," Maurice said raising the gun as if about to hit her, but the woman turned and looked up at him.

"You'd better kill me, if you know what's good for you," she said. "Otherwise, one of these days, I'm going to kill you too"

For a moment Georgiana thought he was going to take her at her word. "No, Maurice!" she begged.

She saw him freeze, then relax. "Don't worry, Mam'selle," he said softly. "I would prefer to be killed than what is going to happen to her now."

Georgiana travelled in the ambulance with Maurice following behind in the car. Sylvie telephoned Charles Gros and he joined them in the corridor outside the operating theatre half an hour after Lunas was admitted, having been tracked down by Paul in one of his favourite restaurants. They were told that as no one could say how long Monsieur Lunas would be inside, they would be more comfortable in the general waiting room, but Georgiana insisted on remaining where they were so she could be informed immediately how things were going.

After two hours the door of the Theatre opened and a nurse came out and walked towards them. She ignored Georgiana completely and glanced at the two men.

"Monsieur Gros?" The Lawyer rose to his feet, followed by the other two. The nurse stopped in front of him.

"We understand you are Monsieur Lunas' Attorney?"

Gros nodded: "That is correct."

"How is he?" Georgiana blurted, and the nurse turned to her with a faintly disapproving expression.

"And you are, Madame?" She said.

"This is Mam'selle Montes," Maurice said with a hint of menace.

"Monsieur Lunas' protege," Gros added hurriedly.

"I see," She turned back to Georgiana. "Please wait here. Monsieur Lunas has asked to see Monsieur Gros."

"Can't I see him?" Georgiana begged.

"Alone," the Nurse said firmly. Then she looked pointedly at Gros. "Please follow me."

"But is he going to be all right?" Georgiana persisted.

The Nurse turned back to her, and her expression softened. "I don't know," she said frankly. "The Surgeons have done what they can."

They watched Gros follow the Nurse and disappear through the doors of the operating theatre.

Georgiana heard Maurice muttering softly under his breath and she glanced at him. "What a bitch!" He commented, which made Georgiana feel better.

They both sat down again. "At least he's come through the operation," Georgiana said after a few seconds, and the Moroccan nodded encouragingly.

She had always been a bit frightened of Maurice, Georgiana thought to herself. But sitting there now, in such circumstances, she could not imagine anyone she would prefer to stand vigil with her.

The end to their wait came swiftly. The theatre doors opened suddenly and Gros came out alone and walked towards them. Georgiana felt her heart almost stop when she saw his expression.

"What has happened?" Maurice demanded as they both started to their feet to face him.

"Monsieur Lunas is dead," Gros said without preamble.

"Oh. My God!" Georgiana felt Maurice's hand on her arm so tightly she would have gasped with pain in normal circumstances, but now it just seemed to add his strength to hers.

"He regained consciousness for a few minutes just before the end," Gros continued. That's when he asked for me."

"Didn't he want to see me?" Georgiana said numbly.

"Of course," Gros assured her. "But he knew his life was slipping away and, above all, he wanted to make sure you would be taken care of."

"I don't care what happens to me."

"We have to get you back to America at once."

"Why?" Georgiana looked at him uncomprehendingly.

"Because once the Court hears that George is dead, your bail will be cancelled and you will be taken back to prison."

"I don't care. " Georgiana closed her eyes. "I don't care about anything any more."

"He had plans for your defence. He was working on some new evidence he was sure would prove your innocence....but I have no idea what."

"But I thought...."Georgiana began.

"Without it, you might be found guilty on circumstantial evidence and have to spend years in prison....at the very least." Gros and Maurice exchanged quick glances, then Gros turned back to her. "His last request was that we get you home." Seeing her expression he added: "You must respect that....for his sake, if not for your own."

Georgiana raised her head. "Can I see him?" She asked. "Just to say goodbye."

But Gros shook his head. "I'm afraid that is not possible," he said gently. "In the circumstances no one else will be permitted to see him until an autopsy has been performed."

Georgiana looked at Maurice, who was still supporting her. He said: "Come along, Madame. I'll take you back to the house. You must leave as soon as possible."

"But I don't have a passport."

Gros took her other arm, and together they led her towards the exit. "Leave that to me," he said simply. Then he glanced across at Maurice. "You have the car?"

"Oui, Monsieur."

"Then bring it round to the front entrance."

"D'accord."

Maurice let go her arm and hurried on ahead of them.

It was just the beginning of the nightmare.

Georgiana allowed herself to be helped into the back of the car. Gros got in front with Maurice and ordered him to call at an address in the Rue le Close at the rear of the Station St. Lazare.

Georgiana twisted round and looked back over her shoulder as Maurice drove towards the main gates. How was it possible that so short a time ago, they had driven past this very same place on their way home together without giving it a glance. She watched the lights of the Hospital diminishing in the distance until they reached the main road and passed through the gates out into the traffic.

Georgiana turned back to face the front. Never to see him again; to feel that adored hand in hers; to take possession of each other, and wake again with the joy of seeing him sleeping quietly beside her, or to find, sometimes, he had been watching her sleep with an expression she only caught in that unguarded moment when she first opened her eyes, of such love. Never to see him again. It was not possible!."

Maurice waited outside with the car while Gros led her up the narrow stairs to the fourth floor where first, some photographs were taken. Then they had to wait. But in a remarkably short space of time Georgiana had a United States Passport in her possession with all the suitable stamps, including a French visa. Then on to the house.

Sylvia had already packed her things. The two women cried as they said goodbye to each other but Welsh was not to be found. Nor Paul, who had possibly gone looking for him.

Georgiana refused to look back this time as Maurice drove her down the drive of Poussan-le-Bas for the last time. She knew she would only survive what was going to happen now by looking forward.

Later, she would have to look back, and grieve. But by then, she would be home.

CHAPTER XIII

Georgiana reached New York unchallenged. She contacted Mary and told her what had happened, but declined her friend's invitation to stay with her, preferring to check into a small hotel instead and explaining that she needed to be by herself for a while to catch her breath.

Mary understood, but not the French Embassy. The authorities in Paris revoked her parole as soon as they learned what had happened to George Lunas, and on discovering she had disappeared, it did not take them long to guess what had happened and for their agents to locate Georgiana and serve papers demanding her extradition back to France.

She contacted the Adams - sooner than she had intended, although Charles Gros had already spoken to Paul on the telephone and they were aware of her return, and they arranged for her to be represented at the Hearing before a Judge of the New York Supreme Court.

The Attorney they chose listened carefully to what Georgiana had to tell her and at the Hearing she painted a picture for the Court's benefit of a naive young American girl being encouraged to go to Paris where she was caught up in events beyond her control and in which she was a totally innocent party. The Judge had no great respect for the legal processes of other countries and, as it happened, relations between France and the United States were going through one of their regular periods of chill at the time. He therefore dismissed the application made on behalf of the Embassy but referred the papers to the New York State Prosecutor's Office in the event that the Embassy might seek to pursue the question of Georgiana's culpability in the death of Jules Lavosin before an American Court; an event, Georgiana's Attorney assured her, as unlikely as the highly respected French Michelin Guide awarding three stars to a burger bar.

Ten minutes later, Geogiana found herself standing in the sunshine on the side-walk outside the Court Building with Paul and John Adams, at least part of the nightmare dispelled.

"Are you all right for money, Georgie?" John Adams said, after they had finished persuading her that it really was the end of the matter - as long as she took care never to return to France.

Georgiana nodded. "Charles Gros put enough in an account to keep me going until I can find my feet."

Paul said : "He said your pictures will be arriving at Newark Airport tomorrow. Would you like us to collect them for you?"

"Please." Georgiana turned to him. "And can you look after them for me until I have a place of my own?"

"Of course."

"We can't wait to see them!" John Adams said smiling.

"They're O.K."

He looked at his watch. "Well, I'd better be getting back." he said. "Mrs La Porte said she might look in this afternoon." He glanced at Paul. "Are you coming?"

"In a minute," Paul said. "You go on."

"O.K." John Adams nodded and turned back to Georgiana. "Well Georgie...you know where we are. We look forward to seeing you as soon as you're settled."

Georgiana reached out impulsively to put her hand on his arm. "You've been wonderful," she said. They both saw she was close to tears. "I don't know what I would have done without you." She glanced at Paul. "Both of you." She released his arm and forced a smile.

Paul wanted to take her in his arms, there and then. She was so beautiful; and so brave.

"Well, I had hoped the next time we met it would be under happier circumstances," he heard his father say gently. "But it has been really great to see you again and to do what we could."

Georgiana swallowed and nodded. "She was afraid to say anything for fear of making a fool of herself.

"See you later, then." John Adams gave her a last encouraging smile before turning and walking away from them, soon to be lost in the lunch hour throng. They both watched him for a few seconds, then Paul turned back to her.

"What now?" He said.

Georgiana swallowed, then she said, in as normal a voice as she could manage: "I'm going to meet Mary for coffee."

"Can I drop you there?"

"No, thank you Paul." She softened her refusal with a smile. "I'd like to walk. When I have a lot of people around me I almost get the feeling I'm a real person again."

Paul hesitated for a moment, then he said: 'Georgie....you know how I feel about you. I missed you so much while you were away."

"I missed you too." She glanced round. "And all this."

"Then...can I see you sometime? Soon?" He shrugged and smiled. "You know,....dinner.... a movie. Whatever!" She looked at him and he gave up trying to sound casual. "Anything, so I can be with you."

Georgiana shook her head momentarily, then she said: "You don't want me, Paul. I'm dead inside."

"I know I can't guess how you must be feeling," he persisted. "You've had so much tragedy in your life. I just want to help you. To look after you...to protect you." He saw her expression but pressed on doggedly. "I don't expect anything else at the moment. But I know, in time, you'll feel differently. I just want to be around when it happens."

Georgiana looked at him. For a moment, part of her own unhappiness was replaced by pity for him. "Do you always carry your heart on your sleeve like this? " She said gently.

Encouraged, Paul grinned. "Never before, I swear." Then he shook his head cheerfully. "I don't care what kind of fool you think I am, but I'm deadly serious." He paused while their eyes held each other, then he said. "I love you, Georgie....and if l have any chance at all, I want it." He shrugged. "You know what they say, no matter what your chances of winning the Lottery, if you don't buy a ticket, you ain't got no chance at all!"

Georgiana saw he was looking at her with such longing. A year ago she would not have understood. Now she understood only too well. He was so gentle, and really good looking. She wondered if she would ever see him with feelings that went beyond gratitude and friendship.

Surely, if not him, she really was dead and might as well curl up in a comer somewhere. She took a deep breath, then she promised: "I'll call you when I've found somewhere to live. I can't think of anything else right now."

Paul nodded: "I'll wait....as long as it takes," he said solemnly.

"You're a good friend," Georgiana reached forward and kissed him briefly on the cheek. ''Now, I have to go. Goodbye Paul." '

"Goodbye, Georgie."

With a last smile she turned and he watched her walk away in the opposite direction taken by his father....was it only five minutes ago? Five minutes, in which time he knew his life had changed for ever - for better or worse. A flood of joy welled up inside him as he moved to the curb and signalled a cab. The driver looked at him suspiciously as he gave the address of the Gallery and jumped inside. He realised he was grinning like an idiot.

CHAPTER XIV

Two Years Later

It was obvious even from the narrow street outside the Gallery that a big 'affair' was in progress. Expensive cars lined both sides defying the alternative parking rule, but no traffic cops were to be seen, and it made it difficult for the limos which lined up to drop late comers to get through.

Inside, everything not needed had been cleared out of the way to make room for the Exhibition and the crush of well heeled visitors which grew denser by the minute.

A banner across the front exhibition room greeted newcomers :

"Montes in France"

Georgiana's pictures were mounted all around this room as well as the larger store room at the rear of the premises which had been opened up to more than double the available space. This was packed too. There were her pictures of Paris; of the gardens and house in the Bois-du-Bologne; Fontainbleau, and others painted during her trip with George Lunas. There were several of Welsh, one of Sylvie, but none of Lunas himself. Waiters moved through the throng as best they could serving champagne and canapes from silver trays, and from the appreciative smiles on the faces on even the most demanding critics present it was obvious already the Exhibition was a triumph.

Georgiana stood by the door between the two rooms talking happily to Mary and her friend's good looking companion. Two years had touched the beauty of both women with a sophistication that made each even more outstanding in their own way. Georgiana had been featured in television and magazine interviews in the run up to today's Opening, and both John and Paul Adams realised that her ravishing good looks had caught the imagination of a much wider audience than would normally have been interested in such an exhibition, and ensured it got off to a flying start far more effectively than anything else they could have done.

After her first exhibition a year back, some of the press had unearthed the story of her accusation in France and her escape back to America. And although both the Adams and Georgiana herself had refused to discuss this, such rumours only added to the interest taken in her work. But, at the end of the day, it had been the uniqueness and quality of her style which had ensured the success of that first exhibition and which had prompted the Adams to arrange another so soon.

John Adams came into the front room from the rear gallery. He and Paul exchanged a quick nod, then the older man stepped up onto a small dais placed so that he could be seen from both rooms and called for attention. This took a little while to achieve, but eventually, the conversation died sufficiently for him to be able to make himself heard.

"Ladies and Gentlemen," Adams beamed round at his audience, then began again as the final splutter of conversation died. "Ladies and Gentlemen, my son Paul and I have already greeted most of you, but if there is anyone here we have not yet spoken to, please accept our very warmest welcome to this, the second exhibition of 'Montes in France."

He paused for a moment as quite a few of his audience broke into applause and Georgiana modestly raised her glass in acknowledgement. She lowered it again quickly as Mary, who was grinning, dug her in the ribs with her elbow, but only those close by noticed this as Adams began to speak again.

"Many of us here already knew and admired Georgiana's work before her first exhibition, but I don't think any of us anticipated the tremendous reception accorded to that event and that it would be necessary to mount another, more comprehensive display quite so soon."

Again, a burst of applause, which continued until Adams raised his hand. "So, here we are," he continued, beaming around. "Paul and I would like to thank you all for coming." He glanced across at Georgiana. "And we would like to thank Miss Montes herself for allowing the Adams Gallery the privilege of presenting her work once again."

Georgiana nodded graciously during the applause which followed this as Adams continued: "And what makes this Exhibition different is that we have been authorised to negotiate the sale of a limited number of paintings....those that have a small red circular label attached to the lower left hand corner of the frames. Of course," he held up his hand. "None will be removed until the exhibition closes at the end of September."

He paused as a buzz of excitement ran through his audience. "There is something else." Adams raised his voice to top this: "Something, which I have to admit, gives me even greater pleasure than everything that has gone before." He waited for the buzz of conversation to die. "It is my great privilege to announce the forthcoming marriage between Miss Montes....Georgiana, and my Son Paul."

There were gasps of astonishment, then applause and laughter as Paul pushed his way to Georgiana's side and kissed her on the cheek.

Only one person did not join in this, and glancing at her friend quickly, Georgiana saw she had some explaining to do.

"But you "don't love him. You've told me a thousand times," Mary challenged as soon as the door of her apartment closed behind them and while her escort to the exhibition went to fix them drinks."

"I can't think of anyone else I'd rather be with." Georgiana said defensively.

"That's not enough."

"I feel safe with him. He's done so much for me."

"But what about him, Georgie? What about Paul?"

"I can make him happy. He loves me."

Mary took hold of both her arms and shook them in exasperation. "But you don't love him, Georgie."

"So?"

"In time you'll meet someone else and fall in love. I know at the moment you don't think it's possible, but you will. I know."

The two women stared at each other for a moment, then Mary's friend arrived at their side and handed them the drinks. "Then she'll split," he said amiably, and raised up his own glass. "Cheers!"

"No, I won't," Georgiana said, taking a sip. "It'll never happen."

"You can't be sure of that," the young man persisted.

Mary turned to him irritably. "Look....stay out of this Handley," she snapped: "It's none of your business."

"Well, pardon me!" Handley turned on his heel in a huff and went to sit over on the other side of the room.

Mary then turned back to Georgiana and said more reasonably : "Why won't it happen?"

Georgiana shrugged: "Because I'll never love anyone ever again. While I was with George it was wonderful. Everything since has been like a slow awakening from a dream."

"But you don't...." Mary began, before Georgiana interrupted her.

"I never want to be possessed like that again," she said forcefully. "I've thought about it a lot. If it had gone on, I don't know what would have happened!"

"So when' s the happy event? Handley called across the room. Despite his feigned indifference he had been listening closely.

Mary smiled, in spite of herself "A happy event is a baby, knuckle head!"

By unspoken agreement, both women drifted across the room closer to where he was sitting.

"We're getting married on August tenth," Georgiana told him. "Just a few friends." Then she glanced back at Mary. "If you're interested?"

"Of course I'm interested." Mary put her hand on Georgiana's arm and squeezed it.

"Don't try and stop me, Mary," Georgiana said steadily. "Making Paul happy is my best chance of being happy again myself."

Mary put her other arm around her and drew her into a hug. "I won't try and stop you, honey," she whispered, "If that's what you want. I want you to be happy more than anything in the world."

Handley looked at them, grinning. "Where are you going for your Honeymoon?" He demanded.

The two women separated and looked down at him tolerantly. "New Hampshire," Georgiana said, then drained her glass. "John has recommended a hotel right on the lake. It sounds really great." Then she held up the glass. "What about another of these?"

"Sure thing." Handley bounded to his feet and took their glasses from them.

* * *

The Hotel was everything John Adams had said it would be. Being the height of the season he had to pull some strings to get them one of the best suites. When they arrived, the Hotel was full, but the ratio of staff to guests was unusually high, and they found everyone cheerful and with seemingly limitless time to make them feel welcome.

Most of the guests were families who exhausted themselves with all the outdoor activities available. After dinner, the lounges emptied as parents followed their younger children upstairs to bed leaving the older ones to take the hotel's complimentary bus into Squamscot (population four thousand) where there was a disco, a movie theatre and a diner with music; none of which, the Management of the Hotel assured any concerned parents, being places where their progeny were likely to get into trouble.

Paul and Georgiana, having arrived just in time for dinner went for a stroll along the lakeside afterwards, then to the end of the jetty where they sat for a while and watched the almost full moon rise between a gap in the Mountains opposite to throw a pathway of gold towards them across the water. They had been told there was no road running alongside the lake opposite, consequently the houses and small farms which existed could only be reached by boat and were few in number. But the shore line on their side had a necklace of lights right down to the end of the lake to their right, where the lights of Squamscot defied the blackness beyond.

Paul was a charming companion who knew when to amuse, and when to be quiet. Georgiana had deliberately not brought any of her paints with her. She was determined to be a good wife and to begin by giving him her undivided attention during their honeymoon. But despite her resolution she found her mind jumping back to the last time she had gone away 'en vacance. ' Even her mind kept slipping back into French.

Georgiana forced the memories away with an effort of will but it was like trying to hold back an unruly crowd; no sooner had one thought been successfully pushed away, than others took its place. But the beauty and atmosphere of this place was quite different and she somehow managed to shut out the past most of the time.

Realising she had not spoken for a while, Georgiana glanced at her husband leaning on the rail of the jetty beside her and saw he was looking at her. "I'm sorry," she said guiltily. "What were you saying?"

Paul smiled, and shook his head. "I was just looking at you," he said softly, "and thinking how lucky I am."

"Don't say that, Paul. It's me who is lucky to have you."

"Then we must be two very lucky people," he grinned.

"That's right."

There was a moments silence, before Georgiana said: "Do you think it's time for our marriage to begin?"

"Are you ready?"

She looked back at him, then she took his hand and held it against her breast for a moment, before raising his fingers to her lips and kissing them.

Georgiana found it easy to forget everything else while they were making love. Paul was both considerate and skilful and raised her to an intensity of passion to match his own; and as she drifted off to sleep in her husband's arms later she thought contentedly that he might even banish all ghosts from her past.

Whether it was just before she finally fell asleep, or that moment when consciousness had just let go, but was still within reach....she suddenly heard a short sharp bark, and her eyes snapped open. She listened intently for a few seconds, and was just about to close her eyes and drift off once more, when there it was again. This time there could be no doubt. She had not dreamt it.

Again: sharp, and demanding. "I'm here," it said.

Georgiana sat bolt upright. The hairs on the nape of her neck were tingling with an electric charge that shot down her spine and made her jump out of bed and run to the window, pulling back the drapes to look outside.

"Georgie, what's the matter?" Paul sat up in some alarm, but now he heard it too.

Most of the Hotel's outside lights had been switched off But by the light of the moon she could just make out the shape of a dog standing under one of the trees looking straight back at her. It barked again. Short, sharp and impatient. "I'm still here."

"My God!" Georgiana swung round to look at Paul. "It's Welsh!"

"Welsh?"

"My dog! Oh my God!" She flung herself across the room, grabbing a robe from the foot of the bed and pulling it on as she tore open the bedroom door and rushed out into the corridor.

"Georgiana....come back." He heard her running away down the corridor.

The night porter was alarmed as a dishevelled young woman came thundering down the stairs then ran across the lobby to the front door to disappear outside. He had no sooner recovered from this when a man also came hurrying down, and set off after her.

Outside, Georgiana sprinted across the lawn towards the tree, but before she was half way, the dog reached her and jumped into her arms almost knocking her over.

Georgiana's robe had fallen open in her haste, but she hugged the warm silky body to her bare flesh while he covered her face and neck with kisses. "Oh Welsh! Oh my darling!" she repeated over and over while the dog whined with delight. "How did you find me?"

Out of the comer of her eye, she saw Paul approaching and swung round to face him, her face radiant with joy.

"It's Welsh," she said... "It's my dog from France. I never thought I would ever see him again."

Paul stopped, looking at them. He looked at his wife's face. He had recently seen her lit with passion as he held her in his arms. But now it was suffused with a different joy. With love. In an instant he realised she would never look at him like that, as long as he lived, and his heart ran cold.

CHAPTER XV

After their return from New Hampshire, Paul's father informed them that he had received an invitation from the National Gallery in Washington who wanted to stage an exclusive exhibition of Georgiana's work the following spring. This was an honour never before accorded to a contemporary American Artist. Even Jackson Pollock had been compelled to share with Mark Rathko, Hans Hartury and Mark Toby back in the forties. The Adams were already charging more than ten thousand dollars a picture, and because so few had been released their resale value was even higher. But this Exhibition would project the demand for her work into the stratosphere and it was time for her to organise herself.

Georgiana looked from one to the other, and shrugged. "Like what?" She said, after a few seconds.

"Well...you should have proper representation." Adams senior told her.

"I thought you were doing that?"

"We are," the other agreed. "But we ought to make it official."

"You know, draw up an Agreement," Paul put in. So there can be no misunderstandings."

"Exactly," his father agreed. "Even more important now that we're related. We don't want anyone to think we are taking advantage of you."

You would never do that," Georgiana said confidently.

Paul nodded. "We know that, and you know that," he said. "But you'd be surprised how many people will try to stick their oar in and cause trouble."

"Particularly, once your pictures start to demand really big prices." His father added.

"So what do we do first?" Georgiana asked.

Her husband and father-in-law began to speak at the same time, but the older man gestured for Paul to continue. "The first thing," Paul told her, "is for you to get an independent lawyer who will advise you on any agreement we might suggest."

"Just what I was going to say!" John Adams said. "You can use our accountant, but you really must have independent advice before signing anything."

"How am I going to find one?" Georgiana demanded. "I don't know any lawyers."

"I've thought of that," Adams Senior told her. "Ask your Bank to suggest someone. But tell them it must be someone who is expert in contracts of the sort we're talking about."

So it was agreed, and a few weeks later a Contract was drawn by Georgiana's new lawyer and a firm representing the Adams appointing John Adams as her Agent and Paul as her business Manager; both contracts revocable by Georgiana on giving three months notice.

Other matters did not run so smoothly. Georgiana had released only a limited number of her pictures for sale, and the owners of most of these - those who could be contacted - agreed to lend them to the Exhibition, but it was necessary for Georgiana to complete at least twenty more in the six months available before the Exhibition opened and that meant she would have to work harder than she had ever done before in her life.

She and Paul found a large, airy apartment on the top floor of an old warehouse overlooking the Hudson, with one huge room which served as both studio and living room. Georgiana then flung herself into completing the required canvas on time. She found herself back in Washington Square; in Central Park, on the Broadwalk of Coney Island and other places where the young painter and her dog soon became a familiar sight. Welsh went with her everywhere, falling back easily into his remembered role of guardian, but now she was sometimes recognised. And whereas most people were happy just to say 'hi', and "didn't I see you on T.V.?" before moving on, some became persistent, despite Welsh's discouraging growls, forcing her, in extreme cases to pack up and abandon a project, and this all added to the pressure.

Paul had done his best to begin with to adapt to Welsh. But he was not a 'dog' person, and given a choice, would never have chosen to have one. It seemed to him also that all the redeeming features he understood dogs to have were reserved for his wife, whom the animal obviously adored, while he was just tolerated.

Paul was well aware of the pressure Georgiana was under and did his best not to add to it. But in his determination not to quarrel, he suffered in silence, with the result they frequently went whole days without exchanging a word. Georgiana became progressively more tired in the evening, and rather than make an issue of it, Paul got into the habit of calling in at one or two of the neighbourhood bars on his way home from the Gallery, with the result he often found his wife already in bed and asleep, with Welsh in his basket, now moved into their room beside the bed.

Things came to a head one night just before Christmas, when Georgiana, despite promising to do so, failed to show up at a reception laid on in her honour by two of her most loyal patrons. Both Paul and his father did their best to make excuses for her, and their hosts were gracious and understanding, but as they were going down in the elevator as the party broke up - most having arranged to go on to the Theatre - John Adams gave vent to his irritation over Georgiana's behaviour, and this did not make Paul feel any better about it.

He had already consumed several glasses of champagne at the reception and stopped on the way home to try and calm down. The result was that, by the time he came through the front door of the apartment and found Georgiana sound asleep on a divan in front of the open fire which she had insisted on before they moved in, he was more than a little drunk. Swaying slightly, he knocked into a chair as he made his way to the hi-fi and turned down some music that was playing. This woke-up Georgiana, and Welsh, who had been lying on the floor beside her, got to his feet with a growl.

Paul turned to face them. "Well,....isn't this cosy," he said thickly. "I thought you'd be here!" He moved a few steps closer as Georgiana sat up frowning. "And what happened to you, might I ask?" He held up his hand before she could reply. "No....don't tell me. Let me guess. You just didn't feel like turning up!

Georgiana swung her feet to the floor. "I had a headache," she said defensively.

"Oh come on Georgie...not that one!" He took another step towards her and would have taken a second if Welsh had not growled again. "You're getting confused," he continued, sourly. "Headaches are what we have instead of sex!"

"O.K. I didn't feel like going out. I'm tired. Is that better?"

"But it was a party in your honour. Doesn't it strike you as just a little bit rude when someone goes to a lot of trouble and you don't even bother to tum up?" Paul watched his wife stand up and move to a side table, where she poured herself a glass of brandy. She took a drink before turning to face him.

"Well, I'm sorry. I'm sick of parties!"

"Oh, you're sick of them. Paul followed her. "Well, it may come as a surprise to you to know that both your Agent and your Business Manager are sick of them too. But we go to them....and we give them for your benefit, nor ours."

Georgiana took another sip. She could see he was drunk. There was a limit to how much she was prepared to take, but when she spoke, it was as calmly as she could.

"I'm grateful, Paul. But I've had enough for the time being. I want a breather. Can't you understand that? You go. You're much better at them than I am anyway. And it will give us a break from each other now and then."

Paul looked at her sharply. "What's that supposed to mean?" He demanded.

Georgiana sighed. Then she said: "You say you love me....that you want me to be a success."

"I do," he began. I do want...."

"But now that I am, you seem to resent it." She interrupted.

Paul frowned and wiped his hand across his face before answering. "I don't resent it, Georgie. But you lock me out. It's ever since this bloody dog turned up," he glared at Welsh.

"Don't be ridiculous!"

Paul took another step towards her. "You used to talk to me about what you were thinking and planning. Now you don't say a word to me from one end of the day to the other.

"It's all in your imagination, I'm tired at the end. of the day, that's all. How can you be jealous of a dumb animal?"

Paul stood looking at her, then it all surfaced. "It's like he was here," he said tensely." "Between us."

"George?"

"George Lunas. Yes."

"George is dead!"

"Maybe. But it's like he's sent that thing from beyond the grave." He pointed at Welsh while Georgiana looked at him in disbelief "His familiar," Paul went on. "I've read about such things, but I never thought I'd see one."

Georgiana looked at him disgustedly, "You're drunk!" She said, but Paul persisted.

"Yes, I'm drunk. But I know the Spirit of that man is here in this room."

Georgiana started to turn away, but he called after her. "How was it he turned up the very night of our honeymoon? We've never had a proper explanation."

Georgiana turned back to face him. "I don't care." She said.

"Well I do. If someone is trying to wreck our marriage, I care very much."

Georgiana finally lost her.temper and stormed up to him. "It's you who's wrecking it," she shouted in his face. "With your insane jealousy, and your drinking. You'd better get a grip on yourself if you want me to stay."

He looked as if she had hit him across the face. Georgiana swallowed to try and regain control, then she went on tensely: "I'll do my job and you do yours. I won't ask you to produce any pictures, and you won't make me do things I don't want to when I'm tired out."

Paul took a step back. And when she continued, it was even more calmly, but her voice sounded strange, even to herself "I appreciate everything you and John have done for me. But in fairness, I've made you both rich. Now I've got this Exhibition in Washington in just over three months time and I'm terrified I'm not going to be ready. So, please.... let me work towards it in my own way, or I'll have to move somewhere else".

Paul went white, but said nothing. He turned on his heel walked out of the front door, leaving it open behind him.

Georgiana heard him come back sometime after she had gone to bed and fallen into a fitful sleep. She knew it was him, because although Welsh growled softly, he did not bark. She waited for him to come to bed, intending to make it up, but fell asleep again; and when she eventually woke up she discovered his side of the bed had not been slept in and guessed he must have spent the night on the couch in the living room.

Paul was nowhere to be seen but she found a note in the kitchen apologising for his behaviour the previous evening and saying he had gone to the Gallery early so as to be out of her way.

On impulse she picked up the phone and dialled the Gallery, but the answering service was still on. She left a message asking Paul to call her, and when he failed to do so by nine o'clock, when the Gallery opened, she phoned again and spoke to Anne, who had just got in. She told her Paul had been in but had left a message on her desk to say he had gone to a meeting at the Hyatt Hotel in Times Square and did not expect to be back until mid morning.

"That's O.K." Georgiana, said. "I'll catch up with him later, it's not important." She put down the phone feeling guilty and depressed. She looked down at Welsh, who was waiting expectantly, then phoned Mary and asked her to meet for coffee.

Afterwards, the two girls took Welsh for a walk down to Battery Park and gradually Georgiana's depression lifted.

She eventually caught up with Paul when she rang again on getting back to the apartment. Despite his protests, she insisted on taking a major part of the blame for what had happened and asked him to come home early so she could make him dinner at home.

The evening was a success. She was touched by how happy he seemed that she should care about him enough to go to some trouble, and after they had done the dishes she put Welsh to bed in front of the fire and led Paul into the bedroom where they made love in a way that seemed to recapture the first time they had come together. Paul eventually fell asleep in her arms. She held him until she became uncomfortable but managed to extricate herself without waking him. She then found she was unable to sleep herself and lay on her side looking at him so peaceful beside her. Suddenly Mary's words, the day their engagement was announced came back to her. It was true she did not love him. She had no wish for anyone else; but what if, one day, she did meet someone else and fall in love? Suddenly she was afraid for him, and for herself She must never allow that to happen.

Despite their making up, during the months that followed, which Paul and his father spent in preparing for the Exhibition in Washington and Georgiana in finishing the paintings they still needed, Paul made himself as scarce as possible during the day, and in the evenings gave her as much space as she seemed to need; leaving it to Georgiana herself to indicate when she wanted more from him. She realised she was being completely selfish in using him like this, but he seemed happy enough, and although she knew he still liked to call at his favourite bar on the way home, he never appeared drunk, and the night they had quarrelled was never repeated.

Several weeks before the Exhibition was due to open Paul went to Washington to co-ordinate the hanging of Georgiana's pictures with the Curator and staff of the National. He phoned Georgiana a week before to tell her that apart from some spaces left for the three pictures she would bring with her just before the Exhibition opened, the hanging was complete and would she care to fly up the following day to check that what they had done met with her approval. But Georgiana told him she trusted his judgement - which, of course, pleased him, so it was not until the day before the Opening, when John Adams drove with her and the remaining pictures to Washington that she saw what he had done for the first time.

CHAPTER XVI

Nothing that had gone before prepared her for the opening in Washington. Across the front of the building was a huge banner which simply said "MONTES" in giant letters, and lines waiting for the ticket office to open stretched round the block.

Inside, Georgiana watched while they filled the empty spaces with the last three pictures; then she walked round the rooms, which seemed vast after the Adams Gallery, looking at the rest which had been positioned and lit to maximum effect. She turned at last to Paul and John Adams who, together with the Curator, had walked round with her, mostly in silence, and gave the first two a hug before turning to the other with tears in her eyes and thanking him.

Then the tension broke, and they made their way to the exit laughing at a story the Curator told them about a previous exhibition when the then President, who had never been in an Art Gallery before in his life, was persuaded by his staff that it would be good for his image to be seen to show an interest. It seemed that after the poor man had been dragged round for over an hour, one of his aides whispered that he should say something to the Ambassador of the Country who had provided most of the pictures and who had walked around with him - taking his silence to indicate awe at the masterpieces on display.

"What shall I say?" The President hissed back.

The Aide shrugged. "Just tell him how much you liked them, Mr President. No need to make a speech."

The President nodded, and turned to the Ambassador beaming. "Great show, your Excellency!" he said, with all the enthusiasm he could muster. "What those guys did before the camera was invented beats the hell out of Mickey Mouse!"

"It is not recorded what the Ambassador replied," the Curator said smiling as they reached the front entrance. Then he looked from one to the other and held out his hand to Georgiana.

"Good luck for tomorrow, Miss Montes."

"Thank you."

The two shook hands, then the Curator bowed slightly and shook hands in turn with Paul and John Adams. "I am sure you will have a great success," he assured them. "Try and get a good night's rest." He turned back to Georgiana. "I always say that, but I know it's easier said than done. Anyway, we will see you at ten o'clock for the official opening." He shrugged. "The usual thing we have to go through. Don't worry about it. There will only be about three people there whose opinions amount to anything and they know your work already. It's what happens afterwards that counts".

Standing on the side walk on the opposite side of the street they looked back at the huge banner which stirred with the gentle breeze. The lines for the booking office seemed to have grown even longer during the time they were inside and now stretched right down the side of the Gallery and out of sight, somewhere round the back.

Georgiana took a breath, then she turned to the two men standing beside her. "I know I thanked you back there," she said, "but I want to say it again: You've both been wonderful. I'll never be able to repay you for what you've done for me." Paul and his father exchanged smiles as Georgiana turned to her husband. 'I'm sorry I've been such a pain, Paul. I don't know how you've put up with me! I'll try and make it up to you."

Paul put out his hands to hold her at arms length, looking into her face. "I love you Georgie," he said softly. "And I'm so proud of You!"

"I'll try and be a better wife."

"Georgie...."

He started to protest, but she interrupted him. "Perhaps we could go away together somewhere, just the two of us?"

"That would be wonderful!"

"Mary will look after Welsh while we're away."

Paul nodded happily.

"We can talk about it back at the hotel."

John Adams, who had been looking from one to the other with a smile said: "Great! I'll leave you to it then. I have to meet some prospective clients at the Plaza for dinner, so I think I'll go and do a bit of shopping first."

Paul dropped his hands and turned to him smiling.. "O.K. Pop. See you later then."

Georgiana gave him a peck on the cheek, then they stood hand in hand while John Adams hailed a cab, got in, and was swept away into the traffic.

Paul then turned to her and said: "It's such a lovely day. Shall we walk?"

Georgiana let go of his hand, then she said gently: "Paul, would you mind going back to the hotel without me? I'd like to unwind by myself for a while. I won't be long, honest!" She smiled up at him, but Paul frowned.

"Well....O.K" he said doubtfully. "But be careful where you go. The crime rate here is four times what it is in New York."

"I only want to walk through the Park," she assured him. "Look at the flowers....and think what a lucky woman I am to have such a handsome husband."

Paul smiled, and suppressed his misgivings. "Well, O.K," he told her. "Maybe I'll drop into a Travel Agent and pick up a few brochures."

"Great. We'll look at them as soon as I get back." She kissed him on the cheek, and seeing his worried look return said : "Don't worry. I'll be perfectly safe at this time of day, with so many people around."

Paul nodded and smiled in response to her assurance. Then he watched her walk away until she reached the comer of the block where she turned right and disappeared. He thought how beautiful she was, and how much he loved her. He never saw her again.

Georgiana reached the Capitol Building but did not go inside. Instead, she walked round the back and down the steps to the top of the Mall, a long straight stretch of grass with paths leading down either side to the reflecting pool set a few hundred yards in front of the huge, needle shaped Washington Monument. This repeated the Column, the blue sky and the few wisps of cloud on the surface of the water. She walked towards it, then stood at the edge of the pool and saw how the reflection lay pointing towards her so the tip seemed only a few feet from where she was standing.

Georgiana stood contemplating this until a well dressed young man came up to her and invited her to contribute a dollar to his lunch. She gave him a quarter, but he started to argue and she moved away as fast as she could, without appearing to panic; glad for the first time of the number of tourists and joggers from nearby Government Offices.

Georgiana walked round the Monument and down another, similar stretch of the Mall to the Lincoln Memorial. She had her antenna out now, but nobody bothered her again, and she eventually sat on a park bench near the Memorial dozing in the later afternoon sun as it dipped towards the horizon on the other side of the Potomec river. She had slept very little the previous night and John had called for her early to load up the car with her pictures.

She started, then realised she must have fallen asleep. She looked round embarrassed, but no one was looking at her. The sun had gone now and she stood up feeling better. The walk and the nap had done her good and she felt completely at peace about the Opening tomorrow. She glanced at the Memorial. She had never been to Washington before, and who knew if she would ever come again.

On impulse, she decided to give climbing the steps to go inside a miss and called a cab instead which dropped her at the entrance to the Arlington Cemetery. After seeking directions, Georgiana found herself standing beside the grave of John F. Kennedy. Her father had thought the world of him and had wept openly when the news of his assassination had been announced. Like many people, Georgiana remembered exactly where she was when it happened, although she had only been little at the time. Later, she had associated her father's sudden death with that of the President, and looking down at the grave now, with Kennedy's Service Cap set in front of the eternal flame, Georgiana remembered her father and wept.

By the time she reached the entrance gates again it was starting to get dark. She got into one of the cabs and gave the name of her hotel. But as they started to cross the Potomac Bridge back into the centre of town she suddenly leant forward and asked the driver to go via the National Gallery.

"The National!" The man protested. "That's miles out of the way."

"I know. That's 0.K."

"What d'you want to do that for?" The man demanded over his shoulder.

Georgiana smiled: "I just want to see if the same banner is still hanging there. Just to make sure I didn't dream it!"

The cab threaded its way through the late rush hour traffic and eventually approached the Gallery. "Slow up, please," Georgiana requested. "I need to take a good look."

The driver sighed. "Look, it's better we pull in for a minute," he said. "I don't want someone going into the back."

"Fine."

There was a space right at the bottom of the steps which led down from the main entrance. The cab slipped into it but the driver kept the engine running.

Georgiana looked up at the banner which was now illuminated by two flood lights. "O.K.?" The driver demanded impatiently, after a few seconds.

She opened her mouth to agree, when suddenly she saw a man had appeared at the top of the steps and was hurrying down obliquely to her right. Whatever she was going to say died in her throat as she spun round to follow him with her eyes.

'It had to be Him! It was Him! She couldn't be mistaken!' Georgiana reached for the door handle but found it locked.

"Let me out....quick," she screamed at the man in front. He spun round in surprise. "It's too far to walk from here."

"Never mind. I want to get out now....please. Hurry!"

The driver glanced hurriedly at the meter. Hysterical passengers he could do without. "O.K. lady," he said. "That's five - fifty."

Georgiana threw a ten at him and flung open the door as soon as he unlocked it without waiting for change. She could see the man had crossed with the lights at the intersection fifty yards back and was walking away from her on the opposite side-.

"Hey....don't you want change?"

Ignoring him, and the angry protest which followed when she failed to close the door, Georgiana began to run. She reached the intersection, but the lights were against her. Despite this she plunged into the traffic and managed to reach the other side without being hit.

Hearing the squeal of brakes and angry horns, the man she was pursuing stopped at the entrance to the subway and glanced back curiously. But seeing nothing, he continued on down the steps. It was just long enough for Georgiana to see which way he had gone.

"George!" She shrieked at the top of her voice, while realising she hadn't a hope of making him hear her. "Stop!"

She ran towards the subway entrance. People who saw her coming stepped out of her way. She banged into a large man who deliberately stepped into her path grinning and was then surprised at the force of the collision, but she ran on, leaving him grumbling behind her and plunged down the steps leading to the platform.

There was a line for tokens. Georgiana saw the man she was pursuing had already passed through the barrier and was walking towards the end of the platform. She heard the rumble of an approaching train. Panic stricken she screamed his name several times, but he did still not hear her over the sound of the approaching train. She turned and ran to the head of the line waiting for tokens, but was pushed away. She ran back to the barrier just as the train arrived and began to cry.

Suddenly, there was an elderly black man standing in front of her holding out a token in the palm of his hand. "Look, Lady," he said, "if it means that much to you take one of mine!"

Georgiana snatched it from him. A moment later she was through the barrier and running onto the platform. There were quite a few waiting to get on the now stationary train and she could see him standing back to let people get off "George.... George....for God's sake wait!. George!!"

At last he heard her and turned. She stopped about twenty feet away staring at him, eyes wide in disbelief. She was panting with effort, and it was a few seconds before she managed. "My God....it is you!" She staggered forward and half collapsed into his arms.

He held her tightly for a few seconds, then she pulled her head back so she could look him in the face.

"You bastard!" She spat at him. "Why aren't you dead?!" Then she started to pummel him in fury.

It took Lunas quite a while to calm her down enough to get her out of the station and into a cab which then took them to his hotel. Georgiana refused to let him touch her and stared at him in silence with pain and fury in her eyes, but she allowed herself to be conducted to the hotel elevator and up to his suite without protest until the door finally closed behind them.

Lunas pointed to a chair. "Sit over there," he said, and went to a small cabinet on which were glasses and several bottles. "We both need a drink!"

Georgiana gave him a look, but obeyed and flopped into the chair indicated, suddenly deflated.

He poured two glasses of brandy then turned and moved back across the room to hand one to her. Georgiana took it without a word. She took a slug then looked up at him, her eyes smouldering.

"Well you bastard....why aren't you dead? I suppose I didn't mean that much to you after all!"

"Georgie, I am so sorry!"

Ignoring this, Georgiana took another slug from her glass, then looked round. "Have you got any cigarettes?"

"Since when did you start to smoke?"

"Now!"

Lunas suppressed a smile. "Well," he said dryly. "I'm glad to see success has not spoiled you!"

"How would you know?"

Lunas paused for a minute, then he said: "If you will listen, I will explain."

"I'm listening."

He pulled a chair up close and sat in it so he was facing her.

"You know, I've often wondered what I would say if l ever had the chance to see you again!"

Georgiana looked at him, unblinking. "For me, it was different," she said flatly.

"Of course. In my imagination, I always started by telling you how much you have always meant to me." He paused, as she continued to stare at him. "But I can see you would take a lot of convincing!" he ended ruefully. He took a sip from his glass, then went on: "When I knew you were to be married, I sent the most precious thing I possessed as a gift."

Georgiana frowned, then suddenly her eyes widened. "Welsh!"

"Yes. How is he?"

"He's fine!" For the first time Georgiana's expression softened. "My friend Mary is looking after him."

"It seemed too late for me. So I wanted someone I loved very much to be part of your life."

"Thank you." Her voice was flat again.

"Back at the Hospital, when I told Charles to get you away, I really thought I was dying." Lunas drained his glass and shrugged: "If you do not believe me, Charles will confirm that for more than a week my life, as you say in English, hung by a thread!"

Georgiana allowed herself a bitter smile as she said: "George, Charles would confirm anything you told him to."

"But it's true, none the less. Either way, I wanted you out of danger. I did not know what was going to happen. I was stupidly careless with the girl. But I have other enemies who might have taken advantage of my weakness to try and destroy me."

"What enemies?"

"It doesn't matter." He leaned forward and touched her knee momentarily. "But you could easily have been caught up again in something you did not understand." He leant back in the chair. "I am sure, for example, that the murder of Jules Lavosin, and your inevitable implication was a way of striking at me through you. Besides, I was no longer in a position to honour the undertaking I had given the Court, and you would have been taken back to prison."

Georgiana looked impatient. "Didn't you know I didn't care about any of those things?"

Lunas nodded. "Yes I do know. And that the only way you would agree to be taken to safety was if you thought I was dead." He looked at her and saw her eyes glistening with unshed tears. She bent forward slightly, and he put his arms around her.

"It was the worst thing I ever had to do," he said softly.

"I'm sorry," she said in a strangled voice after a while.

Lunas shook his head and began to stroke her hair. "No....it is me who is sorry. So many times, when I was lying there, I was tempted to send you a message."

Georgiana pulled back her head so she could look at him. "Why didn't you?" She demanded. Lunas smiled briefly. "And the first thing you would have done?" He said.

"Come to you, of course."

"Exactly."

Georgiana paused for a moment, then she said: "Would I really have gone back to jail?"

"Yes. And what would have happened if the Trial had gone against you?"

"But you said it would be all right," Georgiana protested.

"Of course. What did you expect me to say?"

"Charles would have defended me."

"And he is the best there is. But you must remember that in France the system is different. There, it is up to the defendant to prove their innocence."

"But you being in hospital would not have made any difference to that."

"Only if you were found guilty. Do you think I would have let them keep you in prison?!" He shrugged: "As it was, they could not blame me in the circumstances if you jumped bail!"

He got up from the chair and took the glass from her hand. "Would you like another?"

Georgiana shook her head, and she watched him go to the cabinet and pour himself another brandy before he turned back to face her. "It took me much longer to recover than I had hoped" he said, half over his shoulder, "once I knew I was not going to die, of course. By which time, as I anticipated, certain....challenges had been made to my position, and these had to be dealt with." Lunas walked back to stand behind the chair he had been sitting on. "As soon as I could, I made plans to fly to New York....to explain to you what had happened. But the day before, I had a message from John Adams to say that you were to marry Paul."

"John Adams has known you were alive all along?"

"But not Paul. I forbade him to tell either of you."

"But it wasn't too late," Georgiana said passionately. "Why didn't you come? If you only knew what a mistake it has been!"

"Are you not happy, Georgiana?"

"I've never been happy since I thought you were dead." She looked up at him and he could see the tears in her eyes again. She raised her glass. "Maybe I will have that second drink, after all."

"Certainly."

She watched him fill her glass and bring it back to her.

Georgiana took a sip then, with a shake of her head she said: "No matter where, or who I was with, I was always looking for you."

Lunas sat down again facing her. "I was desperate when I got the news" he told her. "I did not know what to do. Then I spoke to an old friend, one I thought I could trust, and it was she who told me to let go. Youth deserves youth she said."

"She?" Georgiana found herself bridling, although she knew jealousy was absurd in the circumstances.

"We were lovers more than twenty years ago....when we were very young." He shrugged. "Anyway, so much for mature advice....she was wrong! You are the most wonderful thing that ever happened to me. I was a fool to have listened."

Georgiana looked at him, then she said softly: "We were so unlucky."

"Yes."

There was a moment's silence before Georgiana said: "Did you pay for my first exhibition?"

"That much I was able to do. But far more depended on the Adams. I shall always be indebted to them."

"I feel so responsible for Paul."

"And you must go back to him." Lunas got up again and stood looking down at her.

"But I can't," she said tensely. "Not now we've found each other."

"We can't put the clock back, Georgie; however much we might want to." Georgiana stood up to face him.

"If you send me away now I'll kill myself," she said quietly, but in a tone that made him realise she meant it.

After a moment he said gravely. "That would be a great pity. Not only would it bring the work of a great artist to an end, you might damage the most beautiful body it has ever been my privilege to admire."

Georgiana looked at him. Suddenly she knew that, despite what he had just said, he was never going to send her away. All that remained was for him to realise it too. As calm as ice, she took her glass over to the table then turned back to him. "How many women have you made love to since we were together?" She challenged.

Lunas looked at her with surprise. She had never dared to take charge in such matters before. She had certainly grown up! He was a little shocked, but suddenly more roused than he could remember. The truth was, there had been a few, but he was not going to spoil the moment. Instead he shook his head and smiled ruefully.

"I thought not." Georgiana moved half way back to him. "At least, none that you will want to remember." In a moment her dress had slipped to the floor and she was in his arms.

"Georgie!" A last a twinge of conscious reminded him this was the wife of a man to whom, only a short time ago, he had admitted he would always be indebted to. But no man can withstand the power of a beautiful woman in love. She writes the music of the song they sing together and charts the journey they take - which ending is both perfection and a new beginning as long as love lasts.

John Adams knocked on the door of Paul and Georgiana's hotel suite and was taken aback when Paul eventually opened the door to see his son still wearing the clothes he had been wearing earlier in the day 'though, now considerably dishevelled. There was a glass in his hand and he saw his son had already had a great deal to drink.

"Come in, come in," Paul said affably.

"There was a message you wanted to see me."

"Yes. And here you are." He stood back to let his father enter then shut the door noisily behind him.

A glance round the room told Adams senior that Georgiana was absent and he sighed inwardly. They had had a row and Georgiana had gone storming off somewhere leaving Paul with a bottle.

"Would you like a drink?" Paul said abruptly, joining him in the middle of the room.

"No, thank you."

"Well....I think I will....just a nip." He made for the drinks trolley and tipped a liberal slug into the glass from an already opened, half empty bottle of scotch. "How were the Pendleberries?" He asked over his shoulder.

"The Pemberys."

"Yes, of course. Paul turned to face him. "Cheers!"

"They were fine," Johns Adams said carefully. "They are looking forward to tomorrow's Opening, particularly to meeting Georgie for the first time."

"Well now...." Paul took a few steps towards his father, then stopped, swaying slightly."That's. going to be a bit of a problem."

"Why?" Adams senior looked round. "Where is Georgie? What are you talking about?" "One question at a time."

John Adams started to feel angry. "Look, Paul, I haven't got time for all this. If you've had a row fine, but tell me where she's gone. She really ought to get a good night's rest."

The idiot smile left his son's face. Suddenly he looked ill and tired and his father's anger turned to concern. "What's happened?" He said more gently.

Paul pulled a face and shrugged. "She's on her way to Switzerland?" He said.

"Switzerland?"

"With George Lunas."

"Lunas!"

"Whom you forgot to mention was still alive, by the way. Apparently, they ran into each other by chance. Now he's taken her back to Europe."

Adams thought for a moment, then he said helplessly: "If she goes to France she'll be arrested."

"Which is why they've gone to Switzerland. So everyone can live happily ever after."

John Adams looked at his son with pity. "Paul, I'm sorry I never told you. But Lunas swore me to secrecy. It was he who has been providing the money to promote her career."

"And I thought it was you."

His father shook his head. "I never had that kind of money," he admitted.

"You might have warned me!"

"I said I was sorry. Georgie didn't know. She thought he was dead. I had no idea he would contact her."

"Oh he didn't. Georgie has never lied to me. But...what the hell! They're together now, and there's nothing I can do about it."

John Adams thought for a moment, then he brightened. "Well.... it needn't affect the Opening tomorrow. After all, most of the time the featured artist has been dead for years. I'll just explain to the Curator that some urgent family thing has made it imperative for her to fly to Europe. What do you think?"

Paul shrugged, then he said wearily "Frankly, my dear, I don't give a damn!"

CHAPTER XVII

The first thing Georgiana noticed when she opened her eyes was the smell of pine wood. Like most Chalets in Switzerland, theirs was made entirely of it, apart from the huge stone fire place in the living room, and the stone chimney. It was a different smell from the wooden houses of New England, some of which she had visited the few times her father had managed to take them on vacation to Cape Cod.

She and George had lived in the chalet for the past two years and she knew that if they took her to the other side of the world, blind-folded her, then somehow managed to supply that particular smell, she would be back in her imagination in the mountain retreat overlooking Lake Geneva into which they had moved shortly after she realised she was pregnant.

She turned and looked at the empty space in the bed beside her. George had left early to fly to Paris, but he would be back in time for the supper Sylvie would cook for them so they could all sit down together "en famille": She and George, Sylvie, Welsh and little Ricci, the son she had named after her father and who was probably down in the kitchen now being given his breakfast by Aunt Sylvie, who adored and spoiled him ruthlessly.

Never had Georgiana felt so content. What more could she ask of life? She had a family who loved her. She was living in a part of the world where inspiration beckoned from every meadow, tree, stream and mountain top, and with Sylvie in charge of the house, she had the opportunity to pursue her career with a freedom anyone would envy. Exhibitions of her work had been staged in London, Berlin and Sydney Australia since the success of the one in Washington, and she knew George had others planned. Without any financial pressure, she was able to work at her own speed, and George told her that scarcely a month went past when he did not notice some development in her technique. Others tried to copy her, with varying success, but a genuine Montes commanded prices only equalled by Picasso in the artist's life time. She had no idea how much money she had. George told her he was saving every penny she earned so that she would have a nest egg in an emergency, and she was content with this arrangement; not that she could imagine anything which might suddenly put her in need; but when Ricci went to College, or even wanted to get married someday it would be nice to have it to give him whatever he needed. And there would be other children, she felt sure. The only thing that cast the slightest shadow over her life was Paul's refusal to give her a divorce so she and George could get married. But with or without a piece of paper, she could not have felt more truly George's wife, or that he was her husband.

Later, Georgiana worked in the grass meadow which separated the garden of the Chalet from the pine trees. These began at the bottom of the slope which led up out of the valley until the soil became too sparse to support them and scrub took over until that too gave way to the snow line, which had already begun to retreat with the Spring but which never left the mountains above nine or ten thousand feet. She lost count of time, and it was not until Welsh, who was dozing beside her suddenly woke up, then dashed away barking with pleasure that she turned around to see the dog bounding towards George, who was back already and was carrying Ricci on his shoulders to fetch her for supper.

* * *

Paul did his best to pull his life back together after Georgiana left him. John Adams knew that his son blamed him for what had happened.

To salve his conscience, Lunas had sold the Gallery back to them at a price they had no trouble raising from the Bank. But even though this contact was severed, it was impossible not to be made constantly aware of the progress of Georgiana's career, and they would have been fools to reject the envied reputation gained for having launched her career in the first place. Despite this, her pictures rarely passed through their hands; truth being, they were too expensive for them to hold these days, and

Paul had sold the two Georgiana had given him to raise the capital they needed as owners to operate, even at their more modest level.

Ignoring his own part in his son's unhappiness, John Adams had developed a hatred for both Georgiana and Lunas and often spent time thinking of some way he could destroy them as effectively as Paul was destroying himself. But it was not until that tragedy ran its course that the answer occurred to him:

New York could be bitterly cold, even in April, when the advance of Spring can suddenly go into reverse and winds come sweeping down from Canada covering the daffodils and crocus in Central Park with a dusting of snow, if he needed one, to linger in Benny's Bar on Ninth Avenue until closing, by which time he had drunk even more than usual and had been joined by a hooker who could not believe her luck to find a potential client in the bar where she herself had taken shelter and who seem to have plenty of money to throw around..

Benny also enjoyed taking Paul's money, but he felt protective towards his regulars, and the hooker's apartment was not the destiny he would have chosen for any of them. Still, Paul was old enough to look after himself!

"Come on Mr Adams," he said politely, ignoring the woman. "I have to close up." But Paul waved their glasses and gave the barman what he hoped was a winning smile.

"Just do these again, Benny," he pleaded, "then we'll be on our way, I promise."

But Benny shook his head firmly. "You said that a quarter of an hour ago," he reminded him.. "It's time you went home."

"Oh, come on." Paul pulled out his wallet which was still fat enough to draw the hooker's wide eyed attention - not for the first time that evening. " I spend enough in here."

But the barman stood his ground. "The answer's still no."

Paul pulled a face, but before he could say anything, the hooker, who still had one eye on the wallet put in quickly: "Let's go back to my place, honey. I've got a bottle we can share. And, who knows?!" She fluttered her heavily mascaraed eye lashes at him suggestively, but it was the mention of the bottle which caught his interest. He looked at her blearily. "How far is it?" he said thickly.

"Just around the comer."

"Well...." After a moment Paul pushed the wallet back in his inner pocket and started to climb unsteadily off the bar stool he had been occupying for the past three hours.

The barman watched him uneasily. "Why don't I call a cab, he suggested helpfully. "It's late to be wandering around."

"He ain't gonna wander," the Hooker said defiantly, putting her arm under Pauls' armpit to steady him. "He's comin' with me." She gave her charge an encouraging smile. "Ain't you, handsome?"

Paul nodded, then looked at the Barman. "I guess so," he admitted.

"Where you taking him?" The barman demanded, looking at the hooker suspiciously.

"I said....to my place."

"Where's that?"

"Ain't none of your business. But it ain't far." She started to guide Paul to the door. "Come on honey. That's right. Sugar'll take good care of you."

When they reached the door, Paul turned to the Barman who was following with the key. "G'night, Benny. See you tomorrow."

"Good night Mr Adams, take care." He looked at the hooker. "And I'll know you again," he warned. But the woman sniffed contemptuously.

"Why don't you drop dead?!". She opened the door and helped Paul outside.

The barman hesitated; then shrugged. "What the hell," he said to himself defensively. "Worse things can happen - probably wind up with the clap!" He closed the door with self justifying nods, then locked and bolted it behind them.

Outside, the hooker had managed to get Paul to the top of the steps. Cold rain was being driven up Ninth Avenue with the force of a fire hose. They were soaked in seconds, and the hooker shivered. "Come on baby," she urged. "It really ain't far."

"I don't feel good," Paul admitted, as she struggled to keep hold of him.

"You just need a nice drink and a place to lie down."

Paul nodded. "Maybe you're right," he said.

"Come on then." The woman tried to lead him forward, but after three paces he fell over and lay on the side walk.

"Come on honey!" She bent over him but he seemed to have passed out. "Get up," she urged, shaking him. "You're too heavy for me to carry."

It was hopeless. The woman straightened up, looking down at him. She was getting wetter by the second. After a moment, she looked round and saw they were at the entrance to a narrow alley that ran down beside the building. She glanced up and down Ninth, but there was no one in sight except for some cars at an intersection some four hundred yards away. Suddenly she bent down, and with surprising strength, pulled Paul's inert form into the alley. A moment later, her hand was inside his jacket; a moment after that, she had rejoined Ninth Avenue and was walking away as fast as she could with Paul's wallet tucked firmly into her coat pocket.

By the time someone spotted him the following morning, Paul was in an advanced state of hypothermia. He died a few hours later. And because he carried no identification it was several hours before they discovered who he was and called his father.

The Funeral was well attended, but as John Adams stood at the grave side his mind clung obsessively to the two who were not there.

".... I am the resurrection and the Life," intoned the Priest.

John watched his son's coffin being lowered into the grave. Since his wife's death ten years ago he and Paul had supported each other and it had been a matter of pride and enormous comfort that his son had inherited his Mother's good looks and his own love of art. For a while his dream of handing on to Paul a thriving business had been overshadowed by its financial collapse. But then George Lunas had appeared out of the blue and the dream was reborn. His happiness was complete when Paul and Georgiana married.

Apart from his son, George Lunas and Georgiana were the only others he had loved, but since their betrayal, and while he had watched Paul go steadily down hill, that love had turned to hate. There was no doubt in his mind they were responsible for his son's death, and by the time the graveside service came to an end and, as chief mourner, he was the first to sprinkle earth onto the coffin, he promised himself, and Paul, that he would make them suffer for what they had done.

The outline of a plan had already formed in his mind but he was aware of the Chinese proverb that said 'he who sets out on revenge should first dig two graves', and Lunas was a dangerous man. But that was the beauty of it: Lunas would never realise that what happened to them had been planned. They must pay, and go on paying.

When he and his Secretary got to the car he ordered the driver to take them to the Gallery.

Sitting beside him in the back, Anne glanced at him. "Wouldn't you rather go home?" She prompted gently. "I can manage."

"I know you can." Adams nodded. "But we have a great deal to do." Suddenly the depression which had gripped him over the past weeks had lifted, and she looked at him curiously.

"We have?"

"Yes."

He fell back into silence while the car moved slowly to the exit of the Greenwood Cemetery and out into Brooklyn's Seventh Avenue and Anne left him to his thoughts. But once they had joined the Manhattan bound traffic he suddenly turned to her and said: "I have decided the time has come for us to stage a Montes exhibition in Paris." He was, amused by her evident surprise. "But I thought you held her responsible for Paul's death," Anne said eventually.

"I do."

"Then why...." she began, but he interrupted her.

"But I've been thinking, and I have decided the time is right for us to storm the centre of the Universe of modem art on her behalf "

Anne paused for a moment, then she said carefully: "That's very generous of you. But, of course, she won't be able to see it herself. The moment she sets foot in France she'll be arrested. That's why he keeps her in Switzerland."

Adams nodded again thoughtfully, and they each fell back into their own thoughts again until they arrived at the Gallery. Adams then strode to the office at the back with just a perfunctory nod at the young man he had recently hired as an assistant.

Anne followed him, pulling off her gloves. She watched him take off his coat and hang it on a hanger with his customary fastidiousness. Then he turned to her and said: "Contact everyone we know who has bought a Montes and see if they would be willing to lend it for a dedicated Exhibition in Paris....due credit, of course, in the brochure and on a small plaque beside each picture. But first." He moved round and sat at his desk, then glanced at his watch. "What time is it now in Paris?"

"They're six hours ahead. Anne told him, then glanced at her own watch. "That would make it five o'clock, their time."

"Good. Then get me Jean Segeur at the Pompidou Centre of Modern Art. He'll still be there"

"Do you think he will agree?"

Adams nodded emphatically. "He begged, the last time we met, to let them have some Montes. He'll jump at the chance of a full scale Exhibition. It'll be the biggest draw for twenty years. People will come from all over France to see it....and beyond." He paused for a moment, then added softly. "Even from Switzerland."

Anne looked at him then blinked. In that instant she realised what it was all about.

He looked back at her steadily, then waved her away with a small gesture and she turned for the door. "I've got the number in my office," she said over her shoulder.

"Splendid. Please close the door."

As soon as the door was shut, he picked up the phone and dialled a number. A moment later he was connected.

"Is that International information? I want the number of the Chief of Police, central Paris. Yes, I'll wait. Thank you."

CHAPTER XVIII

It was over a year before the Exhibition opened, but then, as John Adams had anticipated, to rave reviews. As soon as he heard it was in preparation, Lunas realised the temptation it would be to Georgiana to risk paying a visit, but she never raised the matter herself, and knowing how obstinate she could be, he decided the wisest course was to assume she had weighed up the risks for herself and decided against it.

Even so, the Exhibition intruded into their lives with a request from the organisers for permission to exhibit any recent pictures Georgiana was prepared to send. And knowing how her work had evolved to an even more compelling level, Lunas encouraged her to co-operate and he helped her pick out twelve paintings completed since they had arrived in Switzerland which he felt illustrated this development. He also arranged their transport. But, much as he longed to, he decided against attending the opening himself, realising it would only be a provocation. In fact, he arranged for them to fly to Greece for a short holiday on a remote island owned by a friend during the run up to the Exhibition and its opening when the arts pages of most newspapers were full of it. This indulgence had to be paid for, however, and as soon as they returned he was compelled to arrange a business trip to Hong Kong and Australia.

The day he left they came out of the Chalet to see him to the car where Maurice was waiting: Georgiana, and Sylvie carrying little Ricci, and Welsh.

Maurice opened the door, and Lunas paused to hug his son for the last time and fuss Welsh before turning to Georgiana smiling. "I'll call you as soon as I get to Hong Kong," he promised. "It's a wonderful City. I so look forward to our being there together sometime....and many other places."

"When Ricci's old enough to be left," Georgiana said.

"Of course."

"But then he'll be wanting to come with us!" She teased.

Lunas glanced at Ricci who by now had lost interest in the proceedings and was starting to wriggle in Sylvie's arms to be put down.

"Much as I love him," he said seriously, "there are times when a man wants his wife to himself "

"No more than I want to be with you," Georgiana said putting her arms around him. "Take care."

"And you take care," Lunas said, before kissing her for the last time. "You are my life."

They waved until the car was out of sight, then Sylvie put Ricci down with relief and watched him run up the flower lined path into the house accompanied by Welsh. She turned to say something to Georgiana, and was surprised when she also turned on her heel and marched back into the house without a word. She followed curiously.

When Sylvie came through the front door, which opened in Swiss style straight into the large living room, she saw Georgiana was at her desk opening one of the drawers with a key. A moment later, she pulled a pile of newspapers out onto the desk and selected one, which Sylvie saw was 'Le Figaro' a French national daily, and tum to the inside pages. After a moment, Georgiana grunted with satisfaction, folded the paper, then turned to Sylvie who had approached the desk, and held it up so she could see.

"I got the paper shop to keep all the reports of the Exhibition while we were away.

"But Madame...." Sylvie began uneasily, until Georgiana interrupted her....

"Look what they say, Sylvie.... 'Montes.... Sensation at Pompidou!... See for yourself " She handed the folded newspaper to her, then stooped smiling to pick up Ricci who had come to her side. "You hear that Ricci? Your Mother is a sensation!"

Not understanding, the child chuckled anyway, catching her mood while Georgiana sorted out another of the papers on the desk one handed. "Here's another," she said excitedly, and read it aloud without picking it up: "Most exciting exhibition at Pompidou since African Primatives!.... here....". Georgiana picked it up and handed it to Sylvie who put Le Figaro down on the desk to take it. " There's more." She rummaged again before reading out: "Nouvelles Republic.... 'why has it taken so long for the Artist's work to be acknowledged here in France?" Georgiana picked through some more. "Le Monde....'not since Picasso has an artist so caught the mood of her time."

She glanced at Sylvie who was now looking at her with a worried expression." "Don't look like that!"

"But...."

Georgiana was not paying attention and snatched another paper off the desk. "Her Ego-centric style involves the viewer as never before, stimulating the senses as if by magic to create the detail logical analysis denies." Georgiana giggled. "Well, well....ego-centric! Yes all right Ricci." The child had begun to fidget and she put him down before straightening up to face Sylvie. "Well...what do you think?. "

"It's wonderful Madame. But why did you not show them to Monsieur Lunas?"

Georgiana shrugged. "I only picked them up a few days ago. I didn't want to distract him just before his trip."

"But he would have been proud!"

"Also...." Georgiana eyes slid away. "I didn't want to worry him."

"I see."

Georgiana turned back to her defiantly. "Besides....I'll bet you anything you like he arranged to have them sent to his office. But he didn't want me to see them. To hear what people were saying."

"Because he was afraid you would be tempted to go while he was away."

"Well....wouldn't you be? To have an exhibition at the Pompidou is the greatest honour anyone could ask for!"

The two women looked at each other for a moment then Sylvie said, as calmly as she could. "You've decided to go, haven't you?"

"Of course."

"I thought so. The minute I saw you with those," she gestured at the papers on the desk. "But it is far too dangerous!"

"I shall put on a wig and dark glasses and they won't know me from diddly!"

"But the Police might think you would try something like that!"

"I don't think so. If I were to go and flaunt myself I would force them to arrest me, but I'm sure it's the last thing they would want to do really. How would it look if the one they're all raving about was put in jail!"

Sylvie still looked unconvinced. "But Airport Computers can link up information in a new way," she protested. "There would be your name on the ticket. If you used another it would not match your passport, and if you used your own...." Sylvie let the sentence hang, ending with a shrug. "Either way, someone could be waiting for you in Paris!"

"I've thought of that." Georgiana smiled confidently. "That's why I'm going to drive as far as Lyons in France then get the train. That way, no ticket, not one with a name on anyway, and no one checks your passport at the Morez border crossing....not if you've got a local number plate!"

"It's still a terrible risk." Sylvie persisted doggedly. "Think what would happen if you got caught!"

"I'm not going to get caught Sylvie.... So stop worrying."

The Police Inspector from the Third Arrondisment in which the Pompidou Centre is situated and on whose desk the orders for the anticipated detention of Georgiana Montes ultimately fell had known a hot chestnut when he saw one. The Exhibition was to be opened by the Minister for Arts, and it was reported that the President himself and his wife, although not able to be there for the opening, intended to pay a visit shortly after their return from the United States, a visit made with the express purpose of improving the atmosphere between the two countries after a period of 'misunderstanding'!

Montes was no longer a poor student. She was famous. She was also a famous American, but she was wanted for murder. It was one thing to have decided not to pursue the extradition, but to allow her to tum up in the middle of Paris and defy everyone quite another - even if, as reported, she probably intended to do so secretly and in disguise. It would be bound to get out later. Then the whole Department would be made to look incompetent. But what would those same people say if they arrested her? Praise for being alert and acting decisively? Not on your life. They would be accused of being brutal and insensitive!

The Inspector sighed. He couldn't win, whatever the decision. But, on balance, it would be better to look brutal than incompetent. That's what people expected the police to be. And there was always the possibility that despite the information given, she would decide not to come. He picked up the phone. The first thing was to get some of his plain clothes people to keep watch on the Exhibition from day one. Fortunately the Consulate in New York had been able to obtain a good selection of stills of Georgiana Montes from Newspapers and Magazines, but it was also important that those he would assign this duty were good at seeing through disguises and would not make a mistake. One false arrest and the trap was blown. He thought he knew a couple who would do admirably.

Despite her bravado in front of Sylvie, Georgiana held her breath as her car reached the head of the line at the frontier, but the Swiss guard merely glanced at her appreciatively before waving her through, while his French colleague a few yards further on was taking a phone call and did not even bother to look as he gesticulated into the phone.

Lyons was a hundred kilometres from the Border. She parked the car outside the railway station then claimed the seat the agent had reserved for her under another name on the GTV for Paris. She was carrying an overnight case and a hat box.

Once the train had reached cruising speed, she got up, took the hat box from the overhead rackand made her way to the toilet. There she opened the box and removed the already dressed blonde wig she had purchased in Geneva for the occasion and spent the next few minutes putting up her own hair and pinning it into position. It took a few moments longer to lighten her eye brows and put on a paler lipstick. Then she stood and looked at herself.

The change was remarkable. With her blue eyes, the wig looked perfectly natural. That such a simple thing could make such a difference! She looked positively Scandinavian! Georgiana wondered if George would still find her attractive! That most men did was evident from the glances that followed her on her way back to her seat; looks, which both amused her but confirmed the wisdom of bringing along some of Sylvie's clothes which, the older woman said, would add ten years to her appearance. She would make another visit to the toilet, with the overnight bag this time, and change into these just before they arrived in Paris.

Georgiana arrived at the Exhibition at four. She decided against the dark glasses which were in her handbag. They might have added to the disguise, but such things always attract attention, as women who habitually wear them know only too well. She had picked her time wisely. There were enough visitors to lose herself in, but not the dense crowds experienced earlier in the day. She found the rooms where her pictures were displayed and for more than an hour walked round slowly, revelling in the reunion and the exhilaration of the moment. Many of the pictures had come from New York. These she had not seen for at least two years. It was like meeting long lost friends and she stood longest in front of those whose ideas she had more recently tried to re-express in her new setting, comparing the reality with her memory of them. If she had left then, possibly all would have been well. But she could not resist standing for a while at the back of the main salon to watch other visitors enjoying her work.

"Excuse me....but aren't you Georgiana Montes?" The woman's voice was loud and unmistakeably American. Georgiana turned quickly to see a middle aged woman smiling at her. "I thought so," the woman went on, without giving Georgiana the chance to say anything. Then she turned and called across the room: "Hey.... Honey, look who's here. Georgiana Montes herself!" It was only later Georgiana remembered the woman had spoken in French and wondered why.

The effect was dramatic. Within a minute, not only the woman's 'husband ' had joined them but she found herself surrounded by a crowd of admirers, making it almost impossible to move. She tried denying it. Shaking her head, and slowly managed to force her way to the exit of the salon, but few people were listening. The news of her presence spread like wild fire throughout the building and crowds followed her wherever she went so that she was grateful at first for her two companions - despite their recognition of her which had set off the whole thing - as, walking on either side of her, they helped her to the main exit and outside. One of them then turned and nodded to a group of police who were waiting with a van parked only a few feet away and these took over, ushering her quickly into the back of the vehicle and driving her away at speed before most of the crowd which had followed realised what had happened.

At first, she clung to the hope that that they were simply helping her get away from those who had been mobbing her. Then one of those travelling with her in the back leaned forward and clapped a pair of handcuffs on her wrists.

CHAPTER XIX

Five months later, Georgiana found herself in the back of a similar vehicle, only this time on a longer journey, to the woman's prison just outside Dijon.

Having been admitted, she was made to change into prison clothes, she was then taken to the Governor's Office and made to stand between two female warders in front of his desk while he examined her with some interest.

The Governor was a kindly man; a professional, who enjoyed his job and believed, despite moments of disillusion, that human beings were intrinsically good, and that given firmness, mixed with compassion, a term in prison could be a healing and educative process. He had learned of Georgiana's impending arrival with an excitement he had admitted to no one, not even his wife, who was more of a realist, certainly where women were concerned, and would have shared none of his sense of pride in having his prison selected to accommodate such an important prisoner; although not even she could have failed to have been aware of the trial which had split French opinion almost equally: those for her acquittal on the grounds of insufficient evidence, and the rest who, like her judges, evidently felt that her running away from French justice gave sufficient additional weight to the circumstantial evidence pointing to her guilt to justify conviction.

The Governor, as a student of jurisprudence had followed the trial closely, long before he knew his life was to become involved with hers, and there is little doubt that, having learned of the previous tragedies in her life, he would have acquitted her without hesitation. But it had not been up to him, and now she was in his charge, it was his duty to treat her like any other prisoner. Despite this, he found himself taking far longer appraising the new inmate than he usually did: that so much had happened to one so young, and despite everything, so beautiful!

190

After a while, one of the warders glanced at the other and the Governor, realising that his routine inspection had turned into a naked stare, pulled himself together. Clearing his throat, he assumed an appropriate expression of authority and began : "You have been sentenced to ten years in this prison, Miss Montes. Frankly,".and now he allowed his expression to soften a little, "if you had stood trial in the first instance you would have got off more lightly...."

"But I'm innocent," Georgiana said wearily. "I didn't do it."

"The French Judicial system is not unsympathetic to crimes of passion," the Governor persisted, ignoring her interruption. "As it was, you chose to run away, and in the course of the extradition proceedings in New York, insulted both France and it's legal system."

"I didn't insult it," Georgiana protested. "What my lawyer said..."

"Be silent when the Governor is speaking," the warder on her right ordered, turning on her fiercely.

"0.K" Georgiana said. "I just wanted to say that I love France, but I doubted if any one would believe me.

"That was certainly borne out by events," the Governor admitted.

"My husband is launching an appeal."

"That maybe." The Governor, took a breath, then he said, "But, in the meantime, you are here, and my advice to you is to make the best of it." He pushed back his chair and stood up. "This is not a cruel place," he said encouragingly. "If they behave themselves, inmates are treated with humanity and respect. It is up to you." After a short pause, he glanced at her escorts. "Take her along now."

"Allright. Come on," the second warder said, but Georgiana stood her ground.

"When will I be allowed visitors?" she asked.

"In a month's time."

"And will I be allowed my paints and brushes? They said...."

"At the risk of repeating myself," the Governor interrupted firmly," that entirely depends on you. The more cooperative you are, the sooner you will be entitled to privileges."

By the time Georgiana was led from the Governor's Office to the main cell block the inmates' supper was in progress, and after being shown her cell, the door of which was left open during the day, she was taken to the main dining hall where the meal was being taken. Most of the women prisoners were sitting at long trestle tables in the centre of the room watched by four warders standing at each corner of the hall. Here and there certain 'trusties' were moving among the tables with baskets of sliced bread and jugs of water. At the opposite end of the hall from which they entered Georgiana could see a hatch where one or two late comers were being served.

"Get your food over there, then pick a place anywhere," her escort said, pointing. "There are no special places."

"I'm not hungry," Georgiana said, turning to her.

"You'd better eat something," the other said, not unkindly. "There's nothing else until breakfast." Georgiana hesitated, then she nodded.

"A cup of coffee then."

"Fine. Go help yourself "

She watched Georgiana go to the hatch, collect a plastic cup of coffee then start to wander along the tables looking for a space.

Her job done, the escort glanced at her watch: she was off duty in ten minutes; just time to write out her daily report. She turned, nodded at the warder who was standing by the door, then left.

Georgiana continued along the tables conscious of the eyes that followed her. Some were dead pan, some hostile, others sympathetic. She wondered how much her future companions knew about her. What was the rule? Did the women here talk about themselves, or was the outside world something everyone tried to forget while they were inside? She'd soon find out, that was for sure.

She made several attempts to sit in vacant places, but each time the women at the table spread out so the place disappeared and she was compelled to walk on. Far from intimidating her, it made Georgiana mad, and that was good. Pure hatred was the best antidote to self pity.

Finally, she came to a table presided over by a huge woman in her mid thirties, sitting down the far end. Here, there were two spaces.

"Are you the American girl?" The young woman nearest her demanded as she moved in.

Georgiana nodded.

"What are you in for honey?" Another asked.

"She stabbed her boy friend," the first said smugly.

"Ah, well," Georgiana thought to herself "That's one question answered."

"I should'a done the same!"

"Come and sit up here next to me," the big woman said with a grin. "Don't pay any mind to them."

Georgiana returned her smile briefly, and moved up the table to where a space was appearing to the big woman's left, as those nearest obediently squashed up to make room, exchanging glances at the same time.

"Thanks." Georgiana put her coffee on the table.

"You're Georgiana Montes the painter, ain't you?" The big woman held out her hand. "My name's Christine, and these here are my friends." Georgiana shook hands and was about to sit down when an older woman sitting to Christine's immediate right said: "We know each other, don't we?"

Georgiana looked at her properly for the first time. There was something familiar. Then, suddenly it hit her, and for a second she was back, standing at the door of George's study staring at Sylvie kneeling beside him on the floor, and there was this mad woman standing over him with a gun in her hand until Paul snatched it away.

"I didn't know she was a friend of your, Marie," the big woman said, looking with interest from one to the other.

"She's no friend of mine," the seated woman answered, staring up at Georgiana with a look of loathing. "She's the whore of that bastard who killed Hans."

Georgiana felt faint with the desire to do the woman facing her some injury.

"And you're the bitch who betrayed him, then tried to kill him because you were too small to accept the responsibility for what you did," She said tensely. It seemed like someone else was speaking for her. She didn't want to talk to this woman, she wanted to kill her.

The big woman and her friends had stopped eating and were now looking from Marie to Georgiana mesmerised by the hatred that crackled between them like high voltage electricity.

"I'm sorry I didn't kill him," the older woman said.

"And I'm sorry it wasn't him that got his throat cut 'stead of your other boyfriend!"

In a second Georgiana picked up her coffee and flung it in the seated woman's face. Then she leant across the table and grabbed her by the hair and banged her face hard down on the table causing blood from her nose to spurt in all directions.

The suddenness of the attack gave Georgiana a momentary advantage, but as the big woman and the others leapt up from the table to get out of the way, Marie recovered and grabbed Georgiana's hair in tum. The knives and forks on the table were light plastic but someone had left a glass water jug and the older woman managed to grab this and smash it into the side of Georgiana's head before both of them rolled to the floor locked in each other's arms.

Christine held everyone back to ensure a fair fight, but it was brought to an end prematurely by the intervention of the four warders, and before either had inflicted any further injury.

The Governor, who had his own dinner interrupted, was both angry and disappointed as he stood facing the two women who had been brought to his office handcuffed to two of the warders, once they had been patched up. Most of all, he was disappointed and angry with Georgiana.

"You haven't been in the place five minutes," he said bitterly. "Is this how you expect to be treated with leniency?"

"I don't expect anything," Georgiana spat back at him. "This is the bitch who shot my husband!"

"He's not your husband," Marie shouted.

"Be quiet," the warder to whom she was handcuffed ordered sharply, and Marie, who had been in prison long enough to know when not to argue fell silent.

The Governor looked to the senior warder present, who was standing to one side. "Is any of this true?" he demanded, and the other nodded.

"Yes, Sir. That is why Gerard is in here."

The Governor gave a grunt of exasperation and half turned away before wheeling back to face her. "What kind of bureaucratic stupidity is it that sends this woman...."he pointed at Georgiana, "to the same prison?!"

"I don't know Sir. But, in any event, the prisoner Gerard shouldn't be here at all."

"Why not?" The Governor looked at her keenly.

The other shrugged. "This is a first offender's prison," she said, "Gerard had only just been released from Lille when she committed the second offence."

The Governor looked at her incredulously, then he had one of his bright ideas. "Good," he said, firmly. "That at least gives us a solution. We'll arrange to have her sent back to Lille tomorrow."

"I don't want to go back there," Marie blurted. "It's a terrible place! I like it here."

"That can't be helped," the Governor said impatiently. His dinner was probably already ruined.

He turned back to the senior warder. "Take them away. And put them in solitary until Gerard has been transferred. On second thoughts, keep the prisoner Montes there for a week. Maybe it will teach her a lesson.!"

When Georgiana came out of solitary she found herself in a cell with two other women. She was allotted a number of routine tasks connected with the running of the kitchens of mind shrivelling repetitiveness and was informed that, in view of her behaviour, visits would be suspended for three months as well as all other privileges.

She was allowed mail however, and George, Sylvie, and eventually Mary, when she found out where she was, wrote to her. She longed for their letters, but the things they wrote about seemed increasingly remote from the life she now led. She longed for news of her son, but the thought that if her Appeal was turned down she would not be released for more than six years at the earliest and he would then be almost nine years old drove her mad. All she thought about all day long was escape.

Her cell mates laughed at her. No one had ever escaped from Dijon. Although for first offenders, it was one of the most recently built, and consequently, one of the most secure Prisons in the country.

When at last George was allowed to visit her, he brought Ricci with him. She put on a brave face for him, but she wept for hours after they had gone, then wrote to George to tell him not to bring the child again. She would lose touch with him anyway as he grew up and she did not want him to remember his mother being in prison. He was too young at the moment to realise what had happened. Better he forget about her altogether until she was able to come home.. Then she would be a stranger to him, and they would have to start all over again. But it might not be too late. Better a stranger than a bad memory.

Lunas was immensely saddened when he got her letter. Sometimes in life bad things and good comes in pairs. And before he had decided what to do, Charles phoned from Paris to say that the Appeal had been turned down. Again, it was the fact that she had run away that had weighed against her.

He sat alone thinking, long into the night. He had failed her utterly. But now he was going to keep a promise she might have forgotten, but he remembered, from when they had been returning to Paris in the car, the night he was shot. He would never allow them to hold her. Now the time had come to make good that promise.

All conversation between prisoners and their visitors were carefully monitored. But on the next visit, when he kissed her goodbye she felt him push a capsule of some sort into her mouth with his tongue. She looked at him startled for a moment, then she managed to tuck it into the side of her mouth and keep it there undetected until he had gone and she had locked herself in a toilet to see what it was.

She found a tiny piece of paper inside the capsule. The message said that she was not to give up hope. She would be back home soon. Be patient. Speak to no one.

The message filled Georgiana with both elation and fear. She guessed he would stop at nothing to bring her home now the Appeal had failed, but everyone said that to try and escape from Dijon was impossible. Besides the female warders, there were armed men guarding the perimeter, and only five miles away was the Regional Headquarters of Gendarmerie where everything from light tanks to anti-aircraft missiles were kept. It was rumoured that some years before a rich man had tried to spring his mistress with the aid of a team of mercenaries and a helicopter, but all of them had died, including the girl and her lover.

It was when there was an accident some days later and one of the prisoners had to be taken to the hospital some miles away that the idea suddenly occurred to her. Twenty-four hour guards were always mounted at the Hospital whenever a prisoner was admitted, no matter what her condition. But transfers to and from the Hospital were made either in an ambulance or police van and these, she learned, were never heavily guarded.

Georgiana dared not wait for his next visit. Somehow she had to stop him before he did something that might get them all killed, and substitute her own idea. But she could scarcely write a letter telling him this. Envelopes were always left unsealed for the prison censor.

She thought of devising some sort of code, or hiding a message in an ordinary letter, but the Prison authorities were not fools. How could she send a message to him, that he alone would understand?

Two days later she put in a request for her paints and the canvas that she had been allowed when her privileges were restored but had not had the heart to use. She asked if she might be allowed to do a painting and send it to her husband for his birthday.

The Governor was delighted to allow this. He had long since recovered from his anger at what had happened the day she arrived and welcomed this sign of her wish to return to normality.

Besides, any picture by Montes would be worth a great deal of money. Perhaps she could be persuaded to paint one for his own birthday?

When the picture arrived at the house in the Bois du Bologne to which he had returned when Georgiana was arrested, Lunas took it upstairs to her studio at the top of the house and mounted it on the easel where she used to work, which still stood in her favourite position under one of the sky lights where she could see the gardens at the rear of the house any time she cared to glance outside.

He stood staring at it for a long time with a mixture of joy at receiving her present and misery that she was not there with him. But he brushed the latter feeling to one side. Already, plans were nearing completion when they would be together again. Ambitious plans true, but with his resources, ones that stood a good chance of success.

He saw at once that the style was different and that in itself made him examine it more closely. In most of her pictures the object conjured by the viewer's imagination appeared in the focus; but hard as he concentrated he could not see that it had one. It was a quite ordinary picture; of a large public building of some sort out in the country; a very ordinary picture, the critic in him noted with some dismay. Certainly not up to her usual standard; but this was due surely to her unhappy frame of mind.

Lunas craned forward and saw that the building had a name painted on the side, so small he had to put on his glasses before he could read: "The Hospital of Saint Joseph - Dijon."

He suddenly straightened up in alarm. Had she been in hospital without telling him? What did it mean? Was she expecting to go into hospital? Was there something wrong with her she had not told him about? He was about to turn away when something else caught his eye: The date underneath her signature in the bottom right hand corner of the picture was larger than usual.

When he looked at it more closely his mouth opened in amazement, then the hairs on the back of his neck started to tingle. It was dated the following month. He glanced at the date on his watch: in exactly twenty-seven days time. She was going to be in the Hospital of St. Joseph, Dijon, in exactly twenty-seven days. If it was true, it changed everything. But how could she be so sure?

CHAPTER XX

Georgiana picked her moment. She knew Christine wanted her, and she gave the big woman the impression that if she liked to get everyone else out of the showers early it might give them time to have some fun together.

It worked like a charm. After a while one after the other of those on their rota left until there was just the two of them.

When the last had gone, the big woman came to her with her arms open and a big welcoming smile, but her joyous anticipation turned at first to puzzlement, then rage when Georgiana said she had done the whole thing to win a bet and there was no way she would want to be petted by an oversized lump of lard. What really did it was when Georgiana laughed in her face.

The big woman beat her up for about five minutes before the warder in charge of the next rota arrived. It took another two minutes before help arrived, and another three before they managed to pull the enraged woman off Georgiana. By then she was obviously an urgent case for the hospital.

It was a big hospital; so big, that few members of staff knew more than a handful of those outside their own department, and as it was before the growing hostility of many members of the public towards those manning casualty departments, security personnel in hospitals outside Paris itself were usually considered unnecessary. Exceptions were made when prisoners were admitted, but Georgiana, in her present condition, was considered of little risk, meriting only one warder at any one time to keep an eye on her while she was recovering, and a great deal of the time the women on duty absented themselves to attend to their own needs and comfort. No one queried the arrival of a new consultant who introduced himself, as "Doctor" Paul Grisson, and who visited Georgiana daily, but whose real task was to report to Lunas via Maurice, who had taken a house close by, regarding her improving condition and the likely timing of her transfer back to the Prison. He also became friendly with the various women whose duty it was to guard Georgiana. These were mostly bored out of their minds with their assignment and eagerly grasped any divertissement such as that afforded by the apparent interest displayed in them by the new young doctor. And, when the moment arrived, one told him in plenty of time for Lunas to set in motion the plan for Georgiana's escape.

The "Doctor" visited his patient for the last time the evening before. He found Georgiana sitting in a chair beside the bed, her face still bruised, but healing fast and with her two broken ribs sufficiently knitted to cease to be so painful. Georgiana had recognised Paul from Poussin le Bas at once, even while drifting in and out of consciousness from the beating she had received. She guessed what his role might be and looked forward to his visits with mounting excitement. As soon as the woman guard took the opportunity to slip downstairs to telephone her boyfriend, Paul produced a make-up bag of the kind female prisoners were allowed, and after transferring Georgiana's possessions, substituted this for her own which he then dropped into the nearest trash can.

Although similar in most respects the new bag was bigger - though not enough to attract attention- and contained in a padded section a tiny but lethal automatic. This was simply a precaution, Paul told her. The Boss's instructions were that she was only to use it as a last resort.

The following day dawned without a cloud in the sky. Georgiana was escorted out of the main entrance of the hospital between two warders. Some people glanced at her curiously as she was led towards the waiting police van, but these were mostly too wrapped up in their own concerns to let their eyes linger for more than a few seconds. Georgiana noticed that, unlike her arrival at the hospital, which had been in an unescorted ambulance, this time an additional police car was waiting, and when she got into the back of the van with the two warders she clutched the make up bag closer to her and hoped George had allowed for such an eventuality.

Once they left the hospital behind, the road ran through partially forested countryside. After about ten miles a large black car with tinted windows came up behind the van. The driver sounded his horn politely indicating his intention to overtake and the driver of the van waved him on. In his wing mirror he saw the car move over to the left and start to overtake. The road was straight and clear in front of them for at least a mile. The van driver expected such a powerful vehicle to accelerate past not only the van he was driving, but the police car in front. But to his surprise, then irritation, the car pulled back in front of him, causing him to brake sharply to stop running into the back of it. He then saw they were approaching a cross-roads. Possibly the driver in front was now going to turn right. Even as the thought formed in his mind, the big car started to slow down.

The police car in front of them shot over the crossing drawing away even further from the two vehicles behind. Instead of turning right, the car which had just passed him slowed to a halt thirty yards short of the crossing. The van driver cursed volubly, but before he could pull out to drive around it, a tractor towing large harvesting machine drove slowly onto the crossing from the right and appeared to stall half way over, effectively blocking the road ahead.

Then everything seemed to happen at once: the doors of the car in front opened and two men jumped out. Both were carrying revolvers and had the lower part of their faces covered by scarves. Following his training the driver sounded the hijack warning knowing the two warders in the back would immediately lock the back of the van on the inside and pull another lever which would immobilise the engine. But driving the van away evidently did not feature in the plans of those advancing menacingly towards him as one aimed his revolver and blew out the two front tyres.

The other snatched open the door on his side and ordered him out. The first, meanwhile, marched to the back of the vehicle and, on finding it locked, came back and gave him ten seconds to unlock it. The driver explained that the security system only allowed the van to be unlocked from the inside, but his captor started to count anyway. The driver shut his eyes and prayed. He heard the count reach eight, then he heard the back of the van open and opened his eyes to see the two warders emerging from the van with their hands up, followed by the prisoner who seemed to have them covered with what appeared to be a toy pistol.

"Georgie!" The man who had been counting moved to sweep the prisoner into his arms. The driver looked round quickly wondering if the distraction was sufficient to try and make a run for it, but he saw the other man had shifted his gun to point directly at him and abandoned the idea with some relief He had not given much for his chances anyway. He saw the driver of the tractor throw what appeared to be the keys into the ditch, then he too produced a gun to join them. In less than a minute, the van driver and the two warders were locked inside the van.

The others quickly got into the car; Maurice in the driving seat with Paul beside him; Lunas and Georgiana in the back. The car skirted round the tractor then accelerated away up the road to the left through the forest just as the police car returned to find the road blocked on their side by the harvesting machine.

After two miles, the black car pulled up where a forest track joined the main road. Paul got out then stood at the road side for a moment watching the car disappearing into the distance. A few yards into the trees another car was waiting, and it was only a matter of seconds before he had pulled off his tractor driver's overall, flung it into the trunk, then donned a dark jacket which had been lying on the front passenger's seat. Paul drove the car onto the main road, then headed in the same direction as the others, but took a left at the next cross roads.

Sitting beside her in the back of the other vehicle Lunas examined Georgiana's face, lightly touching the fading bruises and kissing the fingers of her left hand tenderly. "You have been through a terrible experience, my darling," he said after assuring her that Ricci was well and eagerly waiting for them with Sylvie back at the chalet in Switzerland.

Georgiana shook her head. "It's my own fault," she said. "Mostly, people were kind, even at the prison."

"But your face!"

"They don't send you to hospital for a pain in your big toe, George! Big Christine didn't know it, but she was doing us a favour."

"But now I am going to look after you. No one will ever hurt you, ever again."

"Ever is a long time!". Georgiana sat back in her seat and looked at him directly. "How are we going to get out of here?"

"Don't worry. There is a plane waiting for us. Back in the opposite direction to the one they think we will take."

"You think they will expect us to try and drive to the Swiss frontier?"

"No. I think they will expect us to go to ground somewhere until everything had died down."

Georgiana looked at him frowning. It did not sound as if he was speaking directly to her, but to some invisible third party. She looked at Maurice in front. The Moroccan had also pulled his scarf away from his face, but he seemed to be concentrating on his driving now the road they were on began to climb up through the forest in a series of bends. He probably could not hear what they were saying above the roar of the engine.

They saw the road block half an hour later, a mile further on where the road became visible as it emerged from the trees for a few yards following the contour of the mountain five hundred feet above them. Maurice pulled into the side of the road and pointed. Lunas reached into a compartment and pulled out a small pair of field glasses which he raised to his eyes for a few seconds.

"Well?". Maurice glanced back over his shoulder. "Is there another way to the air strip?"

Georgiana saw Lunas shake his head slightly. Then he said: "There may be. But it would take too long. The longer we take, the greater the danger someone in a helicopter will see the plane waiting for us!"

"I can get through," Maurice said after a few seconds. "It's bad luck they have chosen this road."

"How did they set up so quickly?" Georgiana demanded.

Lunas shrugged: "I don't know." But they are not really expecting us.

"What do you mean?"

Maurice said: "If there are a lot of check points, the chances of any one being the one to have to try and stop us is small."

Lunas nodded. "We must drive up to them slowly and calmly. Like any members of the public not unwilling to be stopped and questioned!"

The Moroccan laughed and nodded. "Until the last minute," he grinned. He pulled his heavy automatic out of his shoulder holster and laid it on the passenger seat beside him. "O.K. Boss?"

Lunas nodded. He took his own gun out and rested it lightly on his knees.

Georgiana looked at him, eyes wide. So this was it. If they broke through, they would reach the plane. If not!

She realised she ought to be afraid. But she didn't feel anything at all. It was like watching somebody else. She was as detached as if she were painting the scene. Here was the setting. These were the possibilities. What would the viewer see in the centre of the picture? She was scarcely aware of Maurice putting the car into gear and accelerating to normal cruising speed.

They came round the last bend, and there were the two police cars drawn across the road.

"Get down!". Lunas put his hand on her shoulder and she slid down obediently behind the front seat. She never saw what happened as a consequence, but one moment the car was slowing down, the next it suddenly lurched forward. Shots were fired both inside and outside the car and the engine screamed as the car gathered speed, leaving the sounds of the shots outside the car behind.

Georgiana struggled back onto the seat and looked back. The policemen seemed unharmed and were jumping into their cars.

"Did you hit any of them?" She asked breathlessly.

"I was aiming at the tyres," Lunas said. "I don't know if l hit any." He opened the chamber of his revolver and fed bullets into it which he took out of his pocket.

Maurice glanced in the mirror, then he said grimly: "They're coming!" After a few seconds Georgiana said: "How much further is it?"

Lunas turned to look back for a moment, then he said: "The track leading to the air strip is about two miles further on. If we can make it and turn in without them seeing us, the chances are they will shoot on past and take several minutes before they realise we're no longer in front. That will give us the time we need."

"This is no good!". Maurice suddenly braked hard and pulled into the side. He jumped out of the car and pulled open the door next to Lunas. "You drive," he barked. "I will see what I can do to slow them down."

There was no time to argue. Lunas took his place at the wheel. Maurice slammed both doors then stood for a moment watching the black car gathering speed, he then took up a position by one of the pines closest to the road with his gun at the ready for the first of the police cars which could already be heard approaching.

When it came into sight, he stepped out from behind the tree, and waved the leading car down. It slowed for a moment, then obeying an order from the man beside him, the driver put his foot down again. Maurice opened fire, but the second car arrived seconds later and a lucky shot from one of the passengers caught him in the shoulder causing him to drop the gun as it accelerated past.

The landing strip consisted of a long narrow sloping grass field which rose to a line of trees to their left as they drove off the narrow forest track which connected it with the road they had just left. To their right the strip descended to the edge of a ravine which then dropped away sheer to the valley floor.

Lunas swung the car to the left in a wheel spinning curve as soon as he reached the grass and began to drive up the centre of the strip to where a small propeller driven aircraft was standing in front of some wooden huts facing down the slope and with its engine already running. Lunas pulled up beside it and the pilot, who was already on board, leaned out of the cockpit and beckoned them urgently.

Moments later, the engine roared and the plane began to move down the runway bouncing on the rough grass, just as the two police cars bursts onto the field.

The pilot had been warned what might happen, and now only he could make the decision.

The two police cars halted for a moment while the two drivers had a hurried exchange over the radio. Then the leading vehicle started to drive up the strip towards the aircraft which was now gathering spced towards them, its engine at full throttle but hampered by the length of the grass. The driver of the second vehicle and his two companions leapt out of their vehicle, two of them carrying rifles, and took up positions.

Georgiana held her breath. Although the advancing police car was also slowed by the long grass, every yard cut down the space available for take off. Surely now it was impossible. One or the other must give way or they would crash into each other.

When it seemed he had left it too late, the pilot, eyes grimly fixed on the air speed indicator which told him he would stall if he tried to take off now, pulled back on the joystick.

The plane rose into the air just skimming the roof of the police car. He had a momentary glimpse of the white faces of the occupants as it shot under him, then he pushed the joy stick forward and the plane lunged back onto the strip, bounced a couple of times, then continued to gather speed as it approached the second car. This was not in the centre of the strip and presented no problems in itself, but as it roared past the two marksmen took careful aim, and just as the plane finally rose into the air both fired.

Having reached take off speed, the plane continued to climb for a few seconds. The two marksmen fired again in rapid succession and now a trail of smoke appeared. The plane soared out over the edge of the ravine, then the onlookers saw the nose suddenly go down, and with the note of its engine rising to a seemingly impossible pitch it disappeared.

They heard the crash before any of them reached the edge of the ravine and saw the burning wreckage strewn over the valley floor.

The marksmen looked down for a long time. Then one glanced at the other and shrugged.

It was almost dark before they managed to reach the wreckage which was still burning and had set fire to several trees, but no other damage had been done and the rescue services began the grim task of searching for the bodies.

When everyone had gone to make their way down to the valley floor and the airstrip was seemingly deserted, Lunas and Georgiana emerged from the cover of the trees which they had just managed to reach before their pursuers had driven onto the field. Looking round to make sure everyone had really gone, Lunas helped Georgiana back into the car, which no one had thought to take away. They crossed into Switzerland four hours later without any trouble at a little used crossing point having rendezvoused with Paul who met them with the other vehicle.

It was not until day light the following morning that the French Search and Rescue came to the conclusion there had only been one person on board the little plane after all.

Although overjoyed to be reunited with Ricci and her home, Georgiana has yet to produce another canvas. Perhaps she never will. The thought of the man who paid for her freedom with his life has left a deep scar.

After several months she told George that she wanted to go back to New York for a while: by herself It was not that she did not love him.

Lunas was wise enough to accept this and lives in hope that someday she will want to come 'home.' There is nothing else he can do.

Although the Police had their suspicions regarding Lunas' part in Georgiana's escape, as in the past, they were never able to prove anything. The Chalet in the mountains overlooking Lake Geneva was closed up, but gardeners visit it regularly so that if she should ever want to return she will find the garden and the window boxes she loved so much waiting for her.

Lunas continues to run his business from Paris and lives in the house on the Bois-de-Boulogne with Sylvie and Paul to look after him. He drives himself these days.

CHAPTER XXI

It was one of those deceptively mild November days when the New York weather tries to fool everyone into thinking the Fall is going on for ever. The Newspapers reported that the trees in New England were past their peak, but in Washington Square the plane trees still clung possessively to their leaves.

Many of the park benches were occupied by students from nearby N.Y. University, laughing amongst themselves between classes. Here and there some older people were doing Chinese exercises in slow motion. One young man was practising juggling, and a pretty girl rode around on a mono-cycle distributing leaflets advertising a drama happening in a nearby 'loft' theatre in which she also happened to be the star.

There were the usual young mothers watching their children at play. Most were chatting to friends but Georgiana was content to sit by herself in the sun with Welsh for company, anticipating the time when Ricci's kindergarten would get out and they would go to collect him. Then 'peace' would be over as he would talk non-stop all the way home, controlling Welsh on the lead with one hand while waving today's art work under his Mother's nose with the other. Welsh, of course, had an entirely different perspective of this, knowing perfectly well that he was guiding Ricci safely home on the lead while his attention was occupied by his conversation.

Two young art students entered the Park deep in conversation and walked straight past the woman who was sitting on a bench by herself with her eyes closed, her face tilted at an angle to catch the sun. The young man glanced casually at her and at the old dog sitting on the ground beside her.

They were about to walk on when his eyes widened and he put his hand suddenly on the girl's arm.

"Sandy....wait a minute."

She paused obediently, looking at him.

"What's the matter?"

Her companion lowered his voice. "Didn't you see who that was?"

"Who?"

"On the bench back there."

They both turned and looked back, and now it was the girl's turn to look shaken. "My God!...Georgiana Montes!"

"It is her, isn't it?"

"Just a minuet." Before he could stop her she had retraced her steps to stand in front of Georgiana. Embarrassed, he followed her.

"Miss Montes."

Georgiana's eyes snapped open, then she held up her hand to shield her eyes from the sun to see who had spoken to her.

"Georgiana Montes....the painter? The girl persisted.

"Who wants to know?" Georgiana realised her words were more defensive than she intended. It was not often she was recognised now. In any event the girl continued to smile at her.

"My name is Sandra Wild," she said. "And this is Billy. We're Art Students. We saw your picture in the programme about modern painting the College put on in the summer."

"I saw you on the late show a while back." Billy offered.

"So did I." Sandy said quickly, not to be outdone.

"Must've been a long time ago," Georgiana said smiling. "I don't stay up late any more."

"It was you, Miss Montes." Billy insisted. "I'd know you anywhere. I'll bet they filmed it earlier."

"May be." Georgiana nodded. "So what can I do for you?"

The young man grinned and started to unwrap a sketch pad he was carrying. "Would you sign one of my pictures?"

"Billy!" The Girl sharply.

"I'm kidding! Just a minute." He turned over to a new page then handed the pad to her with a pencil. "Could I have your autograph.... please?"

Georgiana glanced at the girl who was watching her anxiously. Then she sighed tolerantly and reached to take the pad and pencil. "O.K. Give it here. What did you say your name was?"

"Billy. Billy Wells. My father said I was named after an old time boxer."

Georgiana nodded and glanced down at the pad. But instead of signing it, the pencil began to fly over the pad. "And you want to be an artist?" She said without looking up.

"A painter yes. So does Sandy.... Don't you Sandy?" He tore his eyes away from what she was doing to look at the girl standing beside him.

She was also staring, fascinated at the woman's hands guiding the pencil over the paper at lightening speed and she answered without turning her head. "Yes. But not like Billy. I'd like to get into T.V. You know, Art Director....something like that."

Georgiana nodded and turned for a second to look at Billy. "Then you can keep him while he's struggling!" She looked down again to continue, without waiting for the girl's response. She was holding the pad in such a way now they could not see the drawing.

After a moment Billy said impulsively: "Your pictures sell for thousands of dollars, don't they?"

Again Georgiana nodded without looking up from what she was doing. "I guess so." She said. "I never had much to do with that."

Sandy sighed. "It must be wonderful to sit down in front of an empty canvas and know hundreds of people will want to buy whatever you produce," she said.

Georgiana paused for a moment, then she said in a tone that almost echoed the girls': "I haven't done that for quite a while."

"Why not?"

Georgiana shrugged without answering the question. Then she closed the pad and handed it back to Billy. "Do me a favour," she said.

"Of course."

"Don't look at it until you get home. And don't tell anyone you met me here."

"O. K." He took the pad and put it back in his case.

"I won't tell anyone either," the girl promised.

"Thank you. Oh....you'd better take your pencil as well!" She handed it back to him, but he shook his head.

"Please....keep it. It's a present," he said.

"Well, thank you," Georgiana smiled and tucked it in her coat pocket. "Goodbye, then. And don't forget, you've promised." She leant forward and patted Welsh who evidently felt it was time to go and was standing up, looking at her. "Or my dog will bite you!"

The girl patted him too. "He doesn't look very fierce," she said.

"That's because he knows we can trust you."

Billy pushed the strap of his case over his shoulder, then he held out his hand. "Goodbye, Miss Montes. And thanks a lot." They shook hands solemnly.

"That's O.K." Georgiana said. "Thanks for the pencil. "Maybe it'll bring me luck!" The young man straightened up and gave her a final grin.

"Goodbye, Miss Montes." The girl tucked her arm into Billy's. "Take care of each other," Georgiana said.

"We will." They started to walk away, and Georgiana watched them for a few seconds before responding to Welsh's prodding with his nose and got to her feet.

"Yes....O.K. I know, Ricci's waiting!" The dog gave a short bark and they started to walk away in the opposite direction.

"It's no use." Billy stopped just after they had emerged from the Square into Fifth Avenue and swung the bag round so he could unzip it.

"You promised to wait," Sandy said reprovingly.

"I know. But I've got to look at this." He pulled out the pad and opened it. Sandy craned her neck, as anxious as he to see what the famous artist had drawn.

"It is you, Billy," Sandy said after a few awe-struck moments. "It doesn't just look like you, it is you."

Billy looked at her amazed. "What are you saying?" He demanded. "It's a sketch of you!"

They stared at each other for a few seconds, then back at the drawing. They saw that what was definite was the background against which they had been standing. There were just a few lines in the foreground that seemed to move as they looked at them crystallising into a recognisable shape for a moment, then melting away again, like mist.

"She's signed it," Billy breathed. "Look!"

Sandy looked at him after a moment.. "Our worries are over," she said. "We could get a thousand bucks for this, easy.!"

Billy shook his head. "I'm never going to sell this," he said. "I'm going to put it up in my room.

And maybe one day, I'll do something half as good!"

They looked back into the Square, and saw the bench she had been sitting on was now empty. Billy looked around and then he saw them, the woman and the old dog leaving by the opposite entrance.

He often walked through the Park afterwards; sometimes going out of his way to walk past the same bench. He had a vague idea that maybe he could get to know her properly. At least, talk to her. But she was never there. Maybe she did not believe they would keep their promise he thought sadly. But he still went back.

Sometimes, when the sun was shining he could see her in his mind's eye, drawing for him, while the dog looked on.

Lunas had often heard it in his dreams, but now he opened his eyes and knew he was awake. The short, sharp, demanding bark that told him Welsh was waiting in the garden below to be let in. That could only mean one thing!

---------- E N D ----------